FROM THE ANTHEM CITY

Mike Romeo

Copyright © 2013 Mike Romeo

ISBN 978-1-62646-641-8

All rights reserved. No part of this publication may be reproduced, stored in a retrieval system, or transmitted in any form or by any means, electronic, mechanical, recording or otherwise, without the prior written permission of the author.

Published by BookLocker.com, Inc., Bradenton, Florida.

The characters and events in this book are fictitious. Any similarity to real persons, living or dead, is coincidental and not intended by the author.

Printed in the United States of America on acid-free paper.

Booklocker.com, Inc.
2013

First Edition

Dedicated to:

my parents, Al and Mary Lou,

my wife, Gail,

and Jordan, Matt and John

Prologue
Friday, January 29, 1988

Seven hours waiting for a call. Clint glanced at the telephone on the hotel nightstand for maybe the thousandth time, watching the phone as if looking at it would make it ring. Seconds passed. Nothing happened. He resumed reading the newspaper:

> *Critics and the cognoscenti will no doubt scoff at this book. But readers looking for a fast-paced mystery with a thought-provoking twist won't be disappointed.*

Those sentences triggered two thoughts for Clint. First, he wished he had a book to pass the time, or a magazine. All he had was the newspaper that had been placed outside his door while he slept. Waiting for the call, Clint had read, skimmed or perused every article and advertisement in the paper. He had just finished the last one, the book review in the Weekend section.

Second, what in the hell were the *cognoscenti*?

Three days after leaving the army, Clint was in Pittsburgh. He was searching for the woman who had once saved his life. The last time he saw her she was a detective, happy to be back in her hometown and excited about her new career. Clint didn't see her name in the phonebook, so he took a chance and called police headquarters. He said he was a military acquaintance and wanted to say hello. Police officers were always sympathetic to military personnel. They recognized a similar breed.

It had been a few years. Was she still on the force? If she was, would this officer know her? She might have gotten married and changed her last name.

The desk sergeant sounded like Clint's call was one of a dozen things he was juggling. Not rushed, but trying to handle it with efficiency and detachment.

"Let me see if she's in. Hold on," he said in a deadpan voice.

So far, so good, Clint thought. He recognizes the name.
A minute later the sergeant was back.
"She's out of the office. I don't know when she's returning. I'll leave a note for her. How can she reach you?"
Clint gave him his hotel phone number.
"What's your name?"
"Clint Ronson."
"Okay, Mr. Ronson. I'll let her know you called. If you don't hear from her, you might try a place called Pennington's later on. Her section likes to go there for Happy Hour."
Clint waited and read. He didn't want to leave the room and risk missing her call. He waited and read some more. He turned the TV on for background noise; watched the maid straighten the room and change the towels; ordered room service for lunch. After a few hours, he wondered why she hadn't called. Maybe she was still out of the office. Maybe she had returned but had a bunch of urgent things to deal with. Maybe the note got buried under other paperwork. Maybe she wasn't interested in talking to him.
Clint sat the newspaper aside. He checked his watch. It was 5PM - time for drink special.

Pennington's was a bar and restaurant, recently remodeled but decorated to look like it had been around for years. At Happy Hour, no one was eating. The place was dimly lit, noisy and filled wall-to-wall with drinkers. They were young, professional types - women in smart business suits and men wearing jackets and loosened ties. They stood in tight circles, drinks in hand, feeling relaxed after a week of work; laughing and talking loudly over The Bangles and Belinda Carlisle on the sound system.
Clint ordered a beer. "Big turn-out tonight," he said to the bartender.
"We're always extra busy before the Super Bowl," she said. "It's like a holiday weekend."
"I heard police detectives come here for Happy Hour," Clint said. Maybe the bartender would know their favorite table.
"Wouldn't surprise me," she said. "Everybody's here."

Clint leaned back against the bar. He'd try to scan over the people from here. First, pick out a group that looked like detectives; a group that was a little older, conservatively dressed, more serious-looking. Then sort through the faces. How much had her appearance changed in thirteen years? Did she still have short, blond hair? The athletic build? What about the eyes? Clint knew he'd recognize those eyes if he saw them again.

Scanning wasn't working. The crowd was too dense, the room too dark. Clint started threading his way between the circles. He held his beer close to his chest, his elbow tight against his ribs, to avoid having it jostled. He glanced at faces in the circles as he eased by them. He noticed a pretty blond - not the one he was looking for - and a talkative redhead. A friendly-looking brunette made lingering eye contact with him. Normally that was all the encouragement he needed to introduce himself. Not tonight. More blonds caught his attention, all of them too young to be her.

Clint made it around the bar, slowly picking his way through the crowd. He didn't see a group of detectives. He didn't see anyone who matched his memory of the blond. Maybe they had a quick drink and left. Maybe they hadn't been there at all.

Someone grabbed his arm as he passed by a table. Clint turned. He saw a big guy sitting alone holding a folded newspaper. His head was tilted back and he was squinting, as if he was examining Clint through the bottom of his large glasses. His mouth was partly open in a smirk. The man let go of Clint's arm and pointed at him.

"I know you!" he said. The man sounded surprised and excited, like he had sighted a celebrity among the patrons at Pennington's. Clint recognized him, too. He wasn't eager to get reacquainted.

The man wagged his finger at Clint. "You were the one doing that investigation." He pointed from Clint to an empty chair. "Have a seat. You won't believe what I got to tell you."

Probably not, Clint thought. He placed his beer on the table and sat down. The man laid his newspaper to the side and leaned across, arms tucked under his chest, getting almost face-to-face with Clint. He made wary glances to the left and right. He whispered something.

"I can't hear you," Clint said. The man took a breath and glanced left and right again. He looked back at Clint, his large head tilted to the side.

"I said, you remember those quatrains?"

"Quatrains?"

"You know, those cryptic verses that Russian lady gave you."

"Yeah, sort of," Clint said.

"How you thought they contained clues about your case, but we couldn't figure them out?"

Clint nodded. The man looked away momentarily, then leaned in closer. He locked eyes with Clint.

"I know who those verses are about," he said. "I know who the prince untrue is."

The prince untrue. Clint felt strange to hear that phrase after so many years. Wasn't his identity a key to deciphering the verses?

"I see it's coming back to you," the man said. "You know what else?"

"What?"

"I was right. Those quatrains are prophetic."

Chapter One
Monday Morning, September 9, 1974

"Look! It's Steve McQueen! Where's my autograph book?"

Karen was leaning forward at her desk on tightly crossed arms, a teasing smile on her face. She was a slender brunette, barely out of her teens, youthfully good-looking and full of nervous energy. Clint was surprised she wasn't popping chewing gum. He didn't know what Michael Walsh had seen in Karen when he hired her. She had a lot of rough edges to work in a law office, even as a receptionist. Clint thought she was too sure of herself. She seemed to believe she could get by forever with looks and a flippant attitude in place of poise and knowledge and everything else.

"Well, you look just like him. Same rugged face. Same deep-set eyes under long, thick brows. Same small mouth." She bracketed the corners of her lips with her thumb and forefinger. "Same creases here," she said. "But I think you're taller. How tall are you?"

"Almost six feet."

"I don't think he's that tall. It's hard to tell in the movies. They make 'em stand on boxes and stuff to look taller. And you have green eyes, not baby blues like he does. And your hair's brown. Do you ride motorcycles? I saw a picture of Steve McQueen riding one."

"Too dangerous for me."

"Hey! Did you hear about Evel Knievel trying to jump that canyon yesterday?"

"Yeah."

"I thought he was going to use a motorcycle. He used a rocket."

"It was a rocket-powered cycle."

"What was the big deal? We sent men all the way to the moon in a rocket. He couldn't even get across a canyon. And it wasn't even the Grand Canyon, like he said."

"He couldn't get permission to jump the Grand Canyon."

"He's Evel Knievel. What's he need permission for? Oh well, at least we got football next weekend. The Steelers are playing the

5

Colts. We should win big. The Colts aren't any good any more. I'm putting my money on the Steelers."

"I heard Gilliam might start," Clint said.

"I like Hanratty, but Noll always goes with Bradshaw." Karen's eyes flung open, as if surprised by the realization that Clint might be there on business. "Are you here to see Michael?"

"Do you think I came to talk about Evel Knievel and the Steelers?"

Karen picked up the phone and pressed one of the buttons along the bottom. Her voice suddenly became coolly professional. Maybe this was a glimpse of the potential Walsh saw in her.

"Tell Mr. Walsh that Mr. Ronson is here to see him." A pause. She pressed the button again and looked up at Clint. "He'll see you now."

Michael Walsh, former JAG officer, always projected a crisp air of authority. About eighteen months ago, Walsh had been a guest lecturer in one of Clint's criminal justice classes. He had each student stand up and explain their motivation for entering the law enforcement profession. After class, Walsh called Clint over. "I could use someone with your background," he said. He handed Clint his card. Clint called him. Walsh told him how to get licensed as a private investigator. He put him on his payroll and assigned him as many cases as he could handle with his school work. Clint was in business for himself now. He still got most of his work from Walsh.

Walsh introduced Clint to the others in the office. Anthony Prentiss, Jr., late sixties, wore a gray sports coat over an open-collared shirt. Prentiss had been standing in front of a wall with his arms crossed, examining Walsh's plaques and framed documents – his law degree, his farewell gifts from his army assignments, his Legion of Merit citation. Thomas DeAngelo, mid-thirties, was fit and tanned. DeAngelo was dressed in a navy blue pin-stripe suit with wide lapels and a fat tie. His thick black hair was meticulously styled. "Be careful around DeAngelo," Walsh once told Clint. "He's a shrewd lawyer. He'll charm you; get you to drop your guard. But he'll play rough if he needs to."

FROM THE ANTHEM CITY

"Clint Ronson, I'm pleased to finally meet you." DeAngelo gripped Clint's hand, then drew closer and placed his left hand on Clint's elbow. "Michael speaks highly of you," he said quietly, as if his words were meant only for Clint to hear. "You were Army CID, weren't you? Thank you for heeding your country's call in its time of need."

The handshake that was more like an embrace, the warmth in the voice, the nice words - Clint momentarily felt a fuzzy rush. Walsh was right. DeAngelo could turn it on when he wanted to.

DeAngelo changed his tone to that soft, consoling way of speaking that people use when talking to the bereaved. "I'm here on behalf of City Councilman Stephen Harris," he said. "Councilman Harris' great-uncle, William Harris, was a friend and colleague of Mr. Prentiss' father. When he saw the obituary, he asked me to extend his condolences to the family and see if they needed any assistance."

Clint nodded and opened his notebook. He took a seat in the semi-circle of chairs in front of Walsh's desk.

"Clint," Walsh said. "Mr. Prentiss..."

"Call me Tony," Prentiss said. "I like to keep things informal."

"Okay. Tony asked me to settle the estate of his father, Anthony Prentiss, Sr. It looks pretty straightforward. There's just one thing I need from you. I'll let Tony explain."

Tony Prentiss cleared his throat and shifted in his chair.

"In the early 1900s, my father was the business manager for a newspaper called the *Pittsburgh Sentry*. William Harris was the publisher. The paper organized a football tournament around 1905 or 1906. Somehow the cash prize was left at the newspaper's office. My father held it, thinking he'd quickly get it to the winner."

Clint wrote "Pittsburgh Century" as he jotted notes in his pad.

"Anyway, shortly after the tournament ended, William Harris died," Tony said. "The paper went bankrupt. Its creditors went to court to see what they could recoup. My father did not reveal the existence of the cash. The ledger showed it had been withdrawn for the tournament and everyone believed it had been awarded. He said he intended to quietly present the prize to the winning team after the

7

case was settled. The problem was he didn't know who won the tournament. He opened a personal savings account and deposited the money for safekeeping. Time passed. My father became busy with other things in his life. The money remained in the bank compounding interest. My father told me he always regretted not finding out who won and awarding them their rightful prize. He regretted it so much that he made it a provision in his will."

"Let me read it to you," Walsh said. He picked up a document from his desk. "All surviving members of the football team that won the tournament organized by the *Pittsburgh Sentry* shall share and share alike the full amount in the savings account in my name…" Walsh looked up from the will. "He lists the account number and the name of the bank here." He resumed reading. "If no survivors can be located, an existing team, organization or concern which has a direct connection to the winning team will receive the full amount. If no such team, organization or concern can be located, the full sum shall be shared and shared alike by the charities I previously specified."

"How much was the prize money?"

"The account shows an original deposit of eight thousand dollars," Tony said.

"Now it's almost sixty-four thousand," Walsh said.

"So you want me to find out who won?" Clint said.

"And who was on the team," Walsh said. "And if any are still alive, how do we get in touch with them?"

"There are agencies that specialize in tracking down people," Clint said. "I'll contact one when I get the roster of the winning team." Clint looked over his notes. "What does he mean by an organization or concern with a direct connection to the winning team?"

"My father said teams back then often had an athletic club or a company for a sponsor. If the team no longer exists, which is likely, its sponsor may still be in business."

"Tell me everything you know about this tournament," Clint said.

"I already have."

"Do you know where it was played? What teams were involved?"

"I assume it was played in Pittsburgh or its vicinity since the *Sentry* was the organizer. I don't know anything about the teams." Clint closed his notebook. "If a newspaper organized it, I'm sure they reported on it," he said. "That would be the place to start."

"Do you have any more questions for Tony?" Walsh asked.

"No," Clint said. Prentiss seemed to be out of answers. No sense putting him on the spot.

DeAngelo said, "With Tony's permission, I request you keep me updated on the progress of your investigation and share your findings with me before anything goes public, as a courtesy to Councilman Harris." DeAngelo glanced at Prentiss. Prentiss gave an uncertain nod, like he wasn't expecting the request.

"The execution of a will is a private matter," Clint said. "This isn't a probate case. There's no need to make anything public."

"True," DeAngelo said. "But public notices will be required to find surviving football players. If any are located and they get their prize money, they'll go straight to the press. Or their families will. This has the makings of a great human interest story."

"Why does Councilman Harris care about a football tournament played almost seventy years ago?" Clint said.

"This could be historic," DeAngelo said. "He wants to know what role his great uncle played. And he's a football fan." He gave Clint a sly smile, like he was sharing an inside joke. Work with me, he seemed to be saying. You're a guy, I know you get it: being a sports fan justifies any kind of excessive behavior.

Clint wasn't going to be won over so easily. Councilman Harris' interest in the whole matter seemed out of place. According to Tony, Harris the newspaper publisher died almost seven decades ago. Yet the councilman sent his personal attorney to offer condolences and assistance to the family of his great-uncle's friend. Why the great esteem for such a distant relationship? Who even remembers things like that? Unless there has been something on-going between the Harrises and the Prentisses.

"Tony, how well do you know Councilman Harris?"

"Just what I've heard in the news. I don't know him personally."

So much for the enduring relationship, Clint thought. DeAngelo's presence had nothing to do with Prentiss. He tipped his hand when he was too quick to ask for updates. DeAngelo was here because Harris was interested in the investigation, which could only mean he was interested in the money. How does he even know about it? Did Walsh let DeAngelo see the will? Does Harris know it's sixty-four thousand dollars? If Councilman Harris believed he had a legitimate claim to the money, maybe because he was related to William Harris, why not bring it up now? Why wait to see where the investigation led? Clint wanted to tell DeAngelo to come clean; to tell what Harris knew and how he knew it and why he was trying to interject himself into the investigation. Walsh wouldn't approve of the demand. Anything about Harris was outside the bounds of his assignment. Still, he wanted to put DeAngelo on notice. He wasn't buying all the innocuous-sounding explanations. Clint looked straight at him.

"What are you not telling me?"

"What are you talking about?"

"My gut says there's more to know about this case."

"Mr. Ronson, there's only one more thing to know – who won the tournament? It's your job to find out."

Chapter Two
Monday, Late Morning, September 9, 1974

Forget about DeAngelo and Harris, Clint thought. They're outside your lane. Whatever their motives, they're Tony Prentiss' problem. This assignment was easy money. Clint figured he could wrap it up quickly. All he needed was an independent source that named the tournament winner. An article from the sports page of a 1906 newspaper would do the job. His first stop, probably his only stop, would be the newspaper and periodical archive in the library of one of the local universities - Pittsburgh, Carnegie Mellon, Duquense. Clint picked the closest one, the one that was the legacy of the steel baron. He turned off Forbes Avenue onto the grassy campus. He crept his AMC Javelin past the cream-colored, brick Beaux Arts buildings, keeping it in low gear, until he found a parking spot.

Clint didn't care for this kind of work. He didn't like the tedium of sifting through files looking for a nugget of information. Even so, a big part of his job involved piecing together paper trails. Surveillance wasn't much better; lots of waiting and watching. Until he got the pay-off of catching the subject red-handed in the viewfinder. Clint liked site visits where he went to a location to collect information or reconstruct events. He also liked interviews – the human interaction, the give and take, trying to tease an answer out of a subject, catching an inconsistency in their words.

The archive was a windowless room with rows of gray metal file cabinets under hanging fluorescent lights. The cabinets held reels of microfilm. A table with three microfilm viewers sat against a wall. The archivist looked as dreary as the room. He was a pale man with a gaunt face and penetrating light blue eyes behind wire-frame glasses. Probably not much chance for human interaction with him, Clint thought. Clint said he wanted to see the *Pittsburgh Century*. After a moment of confusion and a brief chuckle, the archivist politely corrected Clint. He then directed him to the drawer containing the *Pittsburgh Sentry* microfilm. Inside, Clint found a tray with eleven small boxes. Each contained a reel that preserved the page images of three months of newspapers. The last box was labeled "July to September 1906". He would start with that one and work backwards.

Clint loaded the film. The newspaper's nameplate caught his attention. The words *Pittsburgh Sentry* were printed in bold, Germanic-looking letters. Beneath them in smaller font it read "Always Vigilant." Th*e Sentry* seemed a strange name for a civilian newspaper. The *Century* was too, but it sounded weightier than the *Sentry*. Now the motto made *Sentry* sound perfect. It said this newspaper was like a soldier pulling guard; always alert, always watchful of the public interest. Clint smiled approvingly.

He began to scroll through the pages. Almost immediately Clint came across an announcement for the tournament: $8,000 winner-take-all prize; all collegiate, amateur and professional teams invited; the staff of the *Sentry* will select the best sixteen entrants; no entry fee; each team is responsible for its travel, room and board; first and second rounds to take place on Saturday and Sunday, September 15 and 16, at the Fayette County Fair in Dunbar; semi-finals and championship the following weekend at the Westmoreland County Fair in Greensburg. The *Sentry* billed it as The World Championship of Football. Clint wrote down the number of the page image and the headline so he could get it printed.

He continued to scroll. In the September 9 edition Clint found the first article. "For the first time since the Madison Square Garden World Series of 1903, there will be a competition to determine the true champion of all of football," the article began. Then it described the format for the tournament. If sixteen teams had entered as intended, the format would have been straightforward: eight games with the winners advancing to the second round, then four games, then two, followed by the championship. But only eleven teams were listed, so the tournament officials had to be creative with the first and second rounds. Five games would be played on September 15. The top-ranked team would get a bye until September 16. The second round would feature four games involving the five winners, the top-ranked team, and the two teams that lost by the smallest margins in round one. The four winning teams would then advance to the third round on September 22. The championship would be the next day.

FROM THE ANTHEM CITY

The article named the eleven competitors. McCann's Fighting Irish of Homestead was the top-seed. The others were, in alphabetical order, Ambridge FC, Clairton AA, East Liverpool (Ohio) AC, Ford City AA, Monessen Terrors, Mount Lebanon AC, New Kensington AC, Waylan AC, Weirton (West Virginia) AC, and the West Virginia Collegians.

Eleven teams, not sixteen like the *Sentry* had announced, and all from no more than a hundred miles from Pittsburgh. Some world championship. Clint noted that with the possible exception of the Fighting Irish, the two teams in the championship would be playing games on consecutive days on back-to-back weekends. Football must have been a different game in 1906. He couldn't picture teams playing that type of schedule today - no time to recover physically from one game before playing another, no time to build a game plan for the next opponent.

From September 11 through the 15th, the *Sentry's* sports pages featured the build-up to the tournament. On Tuesday, Wednesday, Friday and Saturday the paper ran articles about two of the teams. On Thursday, it printed articles about three teams.

The articles sang the praises of each of the teams, touting their credentials as a contender for the world championship. They identified key players and coaches. They glowingly described past accomplishments. All but one of the articles included a team roster. For most of the teams, the articles listed favorable won-loss records from previous years and scores of important games. Clint read things like "Ford City upset Kittanning by the score of 12 to 10 to become the dominant team in Armstrong County." For a few of the teams, Clint noticed there was no mention of past seasons or big games. The articles only identified notable players and where they had played before, such as "George Cannella anchored the fabled Latrobe line for three years before joining Mount Lebanon." Were these new teams? He wondered if they were organized for the sole purpose of competing in the tournament.

The article on West Virginia was the one without a roster. It began: "From Morgantown come the West Virginia Collegians. Last year, West Virginia University posted a record of eight wins and one defeat..." The rest of the article was an account of the games and scores of the 1905 WVU season. Clever opening, Clint thought. Were the Collegians actually the university football team? Why weren't they called the Mountaineers? Why no roster? Were the identities of the players intentionally omitted since they were amateurs playing for prize money?

Every article ended with the same teaser: "The (fill in the team name) expects several college players of renown to join them for this world championship tournament." If the line-up of teams and talent wasn't enough to draw spectators, maybe the prospect of seeing "college players of renown" would be.

Beginning on Sunday, September 16 and continuing over the next five days, the *Sentry* ran stories about the nine first and second round games. These were not the usual dry, factual accounts of games. They were lengthy, vivid narratives; a daily chapter or two in the serialized saga of the World Championship of Football. Each story set the stage with descriptions of the weather and the excited crowds. Then the two contending teams were introduced, essentially summaries of the information reported the previous week. Next came the game action, written in prose that was full of color and hyperbole and quotes. Critical moments in the games were breathlessly dramatized into events of epic proportion.

Clint scrolled through the week, pausing to sample a few of the paragraphs from each of the stories. He learned that Ambridge, Clairton, Monessen, New Kensington and Waylan won their first round games. The Collegians and Mount Lebanon also advanced to the next round since they had the closest losses.

The first round winners were seeded in round two based on their margins of victory. The top-seed Fighting Irish played their first game against the Collegians, who lost their first round game by more points than Mount Lebanon. Waylan, played Mount Lebanon. Third seed New Kensington played sixth seed Monessen, and fourth seed Ambridge played Clairton. The second round winners were Ambridge, the Irish, the Terrors, and Waylan.

The edition of Saturday, September 22 provided a preview of the third round games to be played that day. The Sunday edition reported the results of Saturday's games. The lead story provided the expected lavish account of the win by McCann's Fighting Irish over the Ambridge Football Club. But the second game warranted a single sentence under the heading *Monessen Wins*: "In a third round game of the World Championship of Football tournament, the Monessen Terrors defeated the Waylan Athletic Club."

Strange, Clint thought. Big stories about every game so far, but nothing about a semifinal game. Maybe this game ended too late to file a complete story. The full report would probably be in Monday's paper.

Clint was already congratulating himself for finding the information so quickly, and it wasn't as tedious as he expected. Two teams remained - McCann's Fighting Irish of Homestead and the Monessen Terrors. Who was the winner? They played on Sunday. Monday's edition would carry the full story. He scrolled ahead, turning the knobs quickly, anticipation building. Page images flashed by.

Suddenly the screen showed nothing but white light. No page images for the edition of Monday, September 24, 1906, or any subsequent edition. The rest of the microfilm was blank. Clint checked the tray in the drawer to see if a later reel had been misfiled. They were in perfect chronological order. The one he looked at was the latest. He checked with the archivist.

"The last edition of the *Sentry* was September 23, 1906," the archivist said. He had delicate way of speaking, carefully enunciating each syllable. "The paper folded." The archivist smiled faintly. "Pardon the pun. I meant it went out of business."

"What was the major daily newspaper in Pittsburgh in 1906?"

"There were several back then." The archivist placed a folder on the countertop and turned it so Clint could see. It contained a list, several pages long, of the newspapers the library stored on microfilm. "You can try the *Chronicle Telegraph*, the *Daily Dispatch*, the *Leader*, the *Post*, the *Press*, the *Sun-Telegraph*, The *Gazette Times*, the *Times*. No, the last edition we have of the *Times* is from April 1906."

"You've got to be kidding," Clint said. "Those are all major dailies?"

"The print media was a flourishing business in the early 1900s," the archivist said. "Remember, it was the only media at the time. No TV. No radio. It wasn't unusual for a city to have multiple daily newspapers."

"Okay. We're do I find them?"

The archivist ran his finger down the side of the page. "See these numbers? They're the file cabinets that contain the microfilm for these newspapers."

Clint started with *The Gazette Times*. He quickly scrolled to September fifteenth, then slowly moved page by page to the end of September. No mention of the tournament. He looked at the September twenty-fourth edition. Still nothing. Clint was about to quit when page one of Tuesday, September 25 rolled onto the screen. He didn't do so much as glance at the page, but somehow his eye picked up the word "Sentry". The full subheading was *Sentry Ceases Publication*. Above it, in larger font, was the actual article headline - *Publisher Found Dead*. Clint read it quickly, then reread it to absorb the stunning story: the body of William Harris found in the Monongahela River on Monday morning; wedged between the river wall and a barge; gunshot to the head; a night watchman reported hearing a shot on the Panhandle Bridge around two in the morning; he didn't see anyone leaving the bridge; police investigating; the financially-troubled *Sentry* immediately ceased operations.

Clint leaned back in his chair, trying to assess this new information. Tony said Harris died soon after the tournament. Clint took that to mean days, maybe weeks, later. It was only hours later, and he was shot in the head. Murder? Suicide? Was his death somehow related to the tournament, or was the timing tragically coincidental? Clint went back to the microfilm reader and scrolled through a few more editions, hoping to find a follow-up article. He stopped. The police investigation might take weeks. There might not be a follow-up article. In any case, this piece of information was peripheral to Clint's investigation. He wrote down the page image number.

FROM THE ANTHEM CITY

It was the same story for the other six newspapers. Nothing about the tournament. Front page stories about the death of William Harris and the end of the *Sentry*. Clint took the slip of paper and the reels of microfilm to the archivist. For fifteen cents per sheet, the archivist would print the requested articles.

"I'm trying to find out who won a football tournament organized by the *Sentry* in 1906," Clint said. "The championship game was played on the same day the newspaper went out of business. I thought one of the other major dailies would've covered it. It was billed as a world championship, but it was more like a regional championship."

"It doesn't surprise me," the archivist said, waiting for a sheet to emerge out of the printer. "The competition between so many newspapers was intense, as you can imagine. In its short existence, the *Sentry* always struggled to find enough readers to be profitable. It began as a respectable newspaper but it turned to sensational stories. Anything to improve circulation. Today, we would call it a tabloid. My guess is that the tournament was another ploy to attract readers. Competing papers would have ignored it. Otherwise, they would essentially be promoting a rival's publicity effort."

"Where else could I look?"

"You said it was a regional tournament? A county or small town newspaper might have covered it if they had a team involved. They weren't competing with the Pittsburgh papers, so they might not have cared that it was the *Sentry's* tournament."

Clint went back to the list and found a newspaper from Allegheny County, which covered Homestead, the town of the Fighting Irish. He also found a Westmoreland County paper, which covered Monessen, the other finalist, and Greensburg, the site of the tournament championship. These papers were weeklies and only a few pages long. Scrolling through them would not take much time.

Like the Pittsburgh papers, the Allegheny paper didn't mention the tournament. One edition of the Westmoreland paper contained an announcement about the county fair and listed the tournament as one of the attractions. The next edition ran a brief article recognizing the Monessen Terrors for winning their first two games. Clint noted the paper called the competition "the *Pittsburgh Sentry's* football tournament," not "the World Championship of Football." He didn't find a follow-up on the Terrors' results in games three and four.

"Dammit," Clint said to himself. He thought he had hit the mother lode on this first try, all those stories in the *Sentry*. Now reality was setting in. After hours of scrolling and reading, he was so close, so tantalizingly close. All those stories, all that information about teams and games, but not the one piece of information he needed. Clint squeezed his eyes shut. "Dammit!" he said again. He looked over his shoulder at row upon row of gray file cabinets, all of them full of newspaper microfilm. Was there anything else here worth checking into? Anything he had overlooked?

"Any luck?" The archivist was looking over Clint's other shoulder.

"None."

"I have one other suggestion. There's a young man who's sort of an amateur football historian. I think of him as the football nut, although I would never say that to his face. He comes in here occasionally to research old football topics - games, teams, what have you."

"Someone likes doing this?"

The archivist let the comment pass. He said, "The next time I see him, I could ask him to give you a call."

"How often does he come in?"

"It's hard to say. Sometimes two or three times a week. Sometimes I don't see him for a month or more."

Clint wrote his name and phone number on a piece of paper and gave it to the archivist. He wasn't going to wait to hear from this guy, especially if it might take a month. He would continue to research it. He was still hopeful about finding the answer quickly.

Back in his apartment, Clint made some phone calls. To hold his expenses down, he didn't keep an office. If he needed to see a client, he arranged to meet them in a public place - a restaurant, a library, a mall, whatever suited them. Most of his investigative work required him to be out in the city or suburbs. All he needed an office for was

FROM THE ANTHEM CITY

to make and receive telephone calls, write reports and keep files. He could do those things in his apartment.

First, Clint called the sports department of Pittsburgh's remaining daily paper. He asked a staff researcher if there was any information about the tournament in their historical file. After ten minutes on hold, the staffer said he couldn't find anything. Next Clint called the main library of Fayette County. The university archive didn't have microfilm of the county's newspapers in its collection. By now, a county or small town newspaper seemed like a longshot to Clint. He hoped the Fayette County residents of 1906 had shown special interest in the tournament since the first two rounds were played at their fair. If they had, maybe some newspaper covered it to its conclusion. The Fayette County librarian referred him to the historical society. No one answered at the society's number. Clint guessed they were closed for the day.

He tried again the next day. An elderly-sounding lady cheerfully offered to look through the society's old newspapers for him. She called back a few hours later. Just like in the Westmoreland County paper, she had found an advertisement for the fair that listed the football tournament as an attraction, but no game results. Another dead end.

Chapter Three
Thursday, September 12, 1974

Movie fans eagerly awaited the release of The Godfather, Part II, due in theaters by Christmas. The local TV programmers hoped to tap into the appetite for gangster drama. They pulled out old episodes of *The Untouchables* and showed them at 11:30 after the news. One night Clint came across the show while he clicked through the channels. The reruns took him back.

Clint grew up in Dundalk, a tidy neighborhood of rowhouses in Baltimore adjacent to Bethlehem Steel's massive Sparrows Point mill. His father, a World War II vet with no affection for his service days, worked there. Between overtime, swing shifts and drinking bouts in the local bars, the elder Ronson was rarely home. He was usually asleep when he was. Sometimes his family complained about his absence from their lives. "I put a roof over your head, food on the table, and clothes on your back," he would growl back at them. "What more do you want?"

Clint did want something more. He was envious of all the father and son things he saw his friends doing - playing catch, fixing the car, going fishing. He resented the lack of attention from his old man. Determined to get into the spotlight, he resolved to make himself a force to be reckoned with. In his teenage mind, that translated into being dangerous. The criminal characters on *The Untouchables* became his role models. Clint was infatuated by the fast-living, tough-talking, muzzle-flashing action depicted on the show. He flirted with petty crime and got into a few fights. When his old man told him he wouldn't get anywhere trying to be a badass, Clint finally felt the thrill of recognition. He decided he was on the right path.

But the truth was, his heart wasn't into criminality. His mother had already instilled too much morality into him. How could he be dangerous and be upstanding at the same time? He wrestled with the dilemma. John Wayne gave him the answer. In *Rio Bravo*, the Angie Dickenson character asks, "How does one get to be sheriff?" Wayne replies, "Gets lazy. Gets tired of selling his gun all over. Decides to sell it in one place." Clint had found the high, middle ground. He could take that urge to be dangerous and put it to use, if not for the cause of good, at least as its hired gun. Now he saw *The Untouchables* in a different light. He wanted to be a danger to the bad guys. He wanted to be a special agent.

That's what he told the recruiter. He wanted to be a special agent. FBI, Treasury Department, Secret Service, it didn't matter. To get there, he needed a college education. To go to college, he needed money. He remembered hearing his old man lament about not taking advantage of the G.I. Bill, one of many opportunities missed. Clint wouldn't make the same mistake.

"We have our own special agents," the recruiter said. "Ever hear of CID? Criminal Investigation Detachments? You can get some investigative training and experience." It sounded too good to be true. (Didn't recruiters always sound too good to be true?) Clint couldn't enlist directly into CID. He had to be an MP first. Good enough. Clint signed on the spot.

His mother was surprised and bewildered by his decision. Finally, she offered motherly acceptance. "If that's what you want," she said. His younger brother said, "Just don't get killed." The old man told him he was crazy. "Why do you want to do that when you can get a steady job at the mill?" His father's opposition reinforced Clint's conviction that he had made the right choice.

Clint took to basic training better than he had taken to almost anything else he had tried. Early on, he lost a few contests of will with the drill sergeants. Once he understood that things would go easier if he did it their way, he settled into a productive routine. He liked the whole experience: he was always moving, always with a purpose; getting hot, dirty and dog-tired during the day, then taking a fast, invigorating shower in the evening; slamming down a quick meal in the mess hall before clearing his spot at the table for another trainee; alone with his thoughts at night during fireguard; the pervasive barracks odors of boot polish and rifle bore cleaner and sinus-clearing latrine disinfectants; endless marching to training, sometimes riding back in "cattle trucks," sometimes marching back;

firing his M14; qualifying as an expert; finding he had some natural leadership ability; ending basic as a squad leader. "We like it here, we love it here, we finally found a home, a home, a home away from home," the trainees chanted when they marched. The cadence was meant to be ironic. For Clint, it was the truth.

He came back to Dundalk on leave. The guys greeted him with their usual deprecation, and some wariness. Clint had broken from their pack and had found a new pack to run with. Now the old pack was doing a lot of sniffing, sizing him up, maybe trying to measure themselves against him. The girls were more enthusiastic. He had money and free time. He was a note of excitement in what was already starting to look like a predictable existence. He was familiar, but somehow different, a little exotic, maybe a little risky. He got a few dates. And some Dundalk girls not being the most virtuous, he got lucky a couple of times.

After basic, the army sent Clint to Fort McClellan in Alabama for eleven weeks of Military Police Advanced Individual Training. Clint learned tactical MP skills like traffic control during combat operations, rear area security and prisoner evacuation and processing. He also learned the basic law enforcement functions of MPs. At graduation, he was awarded Military Occupational Specialty 31B.

Clint was sent to the Federal Republic of Germany in early December, 1963. He was assigned to the Third Armored Division, Ray Barracks, Friedberg, the post Elvis had been at a few years earlier. Clint expected to find a bombed-out country and a dispirited population; the Germans grimly dealing with both an occupation and the sinister apparatus of the Cold War - the Wall, Checkpoint Charlie, army convoys on the autobahn, military exercises in the countryside, secret agents and secret police. What he found surprised him. The country had been so completely rebuilt that it looked like a war had never happened. There were quaint, medieval-looking towns with half-timbered buildings and cobblestone marktplazes. There were immaculate woodlands carefully tended to by forstmeisters. There was a staggering variety of richly-flavored biers. And there were frauleins, charming in ways different from American girls, some eager to meet US soldiers.

Clint enjoyed the attractions of Germany, to a point. He had come there with a purpose. On the job, Clint studied the sergeants in his company, asked them questions, and volunteered for extra assignments if he felt he could learn from them. He endured his fellow privates who teased him for being a brown-noser. In his free time he took college classes at the Ed Center.

As soon as he met the minimum requirements for time in service, MP experience and college credit, Clint acted. He collected letters of recommendation from his supervisors. Then he submitted a packet to become a CID special agent. "Don't get your hopes up," the admin sergeant told him. "Most people don't get selected the first time." Most people don't have my recommendations, Clint thought.

Three months later he received his orders. At the end of his tour in Germany, Clint would attend the fifteen-week Apprentice Special Agent Course at McClellan. Upon completion, his enlistment would be extended to allow him to fulfill the minimum thirty-six month service obligation required of CID agents.

In early 1966, Spec Four Ronson reported to his first CID assignment at Fort Jackson, South Carolina. For the next two years he endured Jackson's sweltering summer heat and participated in numerous criminal probes. He investigated the suspicious deaths of army personnel and dependents, rapes, robberies, drug-dealing, misappropriation and fraud. He also fit in a few trips to Myrtle Beach and racked up as many college credits as he could.

In May 1968 Clint, now a sergeant, deployed to Vietnam. Over there he added black marketing, fragging, and drug and contraband smuggling to his resume of investigative work.

The end of Clint's tour in Vietnam coincided with his ETS, the end of his CID service extension. He would be free to leave the army, finish his degree, and apply to the FBI. Clint was in no rush. He liked the army and he liked being a CID agent. He really liked being introduced as Special Agent Ronson. He figured the additional experience would enhance his FBI application. The maximum age to apply was thirty-seven. Clint was only twenty-four. He had plenty of time.

In Vietnam Clint had put in paperwork to become a warrant. He PCS'ed from Southeast Asia to Fort Rucker for Warrant Officer Candidate School. From there he went to Fort Benning for paratrooper school, and then to Fort Bragg. He arrived at the Home of the Airborne wearing shiny new jump wings and a silver bar with a black square designating Warrant Officer One.

Clint was only at Bragg for eighteen months, long enough to get in a dozen jumps, before he came down on orders for another tour in Vietnam. In June 1971, shortly after arriving in country, he got promoted to Chief Warrant Officer Two.

The promotion caused Clint to do some soul-searching. He had started this journey to get the GI Bill, then go to college and become a federal agent. The investigative experience was a bonus. He had worked hard. He had hit his targets like clockwork - college credits, selection to CID, selection to warrant officer. All were marks of success, and success was sweet. Clint was having a hard time leaving it all in pursuit of The Dream. At the same time, he didn't want to end up with any regrets. By accepting the promotion, he incurred a one-year service obligation. Almost all of it would be served in 'Nam. Near the end of his tour he submitted his resignation. His colleagues assumed he had been swept up in the tide of career soldiers heading for the exits, fed up with the war and disillusioned with the state of the army. Clint didn't try to explain his real motivation. He assumed everyone would think it was a cover story.

Back in the states, he was assigned to a transition company at Bragg, a place to put draftees returning from Vietnam who had a few months left on their enlistment. The only requirements were to show up for three formations a day and to carry out whatever details were assigned – grass-cutting, police call, all kinds of area beautification projects. Discipline and standards were lax. Hair was long. Pot use was rampant. It was like the draftees were flipping the bird at the army as they made their way to the door. The First Sergeant was an irritable NCO with a pot-belly that strained the buttons on his olive drab fatigue shirt. He was counting down the months to his own retirement. He had hoped for a cushy job to conclude his career. Instead, he was stuck babysitting a rabble of druggies and slackers. Twenty-five years of honorable service and this was his send-off. When his frustration peaked, he issued mass threats to use UCMJ. He said anyone facing charges might be extended on active duty until their case was resolved. He said that anyone found guilty might receive a less than honorable discharge. That, he warned, might hurt them long after they left the army. The draftees knew they were empty threats.

Clint tried to steer clear of all the drama and keep busy. He volunteered to work at one of the gyms on post. He wore civilian clothes, signed out basketballs and mopped the floors after closing. By the end of July he was out.

Clint chose Frostburg State College. It was the only state school that would recognize all the college credits he earned in the army. They were also agreeable about his GI Bill benefits. Some of the schools he talked to acted like the red tape made him more trouble than he was worth. In late August, Clint bought an AMC Javelin. He drove it to the small campus in the mountainous western edge of Maryland. He leased an apartment, registered for classes, and prepared to be a full-time student.

College life was okay, a little slow-paced and boring compared to what he had been doing. He thought most of the students were childish. It was funny how they acted like they knew everything, but they were as shallow as dinner plates. They hadn't been anywhere or done anything compared to Clint. Clint related better to the non-traditional students, the older ones who had worked for awhile before starting college. They had a grip on what life was really like.

The phone rang. Late calls were part of the job in Clint's line of work. Something about the night, usually in conjunction with alcohol, made people want to bare their souls. But this call wasn't a confession.

"My name is Vince Gleason," the person on the phone said. "The guy in the mircofilm room said you wanted to talk to me. Something about an old football tournament."

Clint gave Vince a rundown on what he knew about the tournament. He told him he needed to find out who won. He also told him about the dead ends he had hit with his newspaper research. Vince sounded eager to dive in. He gave Clint his home address in Monroeville and invited him to stop by. He made one request before he hung up.

"Those pages you got printed from the microfilm, can I have a copy of them?"

"Sure," Clint said. He would give him a copy of everything except the story about William Harris' death.

Chapter Four
Late August, 1906

Patrick's Saloon looked as functional as a factory - brick interior walls, a floor of unfinished planks, a low ceiling with rough-hewn beams, a coal stove. It was the most popular tavern in town because it had the coldest beer. A spring seeped through a basement wall. The owner had built a pool to catch the cold water. He placed the kegs in the pool - ale, porter and a Bohemian-style lager. He ran tubes from them up to the hand-pulled beer engine on the bar. Patrick sold the beer by the mug or by the pail. The cold brew, especially the lager, was a huge draw for the thirsty steelworkers. They packed into the saloon after their shifts in the blasting heat of the mill.

Tom Hammond and Eddie Moore sat on benches on opposite sides of a heavy table. They both wore denim pants with suspenders and plain cotton shirts. Tom was a cheerful bear of a man. He was large and muscular with light brown hair, a lantern jaw and an easy smile. Eddie was the kind of guy who could never sit still, always bouncing a knee or tapping a foot. He was as tall as Tom but wiry, with scraggly black hair, heavy eyelids and a mouthful of crooked teeth. Jesse Mitchell came into the saloon. He worked his way through the crowd slowly, moving with a slight limp, looking for familiar faces among the noisy steelworkers. Jesse had blond hair parted down the middle, a neatly trimmed mustache, and hawk-like blue eyes. He wore a bowler and a black vest over his white shirt. He carried a newspaper and a book. Jesse spotted Tom and Eddie.

"Hello, boys," he said.

"Hello yourself," Eddie said.

"We got an extra mug, coach," Tom said. "How about taking a seat and helping us drink this beer?"

"Business before pleasure," Jesse said. "Look what I came across." He laid the newspaper on the table, folded to show an announcement. "A tournament for the world football championship. All teams are welcome. No entry fee."

"Lemme see that." Tom turned the newspaper and read the announcement. He looked up at Jesse. "You believe it's for the world championship?"

"That's what it says."

"How many teams you think'll be in it?"

"If all teams are welcome, I'd say dozens. Maybe a hundred," Eddie said.

"All teams are welcome to apply. Sixteen will be accepted." Jesse said.

"Who's organizing it?" Tom said.

"The *Pittsburgh Sentry*."

"A big city paper," Eddie said. "It must be legitimate."

"What's this about?" Tom ran his finger along a line in the announcement. "The games will be governed by the new rules."

"The college teams agreed to change the rules," Jesse said. "Passing's legal now."

"We already throw passes."

"Those are lateral passes. The new rules allow forward passes."

"Forward passes? You mean throwing the ball down the field?"

"Yeah."

"That's not football," Eddie sneered.

"Eddie's right," Tom said. "Football's a test of character. You wear your opponents down by running plays as fast as possible. You overpower them with a mass of blockers at the point of attack."

"When the other side has the ball, you meet mass with mass, defenders against blockers."

"And it's a team game. If your ball-carrier gets held up, you get behind him and push; try to knock those defenders off him. Use fists and elbows if necessary."

"Victory goes to the strong."

"I'll drink to that," Tom said. He and Eddie clinked mugs and poured down the beer. Their Adam's apples bobbed with each swallow. They slammed their mugs on the table. Tom wiped his sleeve across his lips.

"Remember that song we heard in Latrobe, Eddie-boy?" Tom began to sing. Eddie joined in.

"After the ball is over.
After the field is clear.
Straighten my nose and shoulder
And help me find my ear. Hey!"

"That's what football's about," Tom said.

"You boys done?" Jesse said impatiently. Tom gripped the lip of the pail with one big hand and tilted it to refill the mugs.

"What's wrong with the rules we got now?" Eddie said.

"Nineteen players killed last year. That's what's wrong. President Roosevelt threatened to ban the game if the fatalities continued. The goal of the new rules is to open the game up, eliminate some of that mass on mass play you two are so fond of."

"The object of the game is to move the ball through the other team. Man against man." Tom said. "Passing's a cheap way to move the ball."

"A team can gain field position through punting. What's the difference?"

"It's a trade-off. You give up the ball for better field position when you punt."

"There's trade-offs to passing, too. I been studying the new rules." Jesse placed the *Spaulding Football Guide* on the table.

"You've got a newspaper *and* a book? What are you? A walking library?" Eddie said.

"Somebody around here's gotta be informed," Jesse said. He opened the guide. He had underlined parts of the text and written notes in the margins. "Halves will only be thirty minutes instead of thirty-five," Jesse said. "Now you need to gain ten yards in three downs to get a first down."

"Ten yards? Not five anymore?" Tom said.

"Ten yards."

"Never happen," Eddie said. "It was hard enough to gain five."

"It'll never happen if all you do is run." Jesse went back to guide. "Blockers can't use their hands anymore."

"How're they gonna block anyone?" Eddie said.

"Like this." Jesse made fists in front of his chest. He held his elbows up, his arms perpendicular to his body.

"At least defense will be fun," Tom said. "I'm going to beat my man the whole game if he has to block like that."

Jesse turned a page in the guide. "There's going to be a neutral zone the length of the ball between the offensive and defensive lines. On offense, you need a minimum of six men on the line of scrimmage, and you can only have four men in the backfield."

"Where's the eleventh player go?"

"At wingback, or you put seven on the line...Here's the part about forward passes. Only the offense can throw a pass. They have to throw from behind the line of scrimmage, and they can only throw one pass per down. The pass has to cross the line at least five yards out from either side of the center. If it doesn't, the offense loses possession." Jesse glanced up from the book. "That means the quarterback has to sprint to the outside to throw." He looked back at the underlined text. "The pass cannot be caught within a zone that's five yards out from either side of the center and extends from the line of scrimmage to the goal line. A pass can only be caught within the field of play. In order to score, the player catching the ball has to run it across the goal line and touch it down."

"What if someone catches the ball across the goal line?" Eddie said.

"It's a touchback," Jesse said. He continued, "Only ends and backs can catch a forward pass. A pass that's not caught has to touch a player on either team before it hits the ground, otherwise the offense loses possession at the spot of the pass. If it goes out-of-bounds without touching a player, the other team gets possession where it crossed the sideline."

"You could throw an intentional out-of-bounds pass instead of punt," Eddie said, "with no chance of a return."

"Except you can kick that melon a lot farther than you can throw it. What do you boys think about passing now?"

"There's a lot of restrictions," Tom said.

"And a big risk of losing possession," Eddie added.

"Can a player make a fair catch on a pass?"

"No. As a matter of fact, the pass catcher himself is fair game. Hold him, hit him, knock him down. Whatever it takes to keep him from catching the ball."

"I don't think this forward pass will catch on," Tom said.

"These rules will be the ruin of the game," Eddie said. "You have to gain ten yards in three downs. Blockers can't use their hands, and the forward pass is crap shoot. No one's going to score."

"Score? No one's going to move the ball."

"There's one more rule change - the on-side kick," Jesse said.

"What's that?" Tom said.

"A back takes a direct snap and makes a low, short punt to an area clear of defenders. If an offensive player can get to the ball first, he can recover it. The ends and backs can get a running start downfield before the ball is kicked."

"Now that sounds promising!"

"That's the only way the offense will move the ball," Eddie said. "It's going to be run on first down, on-side kick on second down, punt on third if you recovered the on-side kick and didn't get a first."

"You think these new rules will change game strategy?" Tom said to Jesse.

"No. If we get the ball within thirty-five yards of our goal line, we punt on first down. Clear it out of our end of the field. Beyond thirty-five yards, we try to keep possession and advance the ball. If we get within thirty-five yards of the opponent's goal line, we should score a field goal, if not a touchdown. Any good team will use the same strategy."

"Lucky for us we got a good punter," Tom said.

"Tad kicks 'em like a rocket," Eddie said.

"Crowell's one of the best," Jesse said. "What do you think? Will the boys be up for this one?"

"You think we'll get selected?" Eddie said.

"I think we have a good chance. We won most of our games last year."

"How's the team look this year?" Tom said.

"Very strong. As far as I know, all of our key players are coming back. Crowell will be back. He's a capable fullback and linebacker as well as an ace punter and place-kicker. Gus Webb will be back. He's a fine quarterback."

"Can he throw the ball?" Tom said.

"He could throw lateral passes well enough. I don't see why he can't throw a forward pass."

"What about Billy Pallister?" Eddie said.

"I hear Billy will be back," Jesse said.

"You can't be sure with him," Tom said.

"I heard he still wants to play," Jesse said. "He's the best halfback I've seen in the past few years. I daresay none can match him in the whole state. He's a mean linebacker, too. If he doesn't come back, we'll still have Jacob Rourke. He would be the top halfback on most teams. He and Gus make a good pair at deep defensive back, too. Then there's you two. Eddie, you give us strength on the outside with your play at end and corner."

"Jesse, who did you say was eligible to catch passes?" Tom said.

"Backs and ends."

"I hope you can learn a new trick, Eddie-boy."

"Don't worry yourself," Eddie said. "I can catch."

"I think your height will be an advantage when it comes to catching passes," Jesse said. "And Tom, I think you're the top linemen in the state. I haven't seen anyone play offensive guard and defensive tackle better."

"Hearing all that, I'm ready to go," Tom said. "When is this tournament?"

"The first round is September fifteenth."

"That's early. Football usually doesn't start until the last weekend in September."

"You think that'll be a problem for anyone?"

"Not for me. The sooner football season starts, the better."

"Same with me," Eddie said.

"Good! Get the word out to everyone," Jesse said. "We start practice next week."

Chapter Five
Friday, September 13, 1974

Vince had provided the address to a narrow, two-story, wood-frame house with a sharply-angled roof. It was built on the side of a hill in a compact row of identical houses. Clint climbed the steep porch steps and knocked on the door. A plain-looking woman wearing jeans and a gray sweatshirt answered.

"My name is Clint Ronson. I'm looking for Vince Gleason."

"Downstairs," she said, motioning wearily with her head. "Use the steps under the porch."

Vince lived in a basement apartment. He was a big-boned kid, about six foot two, with dangling arms, sloped shoulders, a big head and a strong jaw. His long, straight hair covered his forehead, ears and neck like a dark brown helmet. He wore a Steelers T-shirt, jeans, blue Jack Purcells and wire-frame glasses with over-sized lenses. The glasses resembled a visor attached to his helmet of hair. When he walked his upper body rocked from side-to-side, his long arms swinging like pendulums. Vince's build and the way he moved made Clint think of some kind of bipedal creature. A large ape? An upright grizzly?

"Welcome to Cava Vincente," he said. "You get it? It sounds like Casa Vincente but cava means cellar in Spanish. Actually, it means wine cellar. But that's cool, 'cause I've drunk some wine down here."

Cava Vincente looked like the waiting area in an auto repair shop – fake wood paneling, a black vinyl sofa against one wall, a table holding a jumbled pile of notebooks, binders and magazines against the opposite wall, a portable TV on a metal stand in a corner. Through an open door, Clint saw an unmade bed in a darkened room. A set of steps led upstairs.

"I get it," Clint said. He handed Vince a folder with copies of the pages from the *Sentry*. Vince sat down alongside the table. Clint settled onto the sofa.

"So, the newspaper that organized this thing went out of business before they could report who won," Vince said.

"Right," Clint said. "Have you ever heard of this tournament?"

"I heard rumors about a big football championship in this area in the early nineteen hundreds. I've never seen anything in print about it. The other newspapers didn't cover it?"

"No."

Vince scanned over the copies, pausing to read sections. He snorted occasionally.

Big Foot, Clint thought. That's the bipedal creature this kid reminded him of.

"The microfilm guy told me the *Sentry* was in financial trouble," Clint said. "He thinks they organized this tournament to increase readership - a sales promotion. The other newspapers may have avoided it because covering it amounted to helping a competitor."

"Or maybe they didn't think it was a credible world championship," Vince said. "Maybe they didn't think it was worth reporting on." He tilted his head back and squinted at Clint through the bottom of his large glasses, his mouth partly open in a smirk. His expression seemed to say "How about that?" in a way that was more a declaration than a question. Clint was thinking about Ford City, the Armstrong County champions, and all the other small town teams. Even with no background in early football, he already doubted that the tournament had lived up to its world championship billing.

"I don't know anything about the history of football," Clint said. "That's why I came to see you."

This was the cue Vince had been waiting for; an acknowledgement of his expertise, an invitation to strut his stuff. His eyes lit up, the words starting flowing.

"Well, in 1906, there were college teams and there were club teams," Vince said. "Most club teams were amateur. Some paid a few of their players. A few paid all their players. Those teams were the forerunners of professional football. All of the club teams were independent. There were no leagues back then. They played regional opponents. The highest honor for a club team was to be recognized as the state champion. The concept of a national champion was years away. Calling something a world championship, that was just a promotional gimmick."

"The *Sentry* mentioned a football world series played in 1903. What was that?"

"That's what I'm talking about, the perfect example of using the term "world championship" to sell tickets. A promoter created it to have an event for New Year's weekend at Madison Square Garden. It was held in 1902 and 1903, then discontinued due to lack of interest. Four or five teams competed each year, almost all from the New York/New Jersey area. The winning team in 1903 came from Franklin, just up the road from here. Now, back to this 1906 world championship. None of these teams were the heavy-hitters of the era. For a national championship, even a regional championship, I would've expected to see Massillon and Canton. They were considered to be the best teams in the country at the time, and they were nearby, over in Ohio. The best team in this part of Pennsylvania was Latrobe. They didn't play either.

Vince paged through the copies. He held up the announcement for Clint to see. "Something unusual about this tournament, they played in the middle of September. In the early 1900s, football was an October and November sport. The earliest any teams played was the last weekend in September."

He turned the announcement around and read it again.

"Interesting," he said. "They played the games at county fairs." A pause. "An eight thousand dollar prize. Winner takes all." Vince glanced at Clint. "Fifteen hundred dollars a game was a reasonable payment for a team back then." He picked up a pencil and made some calculations. "The tournament champions would have to win four games. An eight thousand dollar prize would have paid them fifteen hundred for each of the games plus two thousand. That's pretty good for the winners. Not so good for all the other teams. They had to pay their own expenses - travel, lodging, et cetera - to compete. And what about the teams that had to pay players? Think about it. The second place team would've played in four games over two weekends, just like the winner, and wouldn't have received squat."

Vince turned through a few of the copies.

"I don't know anything about any of these teams. Ambridge Football Club - never heard of 'em. Clairton Athletic Association - never heard of 'em. East Liverpool Athletic Club - now that's one I might've heard of." Vince picked up a binder and opened it at one of the tabs. "No. The East Liverpool I'm familiar with started playing in 1907. This 1906 team may have been a precursor to the 1907 team, or it may have been a completely different group of players." Vince laid the binder back on the table. He flipped through a few more of the copies. "The Waylan Athletic Club. There's a semi-pro team in Waylan now. I wonder if there's any connection." He turned another page. "McCann's Fighting Irish."

"Inspired by Notre Dame?" Clint said.

"I doubt it. The press started calling Notre Dame the Fighting Irish during the Rockne era. That was the 1920s. This team called themselves that for some other reason, probably a bunch of Irish immigrants." He paused to read one of the copies. "West Virginia Collegians. Don't tell me this was the college team." Vince dug through the pile of magazines. He pulled out a WVU football press guide and opened it to the records of previous seasons. "It could be. West Virginia University played its first official game in 1906 on September twenty-ninth, so they were available to play in the tournament." He studied the scores in the press guide. "I see WVU defeated a club team during the regular season. They beat the Connellsville Independents 37 to 0. Let's see how they did against other club teams. 1905 - didn't play any. 1907...Wow! They beat the Parkersburg YMCA 55 to 0 and the California YMCA 36 to 0. It looks like WVU dominated club teams during that era. What are the chances that they would have lost back-to-back games to club teams in the tournament?"

Vince gave Clint his "how about that" look again. He was enjoying himself, showing off his knowledge of early football trivia. The kid was sharp. Odd, but sharp. Clint liked his little display of deductive reasoning about West Virginia.

"The write-up makes it sound like they were the college team," Vince said, "but they could have been some WVU frat boys, or a composite team of players from more than one college."

"I noticed some unusual scores," Clint said. "Two teams had four points. I thought they might've made a pair of safeties, but the articles report field goals."

"Yup, those were field goals. They were four points back then. A touchdown was only worth five points. The extra point was still a point, and a safety counted for two, just like today. The rules for scoring changed a couple of times over the following years until today's system came into being. The sport was evolving back then. In fact, 1906 is a landmark year. After the 1905 season, President Roosevelt threatened to ban the game due to the number of deaths and injuries. To make football safer, several rule changes were implemented for the '06 season, including the forward pass."

Clint heard a door open, then a woman's voice call down the stairs.

"Vinnie, you down there?"

"Yes, mom," he called back. He sounded annoyed, like a ten-year old answering his mother.

"Is your friend still there?"

"Yes, mom."

"Okay," she said. Clint heard the door close. Now he had a profile of Vince Gleason: a twenty-something who was really an overgrown teenager, pretending to be independent but still living in his parent's basement, probably living off them, spending all his free time researching football history and trivia. He probably never had a girlfriend; probably worked at some mundane job. But he sounded convincing when he talked about football's early days. That's all that mattered to Clint.

"I can see why this tournament only drew eleven teams, and none of the top teams," Vince said. Once again he gave Clint his "how about that" look. It was probably an unconscious mannerism, a physical exclamation point highlighting a profound insight. Clint knew the routine now.

"Why?"

"It had too many things working against it. It was played too early. Only the winner got paid. And if the organizers didn't send out invitations, if they just relied on an announcement in their newspaper, then a lot of teams probably didn't even know about it. You said the *Sentry* was in financial trouble?"

"That's what the mircofilm guy said."

"I'll bet they weren't selling many papers." Vince shook his head. "It's like this newspaper didn't know how to organize a first-class football tournament."

"Maybe they organized it in a hurry."

"It's too bad. It would've been cool to have one of the first football championships played here."

Clint glanced at his watch. He was ready to wrap it up. "You gave me lots of information, just not the piece I need. Can you help with that?"

"Like I said, I never saw anything in print about this tournament until now. But you really got me curious. I can't wait to dig into it."

"You have my number," Clint said. "Call me if you find anything."

Chapter Six
Monday, September 16, 1974

Olivia Foley slowly worked her way into Clint's consciousness. Soon he was thinking about her several times a day - reliving snippets of conversation, picturing her face and body, wondering about her. What was she doing? Was she seeing anyone? Then he found a sheet of paper with her phone number. He was reluctant to call. The paper laid on the coffee table for a few days, pretty handwriting enticing him to pick up the phone. It had been a few months since his last contact with her. Even then he didn't get to know her very well. Their relationship had been strictly business. Finally, he fell back on the old Army credo: "No guts, no glory." He dialed her number.

Olivia remembered him. They chatted for awhile, caught each other up on their lives. She agreed to meet him. She had to give him directions because Clint said he was still learning the city.

"I have to warn you," Olivia said, "I'll be working."

Clint would not have recognized her except for the lithe build and the purposeful way she carried herself. He expected a blonde with a short, stylish haircut. Instead, he found a girl with a cascade of red ringlets and locks on her head. A man had dropped her off and driven away. Standing in the parking lot, Olivia craned her neck and looked for something or someone familiar. She was wearing tiny pink hot pants and a purple tube top under a gauzy blouse that was mostly unbuttoned. She carried a large crocheted shoulder bag. Clint got out of his car and called her name. She teetered toward him on high platform shoes, irritation etched on her face.

"Don't call me by name," she scolded. "When I'm working, call me Crystal."

"Okay, Crystal."

She jerked her head toward the restaurant. "Look, I don't want to go in there. Get something and bring it out."

Clint opened the passenger door for her. "What do you want?"

"A hamburger and a diet drink."

A few minutes later, Clint got behind the wheel. He handed a paper bag and a drink to her. She settled back into the seat and took a long sip through the straw. The aroma of hamburgers and fries filled the car. Her eyes darted around the interior.

"What kind of car is this?" Olivia said.

"Javelin AMX. 1971. Four hundred and one cubic inch V8. Four barrel carburetor. Puts out three hundred thirty five horses at five thousand RPM. It'll do a quarter mile from a standing start in fourteen and a half seconds."

"You selling it to me?"

"Normally I wouldn't tell a girl all that. I thought you could appreciate it."

"I didn't know the Pittsburgh PD hired girls."

Did Clint hear mock indignation or the real thing? He caught himself about to turn her words around, almost making a crack about girls for hire.

"Did I say girl? I meant female."

Olivia took another sip. She seemed content with his quasi-apology. She turned her attention back to the car.

"It looks like a Mustang with bulging fenders."

"You don't see many of 'em. That's why I like it." Clint opened his bag. "How's business?"

"Good."

"I'm not surprised. You're hot bait."

Olivia twisted her mouth. She had large blue eyes, a small chin and cupid's bow lips. Today she was wearing bright red lipstick and heavy eyeliner and mascara that exaggerated the size of her eyes. If she had a soft look in her eyes, Olivia would have appeared waif-like. Softness was something Clint had never seen in those eyes. He had seen mirth, curiosity, impatience, determination, even toughness, but never softness.

"It's part of the job," she said.

"How long you been in vice?"

"A couple of months."

"That was a fast move. You just got sworn in."

"I didn't ask for it. One day my supervisor called me to his office and said they wanted to reassign me. I simply said 'Yes sir' and saluted smartly."

"What's keeping vice busy these days?"

"Prostitution, as you can see. Drugs, gambling, the usual. Gambling's a top priority. Ever since the Steelers started winning, there's been a big spike in business for the bookies. Lately one of the loan sharks has been building a reputation for himself. His goons have beaten a couple of his delinquent customers half to death with baseball bats - and that was their first warning. God knows what will happen to them if they don't pay up. How's PI work?"

"I'm working on a case I got from lawyer named Michael Walsh. You familiar with him?" Clint said.

"I heard of him."

"It's an estate settlement. The guy put the prize money from a football tournament into a personal savings account and forgot about it. His will directs that the money be awarded to the survivors of the winning team. My job is to find out who won."

"How hard can that be?"

"That's what I thought. The tournament was played sixty-eight years ago. It was organized by a newspaper called the *Sentry*, which happened to be struggling financially. Here's where it goes off-track. The publisher of the newspaper died on the day the tournament championship was played. His body was found in the river with a gunshot wound to the head. The paper immediately ceased publication. So there's no record of who won."

"The man with the prize money in his account, he didn't win it."

"No."

"What's it doing in his account?"

"He put it there for safe-keeping."

"Was he supposed to do that?"

"He was holding it until he could get it to the winner."

"Did you check other newspapers?"

"Every one. There must have been ten dailies in Pittsburgh back then. None of them covered the tournament. Apparently they saw it as a publicity stunt by one of their competitors. Also, it was billed as a world championship, but it only drew some local teams. Maybe they didn't think it wasn't worth covering."

"How did the publisher end up shot in the head?"

"I don't know. His death is not relevant to my investigation, other than the fact that it led to the demise of his newspaper."

Olivia finished the hamburger, balled up the wrapper and tossed it in the bag. She lowered the visor and checked her make-up in the vanity mirror. "I look like a damn clown," she said. "You really think I look hot?"

"You've looked better."

She raised the visor. "What else have you tried?"

"I interviewed an amateur football historian. He knows everything there is to know about the early days of football, and I mean everything, but he doesn't know a thing about this tournament. Says he heard rumors about it, that's all. That's how obscure it is."

"How much money's involved?"

"It was eight grand when it went into the bank. It's grown to almost sixty-four thousand."

"That'll be a nice prize for someone."

"There's another angle, but I don't know what it means. The publisher is the great-uncle of a city councilman. He wants to be informed of the results of my investigation before I release them."

"You think it has something to do with the publisher's death?"

"This all happened sixty-eight years ago," Clint said. "How could it matter today?"

"Could he be after the money?"

"The will's pretty clear about who gets it, even if there are no survivors."

Olivia shifted sideways facing Clint and pulled her feet up onto the seat. She wrapped her arms around her knees. Clint noticed the red polish on her fingernails and toenails matched her lipstick.

"So, you got a case that involves one of the big three."

"The big three?"

"Yeah, the big three - substance abuse, money and sex. The motive for every crime is usually one or more of those."

"I don't know if a crime is involved."

"You got a sports tournament - a golden opportunity for gambling, a man with a fatal head shot, and another one who squirreled away the prize money," Olivia said. "You don't think something criminal happened? At a minimum, it sounds like someone committed embezzlement."

"Whatever else may have happened, my job is to find out who won that money, and I'm at a dead end."

"I heard the department uses a psychic sometimes when a case goes cold. They usually go to her for deaths and missing persons."

"A psychic?" Clint said. "The cutting edge of criminal science."

"Okay. How often do detectives use hunches and intuition? Anyway, she's wrong nine out of ten times, but when she's right, she's spot on. Plus she doesn't charge for her services."

A lull in the conversation. Clint quickly finished his lunch. He glanced at Olivia. She looked relaxed, her arms still wrapped around her knees. She seemed to be studying him. He remembered doing a double-take the first time he saw her during police training. Then he gave her a long, admiring look. Things just got interesting, he thought to himself back then. She was built like a gymnast - firm muscles, small breasts, tight round bottom. She carried herself like one, too, holding her shoulders back and her chin up. She was confident, upbeat, a quick talker but not too talkative. Unlike most women, she could trade jibes with the guys. She seemed to enjoy the give and take, judging by the gleam in her eyes. If I wasn't already spoken for, Clint thought...

"Clint, why did you drop out of training?" she said. "You were number one in physical fitness, number one in marksmanship, number one in academics..."

"Number two in self-defense, thanks to the way you threw me."

"It was just a matter of leverage."

"And you having a black belt in some martial art that no one can pronounce."

Olivia smiled briefly. "You had all that experience from your CID days," she said. "You had a great career in front of you. We couldn't figure out why you left. You didn't tell anybody anything. One day you were just...gone."

Clint thought for a few moments. He wanted to give a truthful answer without sounding pathetic.

"I followed a woman to Pittsburgh because I thought we were going to get married," he said quickly. "Becoming a city cop was part of our plan together. When she changed her mind about me, I changed my mind about being a policeman."

"Sorry. I didn't realize it was so personal."

"It's all behind me now."

Another lull in the conversation. Clint hoped Olivia would drop the topic. He wasn't comfortable talking about himself, especially his personal life.

"Why did you call me?" she said.

"I thought we had a good relationship during training," Clint said.

"Former military have to stick together."

"I felt it was more than a service bond."

Clint noticed the momentary look of surprise on her face.

"Why didn't you call me sooner?" she asked.

"I just found our study group list.

"I'm in the phone book."

Clint stared through the windshield at some distant object. He tapped his fingers on the top of the steering wheel, revisiting an event he had not yet come to grips with.

"I needed some time…"

"I understand," Olivia said softly. "Believe me, I understand."

Suddenly she uncurled and put her feet back on the floor of the car.

"Is it one yet?"

"Almost."

"I gotta get back to my corner. Can you take me there?"

Clint started the car, pulled out of the parking lot and worked his way through the mid-day traffic. He clicked on the radio. The sports report was on: "In NFL action yesterday, the Steelers opened the season by defeating the Baltimore Colts 30 to nothing. Quarterback Joe Gilliam completed 17 of 31 passes for 257 yards and 2 touchdowns…"

"Go Steelers!" Olivia said.
"You like football?" Clint said.
"I'm a Pittsburgh girl. I like the Steelers. What about you?"
"I'm not a Steelers fan, and I thought the Pittsburgh PD didn't hire girls."
"I'll call myself what I want. Woman's prerogative. You should know that. Do you have a team?"
"I'm from Baltimore."
"Well, you've had plenty to cheer about. Now it's our turn."
They arrived at the seedy intersection where the police had set up the sting operation.
"This is perfect. I've been gone about an hour. Everybody'll see me get out of your car..."
"They'll think I'm a customer."
"You're lucky we didn't meet a few weeks ago. Some moral crusaders were out here taking pictures of the prostitutes and johns. They screwed up the whole operation."
Olivia reached into her bag. She started talking loudly, like there was someone besides Clint in the car. "Leave this one alone," she said. "He's a friend."
Startled, Clint glanced at her. Was she was losing her mind? Suddenly confronting an inner demon or something? Then it clicked.
"You wearing a wire?" he said.
"It's in the bag."
"Did they hear what we were talking about?" Clint pictured a couple of bored vice cops sitting in a car eating homemade sandwiches, being entertained by the details of his investigation, snickering at his break-up woes and small talk with Olivia. He was glad he didn't talk much about the break-up.
"No. I just turned it back on."
Clint looked for the car that dropped Olivia off at the restaurant. He spotted it parked along the curb, a discrete distance from the corner but with a clear line of sight.
"I'll call you with the phone number for the psychic," Olivia said as she opened the door. "She might be able to help."

"If she's any good, she'll be expecting to hear from me," Clint said.

Chapter Seven
Monday Evening, September 16, 1974

Clint returned home and checked his answering machine. The recording a caller heard stated the number they had reached and requested they leave a message. There was no mention of Clint's name or a private investigation service. Sometimes concealing his identity was an effective investigative tactic. Clint generally had Mike Walsh's cases call him at the law office. He would stop in or telephone Karen a few times a day for updates.

The first voice was a male who seemed confused by the vagueness of the answering machine recording.

"Hello, uh, Mr. Ronson. I assume this is Mr. Ronson's number. This is Thomas DeAngelo. I trust you're busy working on the Prentiss case. It's been a week and I haven't heard from you. I'd like to know how the investigation is going. Please call me back."

Don't hold your breath, Clint thought. The next few messages were related to Clint's other cases. He listened. He took notes. Then he heard a female voice.

"Hi Clint. This is Olivia. The psychic I mentioned is named Elena Ivanova. She's a Russian Orthodox mystic. Apparently she's very religious. She believes her psychic powers are a gift from God. As I said, she doesn't charge for the service she renders to the police department."

Olivia provided Elena's phone number and address. The message ended. Clint opened a drawer under the counter to get piece of paper and something to write with. He picked up a few pencils before he found one with a point. Something shiny and sparkling in the drawer caught his attention. Clint rewound the tape for a few seconds so he could copy Elena's contact information. Then he picked up the engagement ring.

It was a pretty thing. The diamond was almost a half carat, round brilliant shape, set on a simple gold band. The jewelry store salesman assured Clint the cut, color and clarity were exceptional. Clint nodded as he studied the stone through the loupe. He didn't know anything about the 4Cs, but the diamond's kaleidoscopic sparkle was cool to look at under magnification. He was sure Gina would be thrilled.

Clint had met Gina in one of his classes. She was a junior, like him. She was friendly and talkative, a coed with big breasts, full hips, thick brunette hair, a toothsome smile and brown eyes that melted Clint's heart. Like Clint, she was a criminal justice major, but with a vague ambition of becoming a lawyer. Small talk quickly progressed to dating and then to sex. It was sex unlike anything Clint had experienced before - furious, clothes-tearing, devouring, bed-wrecking carnal grappling. Gina found it as irresistible as Clint. Before he knew it, she was spending almost every night at his apartment.

Gina was a conventional girl. Going to college at Frostburg, out-of-state and a hundred plus miles from her home in Pittsburgh, was the range of her rebellion. She was relishing her freedom from what she called her "smothering family," and she was dipping her toes into forbidden waters. Clint - seven years older, worldly, ex-paratrooper, ex-special agent, Vietnam vet - had the aura of excitement that made her heart patter. For his part - call it love, lust, whatever - Clint was head over heels for the vivacious, voluptuous beauty. The hell with being a federal agent. All he wanted now was to follow her to Pittsburgh or wherever she wanted to go and live happily ever after. Over spring break of their senior year he proposed. She accepted. He applied to the Pittsburgh Police Department. He would put his criminal justice education and CID expertise to work as a city cop.

Gina moved back in with her family while she looked for a job. Clint found an apartment on the edge of the city. They put their wedding plans on hold until Clint finished police training.

Clint began training in June, back to a regimen that was familiar but growing tiresome. The cadets showed up at 5:30 AM to prepare their facility for inspection at six. Physical training came next. The first few weeks, PT lasted for hours. It was the same as army PT - calisthenics and strength-building exercises in formation, an obstacle course, running in formation with jody calls, general harassment. For some of cadets the experience was close to overwhelming. For Clint, it was a replay of basic, AIT, the Apprentice Special Agent Course, and WOCS. After a short break for personal hygiene and breakfast, training resumed. There was firearms and marksmanship, self-defense and law enforcement classes. Throw in some formations, tests or quizzes, a uniform inspection and some standing around and waiting (just like the army) and the day stretched on until 6 PM, sometimes later. In the evenings and on the weekends, Clint had homework assignments to complete and studying to do.

In the meantime, for Gina, their once torrid affair seemed to evaporate like a vacation fling. Was it the change in their situation? Her smothering family? Buyer's remorse? An old flame? Clint encouraged her to hang on. They could talk things out when the pace of training slowed, when he had the time and energy.

One evening he came home and found a letter from her with a small lump inside. She had sent him a Dear John and returned the engagement ring, wrapped in tissue paper. A Dear John letter from his fiancée. Not a face-to-face break-up. Not even a phone call. The letter was longer than it needed to be, full of heart-wrenching apologies and reassurances that it was all her fault, that it wasn't anything Clint had done. He read it once and tossed it in the garbage. He dropped the ring into the kitchen drawer.

Clint grimly soldiered on through the rest of the week's training, oblivious to the gaping wound. On Saturday morning he lay in bed, hands interlaced behind his head; staring at the ceiling and wondering what to do next.

On Monday he resigned from police training.

Clint held the ring between his thumb and forefinger, turning it to look at it at from different angles. He told himself he needed to sell it back to the jewelry store or pawn it. He had too much money tied up in it to let the ring lay in a drawer. He glanced at his watch. Clint decided to call Elena the following morning.

Tuesday, September 17, 1974

At 9:30 AM Clint dialed the number. A woman answered. Clint identified himself and said he was calling for Elena Ivanova. He explained that the Pittsburgh police department had suggested he contact her, that she might be able to help with his case.

"The police department recommended me?" Elena said suspiciously. Her soft Russian accent was pleasing for Clint to listen to. It reminded him of the way German girls spoke English back when he was in the FRG.

"Yes. I work with them on some of my cases." Clint knew he was stretching the truth. The police department did not recommend her; one of its employees did - unofficially. And he had never worked directly with them. Sometimes one of his investigations ran parallel to one of theirs. Sometimes they intersected. It all depended on how you defined the word "with." Clint wondered if somehow she knew all this.

"Is this police case?"

"It's a legal investigation."

"How can I be of help to you with this...legal investigation?" Clint heard disdain in the way she pronounced the last two words.

"I'm trying to find the rightful recipients of a sum of money," Clint began. He then told Elena about the provision in Prentiss' will and the tournament and how the *Sentry* ceased publication on the day it should have printed the tournament results and how no other newspaper covered the tournament.

"Your investigation is very different from the usual police requests," she said.

"Yes, it is." Clint tried his best to be tactful. He was looking for a favor. Elena already sounded skeptical. He didn't want to come across as a pushy client or add to her doubts in any other way.

"You think I can tell you who won this football contest?"

Clint detected irritation. Did she think his request trivialized her gift, reducing her to a sort of sports prognosticator? Did she see through the half-truths he used to make it sound legitimate?

"I would greatly appreciate any help you can give me," he said with all the humility he could muster. There was a long silence on the other end of the line.

"Very well," Elena said in a voice that sounded like a sigh. "Come to my house. Bring something with you that's related to the case. Anything. A photograph. An article of clothing. Somehow that seems to help."

Enroute to Elena's home in Squirrel Hill, Clint stopped at a library to make copies of the relevant newspaper articles - the announcement for the tournament, the reports on the Fighting Irish and the Monessen Terrors, and the article on the semi-final game between the Fighting Irish and Ambridge with its brief mention of Monessen defeating Waylan. As an afterthought, he copied the story about the death of William Harris.

Talking to Elena on the phone, Clint pictured her as a babushka, a dumpling of a grandmother, probably wearing a shapeless dress, heavy black shoes and a head scarf. Her accent and reputation for religious fervor likely created the unflattering image. The woman who answered the door did not match the stereotype at all. She was fortyish, tall and attractive. She had strong cheekbones, long dark hair pulled back, and cat-like green eyes under thick eyebrows. Elena invited Clint into the living room. As he followed close behind her, he noticed the faint fragrance of her perfume, exotic and intoxicating.

Clint felt like he had walked into a Middle Age monastery. Dense drapes blocked most of the daylight. A bookcase stood against one wall, the books and ornaments meticulously arranged. A sofa and a pair of chairs and end tables were arranged around a thick oriental rug with a coffee table in the middle. The tables were made of heavy, dark wood. The chairs and sofa had legs that looked like lion's paws gripping globes. Four large icons hung on the walls. Solemn, medieval-looking faces seemed to stare at him from around the room - Madonna and Child, Jesus with a thin nose and vaguely oriental features, two figures Clint couldn't identify, probably saints. An ornate crucifix hung near a corner with a stand of votive candles and a kneeler beneath it.

"What did you bring?" Elena said. Clint handed her a folder with the copies. She quietly read them. Clint breathed in her scent while he waited. He noticed her perfectly manicured hands, her nice figure. Clint liked how women in their forties could be so poised and self-assured. If they retained their looks, like Elena had, it was an appealing combination. Clint was twenty-nine. With women like Elena in the world, he had something to look forward to. Then he wondered if he would see some indication of her psychic powers. Would she close her eyes to conjure deep thoughts? Would she go into a trance?

Nothing like that happened. She was completely calm and expressionless as she read. Elena turned to the last article, the one about Harris' death. Surely, Clint thought, she would express some emotion now - a look of surprise or shock, at least a furrowed brow. But she remained impassive. She finished reading and placed the folder on an end table.

"If I have information, I will contact you," she said calmly.

Clint was surprised. The meeting was so quick and seemed so insubstantial. Elena didn't even ask any questions.

"How long will it take?" he asked eagerly. She led him to the door.

"Sometimes, not long," she said. "Sometimes, nothing."

That afternoon, Clint stopped by his apartment to check his phone messages. When he heard the soft female voice with the Russian accent, excitement surged through him. He immediately dialed Elena's number.

"Have you considered visiting McCann's Bar and Grill?" she said.

"Why?"

"Your newspaper story, it said one of the teams belonged to a tavern called McCann's."

"Did you receive a message about it?"

"What do you mean by message? No. I looked in phone book. There is a place with such a name. It's worth a try."

Chapter Eight
Thursday, September 13, 1906

"Look what the cat drug in," Sam said to the two men settling down on barstools. One was built like a bear. The other was rail-thin with hooded eyelids, a tangle of black hair and a nervous knee. The big man dug into his pocket. He dumped some change out of his thick hand onto the bar. Sam put mugs of beer in front of them. The man looked around the saloon. The place was gray and quiet. Fading daylight barely shone through the windows. Sam already had some kerosene lamps burning to provide illumination. A few millworkers sat in the shadows, holdovers from the crowd that had poured in earlier.

"Haven't seen you two in awhile," Sam said. He had a round face with ruddy cheeks, small dark eyes, and a wide, bushy mustache. He wore a white shirt with a narrow black bow tie. Tom once asked him why he always dressed like that in a workingman's saloon. Sam said his customers deserved some high class service with their cold beer.

"We've had football practice," Tom said.

"Football? It's still baseball season."

"It's baseball weather, that's for sure," Eddie said, barely lowering the mug from his lips.

"Jesse entered us in an early tournament."

"I heard something about that," Sam said. "No practice today?"

"We just finished." Eddie said.

"We're leaving tomorrow," Tom said. "Jesse put us on a ration; one beer on days before games. We have to get our fill for the weekend tonight."

Eddie plunked his mug down on the bar. "I'm ready for another."

"You thirsty, Eddie-boy?" Tom said.

"Tired, too. You saw how hard Jesse ran me."

"If you'd have caught more of Gus's passes, we wouldn't have practiced the play so much."

"Did you see where he was throwing them? Over my head, way to my left, way to my right, at my shoe laces. Nobody could catch those."

"You think it's going to be any different in a game?"

"Gus would be crazy to try a pass in a game."

Sam pulled the handle on the beer engine and angled Eddie's mug under the tap. He tilted his head to the side to watch the flow of brew. "Where's this tournament being played?" he said.

"In Dunbar," Eddie said.

"Dunbar? Why not a bigger town?"

"We're playing at the county fair," Tom said. "First round's on Saturday. Five games. One every two hours starting at eight. We play at noon. Second round's on Sunday."

"Sunday's the championship?" Sam sat Eddie's beer in front of him.

"No. The semi-final and final rounds are the following weekend. At the Westmoreland County Fair."

"Who's playing?" Sam said.

"There's eleven teams," Tom said. "Eight from western Pennsylvania, two from West Virginia, and one from Ohio. They wanted sixteen teams."

"We heard of about half the teams," Eddie said. "All of them small-time clubs."

"One's a college team," Tom said. "None of the big teams, like Lyceum and Latrobe, are playing. No big colleges either."

"Yeah - Lyceum, Latrobe, Greensburg, Massillon - none of them are in it," Eddie said.

"They're calling it the world championship," Tom said. "That's a bold claim for a tournament of ordinary teams."

"Anything to sell tickets," Sam said.

"You won't believe what the prize money is," Tom said. "Eight thousand dollars. Winner takes all."

"You're kidding."

"I'm not kidding. Eight thousand dollars."

"I'm surprised more teams aren't in it, just for a chance at the money," Sam said.

"Me, too."

Tad Crowell and three other players piled into the saloon, talking and laughing loudly. Tad saw Tom and Eddie.

"How'd you two get here so fast," he shouted.

"I know a shortcut," Eddie shouted back.

"Well, find a shortcut to this table and bring a couple a pails with you."

Sam filled two pails and gave them to Eddie, one in each hand. Then he reached under the bar and sat four mugs on top.

"Lemme help you there," Tom said. He scooped up the mugs along with Eddie's and followed him to the table.

"You're not drinking with us?" Crowell said.

Tom pointed a thumb over his shoulder toward the bar. "I'm talking to Sam."

"Give him our regards," Crowell said.

Back at the bar, Tom said to Sam, "The reason more teams aren't entered, Jesse thinks either it's too early for most of 'em, or it wasn't advertised well enough." He took a sip of beer. "You see the *Pittsburgh Sentry* this week?"

"No."

"They got exclusive coverage on the tournament. They had stories on all the teams. Did a nice write-up on us."

"I'll make a point to look at it while this thing's going on."

"Get a few copies in here. Some of your customers might be interested."

"Yeah, the one's that can read."

"Jesse thinks we're better than any of the teams he recognizes," Tom said. "All things being equal, he figures we have a seven out of ten chance of advancing. He said that was good enough odds to justify booking hotel rooms for two nights."

"Where you staying?" Sam said.

"In Connellsville. Closest big town to Dunbar."

"I been looking forward to football season. If you make it to the semi-finals, maybe I'll go up and watch you play. Let my daughter run the saloon for a day...Excuse me for a minute."

Sam moved down the bar to some new customers. Tom watched him serve beers, make change, act like he was interested in something one of the customers was saying. Being a saloonkeeper meant being a good listener, which meant listening to some dull talk - meaningless chit-chat, topics Sam couldn't give a hoot about, the incoherent rambling of drunks. "Everyone who sits at this bar thinks I want to hear their story," he once said to Tom. "It's amazing it don't drive me to drink." One thing Sam liked to talk about was football. Tom knew it. He also knew that if the conversation was interesting, Sam would serve free drinks to keep it going. Anything to avoid the dull talk.

Behind him, Tom heard bursts of laughter coming from Eddie and the other three players. He saw Tad, red-faced and nearly hysterical from a story he was telling. Another wild burst of laughter. Tom turned back and nursed his beer. After awhile, Sam came back.

"One game last year," Sam said, "I remember the big back...what's his name?"

"Billy Pallister."

"Yeah, Pallister. He was carrying the ball. He was surrounded by the team, pushing him forward, holding him upright. Seemed like the whole other team was pushing back, trying to stop him. Just a big pack of players pushing against each other with Pallister in the middle. I was thinking 'Oh my God, he's going to get crushed.'"

Tom nodded, trying to think of the game Sam was talking about. A big scrum like that happened in almost every game.

"Then you plowed into the pack. I mean you hit it with such force you pushed the whole thing forward a couple a feet. A few defenders fell down. Then a few more fell over them. Suddenly Pallister broke free. I can still picture him: twisting his shoulders, throwing his elbows, knocking friend and foe away. Then he was off to the races. I tell you, that was exciting to watch."

Pallister breaking free and making a long run to score, that only happened once last year.

"Sounds like the California YMCA game," Tom said.

"Coulda been."

FROM THE ANTHEM CITY

"You won't see anything like that this year. They changed the rules. Players can't assist the ball carrier anymore."
"What?"
"You can block for him, but you can't push him or hold him up when he's being tackled."
"How come?"
"Too many players did get crushed," Tom said.
"Too many players were getting injured?" Sam said.
"Too many players were getting killed. Roosevelt said make football safer or he would ban it. So the college teams got together and rewrote the rules."
"If the President got involved, things must've been bad."
"You can't assist the runner anymore, but now you can throw a forward pass," Tom said.
"A what?" Sam said.
"You can throw the ball to one of your players across the line of scrimmage. It's supposed to open the game up. Keep the players from packing around the runner, like you were talking about."
"If a forward pass looks like a kick-off or a punt, that'll be exciting - watching the man who catches the ball try to dodge all the tacklers."
"Let me show you how the new rules changed the game," Tom said. "Give me some coins."
Tom knew Sam was fascinated by football formations and plays. Maybe diagramming a few would inspire him to serve that free beer. Sam went over to the till and scooped up a handful of nickels. He poured them in front of Tom. Tom flicked eleven to one side. He turned them so they all had the Roman numeral "V" facing up. Then he sorted out eleven more and turned the liberty heads up. He made sure the liberty heads and V's were all aligned in the same direction. Sam leaned in to see better.
"We use two offensive formations," Tom said. "We call this one the regular formation." Tom moved the V-sided coins into a "T" formation with seven men on the line and the three running backs positioned behind the quarterback.

"The other one is the tackle-back formation. One tackle moves into the backfield as the lead tackle. He's mainly a blocker for run plays, but he can carry the ball, too." Tom slid a halfback wide, outside the line. "If you only have six men on the line, you have to move a halfback to a wingback position."

"That looks like a more powerful formation if you're running the ball to the side where the wingback is."

"You're right."

"And the other formation looked more balanced."

"You're right again...On defense, we have seven linemen." Tom placed the liberty head nickels against the tackle-back formation. "Backing the line are two defensive backs. Two more backs play about twenty-five yards deep. Last year, we had three defensive backs behind the line and only one deep. Jesse changed it this year to help protect against those forward passes."

The tackle-back formation and the defense looked like this:

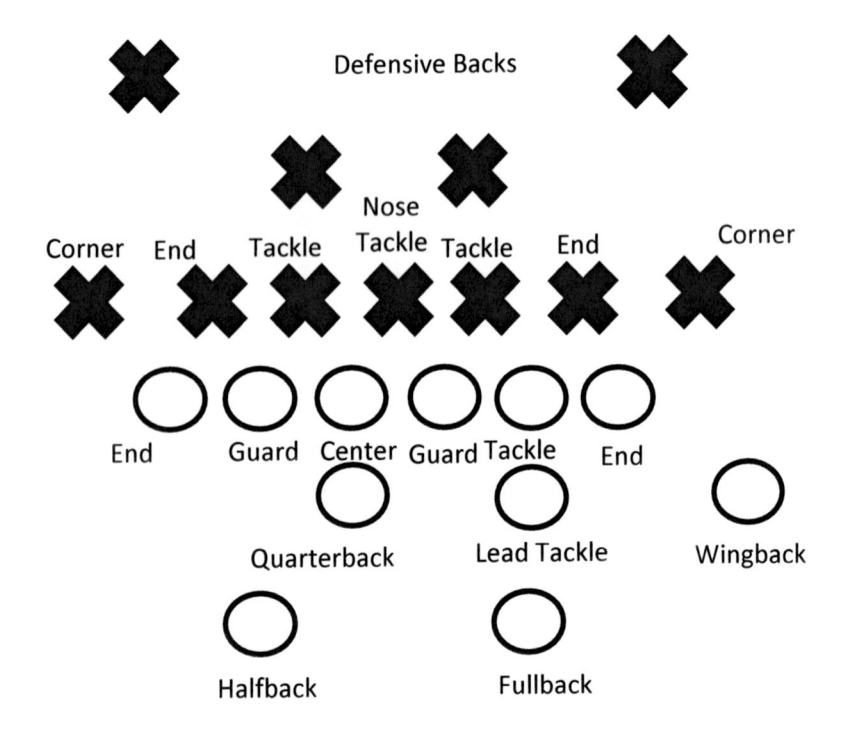

```
     ✖              Defensive Backs              ✖

                    ✖         ✖
                          Nose
Corner   End    Tackle  Tackle  Tackle   End           Corner
   ✖      ✖       ✖       ✖       ✖      ✖              ✖

          ◯      ◯      ◯      ◯      ◯      ◯
         End    Guard  Center  Guard  Tackle   End
                                        ◯              ◯
                   Quarterback       Lead Tackle    Wingback
           ◯                          ◯
         Halfback                   Fullback
```

"Our strongest play is the mass run," Tom said. "We only do this play from the tackle back formation. The idea is to hit the defense on the end of its line, that's where they're weakest, and overwhelm them. Last year, the other backs ran alongside the ball carrier to assist him." Tom slid the coins to depict the play. "This year, the other backs run in front of him to block."

Tom repositioned the nickels into the regular formation. He went through the plays, sliding the coins to show player movement.

"There's a plunge, in which the ball carrier runs straight ahead into the line. The linemen block their opponents out of the way to make a hole. A buck is like a plunge, except another back leads the ball carrier through the hole. Then there's a cross-buck. Gus, he's our quarterback, fakes a hand-off to the fullback who plunges into one side of the line. Then he hands the ball to a back running a buck into the other side."

"A little trickery there," Sam said.

"Exactly. The end run is like a cross-buck, except Gus pitches the ball to a back who runs to the outside. We have two more plays that we only run out of the tackle back formation." Tom quickly moved the coins with his index finger. "One is the pass play. The other is the on-side kick."

"How does everyone know which play to run?"

"Signals," Tom said. "Each formation has a letter and each play is numbered. Gus calls out the letter and then four numbers. Before the game, Jesse tells us which of the four numbers is the live number. That's the one for the play."

"Clever," Sam said, shaking his head.

"Sometimes Jesse gives us a sequence of four or five plays to start the game. Gus doesn't need to call the signals. We just line up and run the plays as fast as we can. Gets the game flowing our way."

"There's more than meets the eye with this game," Sam said, "The strategy, the tricks, how every play is designed like a little battle plan."

"That's why I like it," Tom said.

Tom heard a loud noise over his shoulder. He turned on the bar stool. Eddie had stumbled over a chair.

"Welcome back, Eddie. The party over?"

He held up the two pails. "The beer's gone. The boys're going home."

"Look at you, all wobbly-legs and red eyes, tripping over chairs," Tom said.

"I didn't see it," Eddie said. "It's kinda dark in here." He put the pails on the bar.

"Let me get you one last round," Sam said. "My treat. How 'bout a black and brown. I'll have one with you. It's almost closing time. We'll drink a toast to your success."

As he pulled the beers, Sam said, "My neighbor's son wants to play on your team next year."

"How old is he?" Tom said.

"I think he's seventeen. He's a big fellow. Built like his mother. My brother's talking about playing, too."

"Isn't he kind of old for football?"

"Ever since he started hanging around with that woman, he's been acting half his age."

"Isn't she half his age?"

"At least."

Sam placed a mug in front of Tom. Tom held it up and examined it. Two layers of beer with barely any blending where the layers met. The bottom one, the ale, had a dark copper color, like strong tea. The porter on top was black and silky-looking. Sam came back with two more mugs.

"How do you pour one beer on top the other and not mix them up?" Tom said. Eddie laid his head on the bar to peer at the layers in his mug.

"Trade secret," Sam said. He held up his mug. "Let's drink to a good tournament."

"To big wins and a big prize," Tom said. The three clinked mugs and took long sips. Tom held up his mug again. The two layers were now swirling together. He savored the taste.

"That's nice," Tom said.

Sam wiped his lips. "What do you do to get ready for a competition like this?"

"Practice," Eddie said. "We been practicing for about three weeks."
"Everyday?"
"No. Three days a week, for about two hours."
"We have seventeen players," Tom said. "Jesse gets mad because only two-thirds of 'em show up regularly. He says we'd be a better team if we had more dedication."
"He takes it out on the ones who do show up," Eddie said. "He works us like dogs."
"Turn out was pretty good this week since we got a game coming up," Tom said.
"What do you do at practice?"
"We start with some stretching and calisthenics," Tom said. "Then Jesse has us rehearse those plays over and over until we run them perfectly."
"The best part is scrimmaging," Eddie said.
"But Jesse doesn't like to do it too much," Tom said. "He's afraid someone will get injured."
"We pester him until he gives in," Eddie said. "We tell him we need to do some real blocking and tackling or we won't be ready."
"Sometimes we hit the charging machine," Tom said.
"What's a charging machine?"
"Picture a low wall, about twenty feet long, securely mounted on the front of a sled that's about five feet deep," Tom said. "The sled has rollers. Jesse lines six players up facing the wall. At his signal, they charge out of their stances, hit the wall with their arms straight out, and push the machine back."
"There's some other players sitting on the sled as ballast," Eddie said. "You have to really drive with your legs to push all that weight."
"Toughens you up, huh?" Sam said.
"It really works the legs."
"And the arms and back," Tom said. "It teaches us to use our arms to break through the blockers when we're on defense. When we're on offense, it drills us to explode out of our stances, hit the defensive line in unison like one big punch, and push them back."

"Jesse makes us do it over and over again, yelling at us all the while," Eddie said. "Telling us to stay low and keep our legs pumping. It gets to be torture."

"It pays off," Tom said. "We built the machine and used it for the first time last season. We dominated the line of scrimmage like never before. Then there's the tackling dummy. That's another contraption Jesse had us build."

"It's a big canvas bag stuffed with rags," Eddie said.

"So you can practice tackling," Sam said.

"What else?" Eddie said. Tom noticed Eddie's mug was almost empty. He could drink a lot for being so lanky. When Tom said they were there to drink their fill for the weekend, he was just talking. He really didn't plan to overindulge. From the looks of things, Eddie took it literally.

"This dummy's a moving target, like a real ball carrier," Tom said. "The bag's suspended from a wooden frame by a rope that runs through a pulley. Jesse has one player pull the rope so the bag is hanging free. Then he pushes it to make it to swing."

"He has us get a running start and dive at the bag, ram a shoulder into it and wrap our arms around it," Eddie said.

"You gotta put some force behind it or else you'll make a weak hit," Tom said. "A ball carrier could break free from that kind of tackle."

"Jesse does a lot of yelling for this drill, too," Eddie said. "But I don't care. It's fun. It feels good when you make a clean hit and ride it to the ground."

Eddie put his elbow on the bar and propped his head up. He was starting to look limp.

"Where does Jesse get all these ideas?" Sam said.

"I'll tell you where," Eddie said. "He reads. Every time I see him, he's got a football book."

"He got the idea for the charging machine and the tackling dummy from a book by some college coach," Tom said.

"From Michigan, I think," Eddie said. "He liked that book. He talked about it a lot."

"He doesn't just read the books, he studies them. Even writes down notes," Tom said.

"Jesse's got the new rule book. I guarantee you…" Eddie raised an unsteady arm and pointed at Sam. "I guarantee you he'll know the rules better'n anyone on the field."

"Even the referees?" Sam said.

"Oh yeah." Eddie dropped his arm. "He'll give them hell if they make a bad call."

"And he changed the way we play," Tom said. "Not just to abide by the new rules, but to use them to our advantage."

Eddie pushed his mug toward Sam.

"Another one?" Sam said.

"You gonna fall off that stool, Eddie?" Tom said.

"I'm getting my fill for the weekend."

Tom moved the mug to the side. "You don't want to feel sick tomorrow. That'll make for a miserable train ride." He swallowed the rest of his black and brown. Then he grabbed Eddie's arm and yanked him to his feet. "Let's go."

"Good luck with him," Sam said. "Good luck with the game, too. I expect to see some of that prize money in my saloon."

Chapter Nine
Tuesday, September 17, 1974

Clint hung up the phone. "How could I have been so stupid?" he muttered. McCann's Bar and Grill. That wasn't some sort of psychic revelation. That was just thorough investigative work. He wasn't looking into all the possibilities. He was too fixated on finding a newspaper account. This McCann's might not be connected to the tavern that sponsored the Fighting Irish. If it is, the current proprietors might not know anything about the football team and the tournament. Whatever the case, Clint wouldn't know until he checked.

McCann's was an easy place to overlook. From the street, it was just a door and a window in a one-story row building in the middle of a block. Fluorescent tube lighting in the window spelled out "McCann's Bar and Grill" in red cursive lettering. Clint parked the Javelin and went inside. The interior was just as plain. A bar ran along one side of the room. A dining area consisting of several round tables filled the opposite side. Cheap, dark paneling covered the walls. A few sports posters - Steelers, Pirates, and Penguins - decorated the dining area. The only patrons were three men having a late lunch together. One appeared to be in his seventies, a mean-looking man with thin gray hair, hollow cheeks and glasses. The other two were much younger. One was heavy. He had a round face, perfectly combed dark hair and a mustache. The other had a bald, bullet-shaped dome of a head with a fringe of hair and thick sideburns that extended down to his jawline. The men gave Clint a long stare when he entered - the kind of half-suspicious, half-curious look that regulars give to unfamiliar people who wander into their watering hole. The bartender sat on a stool with a lit cigarette between his thumb and index finger. He held it a few inches from his face, looking like he was studying it.

"Hi. I'm writing a magazine article about a football tournament that was played in the early 1900s," Clint said. There was a grain of truth in his words. Clint had been thinking this case would make a good article, or maybe a book: the story of one of the earliest football championships, the games played in western Pennsylvania, the tournament almost lost to history, the winner unknown. Surely someone in football-mad Pittsburgh would want to read about it. He might make a little money.

The bartender looked unimpressed.

"One of the teams was sponsored by a tavern called McCann's," Clint said. "Back then it was located in Homestead. I'm wondering if there's any connection to this place."

"Could be," the bartender said. "We used to be located in Homestead. We moved here about ten fifteen years ago. And my grandfather had some kind of football team." The bartender slid the cigarette between his index and middle fingers and pointed with it to a framed photo on the wall in the dining area. "That's his picture over there."

Clint walked over to examine the black and white photograph. From the corner of his eye, he noticed the three men watching him.

The photo showed a lean man in a primitive football uniform. He was standing with his hands on his hips, his head cocked slightly to one side. The man looked to be about sixty or sixty-five. He had a taut, weathered face, thick gray hair and fiery eyes. The jersey didn't have sleeve stripes or a number. The only decoration was a harp sewn onto the front. The words "Faugh a Ballagh" were hand-printed along the bottom. Clint wrote them in his notebook and returned to the bar.

"He looks too old to be a football player."

"He's a legend in our family," the bartender said. "He came to New York from Ireland when he was a kid. He fought in the Civil War in some sort of all-Irish unit. Late in his life he moved here, where he had a helluva second act. He opened the tavern in Homestead, took up football, married a woman half his age and started a family."

"What's his name?"

"Patrick McCann."

"Do you know when that picture was taken?"

"A long time ago, that's all I can tell you."
"Do you have any information about his team? Any newspaper articles or anything?" Clint asked.
"What I told you is pretty much all I know."
"What's 'faugh a ballagh' mean?"
"What?"
"'Faugh a ballagh'. The words on the bottom of the picture."
"Oh...I guess it's Irish for football."

The Homestead Fighting Irish of the tournament and Patrick McCann's team were probably one and the same, Clint thought. What were the odds that there were two taverns in Homestead named McCann's, both sponsoring football teams? To confirm the connection, Clint needed to know whether Patrick McCann's team played in 1906. If Patrick had been a soldier in the Civil War, Clint figured he would've been about twenty when he served. That meant he would've been sixty or older between 1901 and 1905. He certainly looked that old in the photograph. The uniform he was wearing looked like it was circa 1906 - coarse baggy pants, high hip protection, a harp hand sewn onto the front of the jersey, lumpy padding underneath. Then Clint remembered that some of the team descriptions in the *Pittsburgh Sentry* contained rosters. The game accounts named key players. If Patrick's name appeared, then the bar and grill had a direct link to the tournament team. He could check later. In the meantime, Clint assumed it did.

"You know anybody else who might know something about your grandfather's team?"

"Nah." The bartender frowned and shrugged. Then he said, "Well, maybe my aunt. She's his oldest child."

"How can I get in touch with her?"

"Well, it's not like I ever heard her talk about it. I never heard anyone talk about it."

Clint knew that nothing inspired improvement like money. Memory, motivation, cooperation. They all got better when money was involved. He didn't want to advertise that he was looking for the rightful owners of a large sum of money. Clint didn't want to attract a bunch of bogus claimants. But this was the most promising lead he had so far. Somebody in the McCann clan might know something.

"There's an interesting subplot to this tournament," Clint said. "The winning team might not have received its prize money. That's one of the stories I'm researching. Anyone with a connection to the winning team might be able to collect."

The bartender paused in the middle of lighting another cigarette. "How much is the prize money?" he asked.

"I'm trying to find out," Clint said. "It could be quite a bit."

The bartender squinted suspiciously.

"Why you telling me all this?"

"Because the McCann's team played in the final."

"Did they win?"

"I'm trying to find that out, too."

"You got a lot of unanswered questions," the bartender said.

"That's why it's going to be a great article," Clint said. "It's a mystery. People love mysteries."

The bartender lit the cigarette, snapped the lighter shut, and took a long draw. Clint caught the crisp scent of freshly burnt tobacco. The bartender exhaled slowly, watching the smoke stream in front of his face. Then he looked at Clint.

"What magazine you writing for?"

"Whichever one pays me the most."

The bartender straightened up and looked over Clint's shoulder.

"You guys need anything else?" he said loudly.

Clint turned slightly so he wasn't blocking the bartender's line of sight. Now he could see the table.

"Nah, we're about done," the old man said in a craggy voice. The round-faced guy and the one with the bullet-shaped head sat quietly, like they were content to let old man speak for them. Maybe he was picking up the tab.

Clint turned to the bartender. "Look, you said your grandfather's a legend in the family. Someone, one of your relatives, might know about his football team. Or they might have old newspaper clippings or something. Talk to them for me. Let them know what I'm looking for. If anyone has anything, they can call me. Here's my number."

Clint tore a sheet of paper out of his notebook. He wrote down his name and phone number, the number with the answering machine that didn't tell callers they had reached a private investigator. He slid it across the bar. The bartender picked it up and examined it.

"Clint Ronson," he read aloud. He looked at Clint. Suddenly he seemed friendlier. Maybe knowing his name meant Clint was no longer a stranger. "My name's Terry McCann. I'll ask around, see if anyone can help you. All I ever heard is that he had a team. I never heard anyone talk about any of their games. But you never know…"

"Thanks," Clint said. "I appreciate it."

Back in his apartment, Clint looked at the newspaper article describing the Fighting Irish. The article contained a team roster. The first name was Paddy McCann.

Chapter Ten
Friday, September 14, 1906

The day before the tournament, Jesse and his team and some supporters boarded a train bound for McKeesport. Most wore their Sunday finest – starched white shirts with ties, jackets, and bowlers. An overnight trip was a special occasion. Eddie curled up in a seat, his bleary face pressed against a window. He fell asleep before the engine pulled away from the platform.

The train clacked along a winding railway between the greenish-brown sluice of the river and mountainsides dense with trees and studded with gray rock outcroppings and cliffs. The players glimpsed steam tugs laboring with barges full of coal or logs. They passed cramped riverside towns similar to their own. Approaching McKeesport, the bucolic landscape quickly turned gritty, urban and industrial.

The team changed trains and chuffed southwest along the Youghiogheny River to Connellsville. They checked into a hotel, two to a room. Tom and Eddie were roommates. Jesse called a team meeting after dinner. Then he imposed a curfew for the evening. No fun for the boys in Connellsville tonight, Tom thought. Jesse was taking this tournament very seriously.

Saturday, September 15, 1906

In the morning, the team travelled to Dunbar by rail. They took a local train that was running a special schedule for the fair. From the train stop, they joined the parade of people making the half mile hike to the fairgrounds.

The team drew stares - seventeen strapping young men wearing sweater-like black jerseys, light brown canvas pants and black stockings. Their pants, stuffed with padding, looked several sizes too large on most of the players. Some of the players had leather panels stitched onto the shoulders of their jerseys for added protection. They dangled their cleats by the laces or draped them around their necks.

A few carried soft leather helmets. Jesse wore his bowler and a jacket, a bag of footballs slung over a shoulder. They called themselves the Black and Brown. The name was partly a reference to their uniform colors, partly homage to the ale and porter concoction at Patrick's Saloon.
"Where you boys from?" a couple of fairgoers asked. Others wished them good luck. Little boys looked on in open-mouthed astonishment as the team walked by. Entering the fairgrounds, the team heard a band playing under a tent. They passed a carousel and a big wheel powered by small steam engines, a dealer selling rides in a motor car, a pony ride, and barkers calling out to lure customers to games of skill and chance. They smelled the aroma of hot dogs, sausages, popcorn, and funnel cakes, the coal smoke from the steam engines, and livestock odors. At the far end of the grounds, a makeshift fence surrounded the football field with a ticket booth at the single entrance. A second fence encircled the field about five yards out from the sidelines and goal lines. There were no stands for the spectators. The organizers hoped the people standing along the inner fence would obstruct visibility enough that the curious would have to buy a ticket.
Tom and Eddie checked out the field. It was regulation - three hundred thirty feet long by one hundred sixty feet wide, and it looked like a checkerboard. Between the goal lines, twenty-one numbered lines ran the width of the field at five yard intervals. The fifty-five yard line marked the center. Eleven more lines ran the length of the field. The two outermost lines were five feet in from the sidelines. The rest were five yards apart. An H-shaped goal post stood at each end of the field. There were no endzones.
"What do you think," Eddie said.
"Not bad for a pasture," Tom said.
"Hope they cleaned it up."
They changed into their cleats and did some stretching. The opposing team warmed-up at the other end of the field. They wore crimson jerseys and stockings with the standard light brown pants.
"A lot of big boys down there," Eddie said.
"They don't look strong," Tom said. "Most of 'em look fat."

Jesse circulated among his players. He stopped at individuals or groups and tried to pep them up.

"Make sure your arm is loose," he said to Gus. "You might get a chance to throw a pass today."

"Hit 'em hard from the first play," he said to some linemen. "We beat them on the line, we beat them in the game. It's that simple."

"Coach, what do you know about these guys?" Tom said when Jesse came near.

"Never heard of 'em," Jesse said. He looked down the field where the Crimson were going through their pre-game routine. "Never heard of 'em," he said again. Then he moved to another group.

"Wait 'til Billy comes running at 'em," Eddie said.

"Then we'll see what they're made of," Tom said.

Halfback Billy Pallister warmed up by himself, jogging across the field with a high-kneed stride. He was stout, with thick, muscular thighs and arms. He resembled a pit bull with his small eyes, flat nose and strong jaw. He wore his hair in homemade bowl cut. Off the field his appearance, build and sullen attitude could be intimidating. On the field, Billy was quick and powerful, instinctive, animalistic. He was the most dangerous Black and Brown player.

The Crimson lined up at the fifty-five to kick off. Fifteen yards away, the Black and Brown eleven spread out over the field to receive. Tom took his place on the forty yard line. He noticed Jesse holding a stopwatch on the sideline, his thumb ready to start the time as soon as the kicker's foot hit the ball.

The ball wobbled through the air toward left side of field, hit the ground, bounced and rolled. Quarterback Gus Webb picked it up and returned it to the forty yard line. Both teams quickly went into their formations. No need to call a play. Jesse had given them a sequence of four plays to open the game. The first was a mass right. The Black and Brown lined up in their tackle-back formation with the wingback on the right. Tom played right guard. Eddie was the end to his right. The tackle was between them. The Crimson put five men on the line with two corners protecting the outsides. Three defensive backs spread out just behind the line, a position that would eventually be called linebacker. One more played deep to provide a margin of safety in case a ball carrier broke through. Gus crouched an arm's length behind center, his hands open and ready. The center passed the ball between his legs. Eddie and the tackle hit the defensive end with an explosive double-team block. All three thudded onto the ground behind Tom's man. Tom fired out from his stance. He drove the defensive tackle backwards until he tumbled over the players on the ground behind him. Tom stayed on his feet. Looking over his right shoulder, he saw the play unfold perfectly. The corner charged across the line to contain the play. The lead tackle and fullback sent him flying with simultaneous hits. The wingback raced through the gap between the double-team blocks to seal the linebacker to the inside. Hard on his heels was Billy at full speed, arms and legs pumping furiously. The Crimson defensive back, their last man, tried to grab a leg. Billy kicked him aside and drove down the field, angling for the center of the goal posts. Good idea, Tom thought. For the kick after goal, the ball would be placed on a line that extended back parallel to the sideline from the point where the ball crossed the goal line. Billy was setting up Tad for an easy attempt.

The Black and Brown's supporters lined the fence behind their bench. They broke into a fight song that sounded like a sea chantey. The one nicknamed The Cheer Leader punched the sky with his bowler and shouted, "Billy's our man, he's full of fight." The others responded with "Hail, hail, the Black and Brown." The Cheer Leader sang, "He hits the line like dynamite." The others replied, "Hail, hail, the Black and Brown." Then all waved their bowlers and joined in the chorus:

Hail, hail, the Black and Brown.
Finest team, all around.
Hail, hail the Black and Brown.
Hold the line, knock 'em down.

Next play: Tom plowed his man onto the ground, falling over him in the process. On hands and knees, he heard the thump of the

kick. He looked up to see the ball sail wide of the uprights. He heard Billy swearing at Tad.
"I put the ball right in the middle of the posts for you."
"And I missed it. So what? I'll hit the next one."
"You better hope we don't lose by a point."
The score was 5 to 0.
Tad's kick-off was an end-over-end beauty straight down the middle of the field. Tom galloped toward the Crimson return man, brushed away a blocker, and arrived a moment after the tackle.
First down at the twenty-five. Breathing hard. Now playing defensive tackle, Tom faced the same Crimson lineman. At the snap, Tom hit him hard, then slid into the gap. Instantly a Crimson player was there, shoulder down, both arms securing the football against his body, legs driving. Tom rammed a shoulder into the player's waist and wrapped his arms around him, just like in the tackling dummy drill. The runner's power drove him backwards. Players immediately swarmed on Tom and the ball-carrier – the Black and Brown trying to finish off the tackle, the Crimson trying to knock them away. Tom was buried inside the crush of bodies, his head and arms pinned against the ball-carrier. He was off-balance; his body twisted awkwardly. The mob rocked back and forth, like a tug-of-war with the opponents pushing instead of pulling. The struggle seemed unending. Tom heard panting, grunting and cursing. He battled to keep his feet digging, to keep up his share of the pushing. The mass of weight and force surged beyond control. Tom lost his footing. The mob crumbled on top of him. After everyone untangled, Tom saw the play had gained nothing.
Second down. Tom blasted past his hapless blocker. The ball-carrier was running across his path, led by two blockers. Tom grabbed him. Using his momentum as leverage, Tom lifted him, spun backwards and hurled him to the ground. The ball squirted free. It bounced crazily toward the goal line. Tom scrambled for it. He scooped it up and dashed fifteen yards to cross the line. He quickly took a knee and touched the ball down. His first score ever.
Tom felt a surge of elation. He wanted to savor the moment, relive it in his mind to preserve every detail, to feel the emotion

again. He wanted to bask in his teammate's adulation. But the game kept moving. The Black and Brown quickly lined up for the kick after goal.

This time Tad's kick was true. The Black and Brown led 11 to 0.

Jogging down the field to line up for the kick-off, Tom's teammates circled around him, congratulating him with handshakes and pats on the back. "That's the way to do it, Hammond," Jesse shouted from the sideline. Tom felt a shiver when he heard the fight song:

Tom's our man, he's full of fight.
Hail, hail, the Black and Brown.
He hits the line like dynamite.
Hail, hail, the Black and Brown.

The thrill of the touchdown was reinvigorating. Tom no longer felt tired. He felt strong. He felt invincible.

On the fifty-five yard line, waiting for Tad's kick, Tom noticed the downcast Crimson players.

"These boys have had enough," Tom said to Eddie.

"What they have is fifty more minutes to play," Eddie said.

Tom's opponent was a big kid with a round face and a body of blubber. He wore a helmet that looked two sizes too small - a leather bowl with ear flaps and a strap that squeezed his chubby cheeks and chin into a jowly bulge. The exertion was killing him. With each play, his cheeks turned redder and redder. His panting grew heavier. Perspiration streamed down his face and ran off his chin. A deep brown sweat stain formed along the front edge of his helmet. Tom hit him with some hard body shots early on to rough him up a little, see how he'd react. The kid was soft. Tom felt like he was running into a dense pillow. The player responded by trying to protect himself - rising up out of his stance instead of firing out if it, using his hands to fend off Tom, giving ground easily.

The kid personified the whole Crimson team, Tom thought. They weren't full of fight. They weren't hitting the line like dynamite, not even like a firecracker. When they had possession, they couldn't move the ball. They would gain only one first down in the half. When the Black and Brown had the ball, they savagely pummeled the Crimson with run after run. Jesse relented on the dogma of punting on first down when his team took possession inside their thirty-five. The Black and Brown could advance the ball from anywhere on the field. Today, Tad would punt far less than his usual thirty kicks per game.

Billy scored another touchdown. More singing and hat-waving from the supporters. Then Gus scored. The Cheer Leader led off with "Gus is our man, he's full of fight." Surprisingly, one of the Black and Brown's drives faltered near the goal line. Tad drop-kicked the ball for a field goal. Another round of the fight song.

Tom jogged up the field to get in position for another kick-off. With the easy scoring and singing the game would be fun, he thought, if it wasn't for the blasted heat and all the running.

On their next possession, the Crimson lost another fumble. A few plays later, Billy scored his third touchdown. By now, the fight song sounded tired. The score at half-time was 33 to 0.

On the sideline, Tom slurped down a ladle of water from one of the buckets. His heart was pounding. He was out of breath. His jersey was sopping wet with sweat. He sat down next to Eddie, who was sprawled on his back.

"Six kick-offs in one half," Tom said.

"I've never heard of six kick-offs in one half," Eddie said.

"I've never been in a game with six kick-offs, not from one team. I'm worn out from running downfield covering those all those kicks."

"I'd be worn out even without the kick-offs. It takes a few games to get into playing shape."

"It's too soon to play football. Like you said, this is baseball weather."

"Maybe Jesse will take us out," Eddie said.

"Normally I'd protest," Tom said. "Not today. We've done our duty."

"And we have a game tomorrow."

"Gather around, boys," Jesse called to the team. Tom and Eddie slowly stood up and joined the rest of the players.

"This game is as good as won," Jesse said. "But we still have a half to play. Let's use it to work on the new plays, the forward passes and on-side kicks."

The forward pass had been a work in progress during the Black and Brown practices. "All we're doing is throwing a lateral in a different direction," Jesse said, "down the field." The execution turned out to be more difficult than the explanation. In the first few attempts, the ends and wingback sprinted to random locations, stopped and turned to face the quarterback. The rest of the backs stood and watched.

"Gus won't have time to look for you," Jesse shouted. "He's got to know where you're going."

The pass catchers trapped the ball against their chest or belly with both hands. Since this technique required them to be facing the quarterback, curl routes made the most sense.

After several trials, the Black and Brown developed a standard pass play. Gus called for the tackle back formation to the side he wanted to throw from, then he called the pass play as the live number. At the snap, Gus ran toward the strong side. The fullback and lead tackle provided blocking. The halfback stayed in position for a possible misdirection lateral. The wing side end ran a curl five yards downfield. The other end cut across the defensive backfield to a point about ten yards past the line of scrimmage. The wingback ran at an angle toward the sideline. When he was three yards across the line, he stopped and turned toward the quarterback.

For short passes, five yards or less, Gus was accurate with a basketball-style chest pass or an underhand toss. For passes over five yards, he tried a side-arm throw. He experimented with cupping his hand on the end of the fat ball as he threw it. He also tried palming the ball at its widest point in the middle and flinging it with the long axis perpendicular to the line of flight. Holding the ball on the end generally caused an inaccurate, pinwheeling throw. Palming it in the middle resulted in a lob - accurate but without distance or speed.

Gus was right-handed. He could easily set up to throw after sprinting the mandatory five yards to the right. When sprinting to the left, he had to turn his body ninety-degrees for the side-arm throw.

For the on-side kick, the Black and Brown lined up with the wingback to the wide side of the field. The ball only had to travel the distance needed for a first down. But it had to be kicked far enough from any defenders to give the wingback and end a chance to run it down. In the practices, Gus would receive a short snap and kick a flat punt toward the sideline. The end and wingback simply made a dash for the loose ball.

The Black and Brown had to wait a few extra minutes to test their new plays. They kicked off to the Crimson to open the second half. The Crimson ran two ragged plays, then punted. Billy fielded the ball and ran a swerving slalom through listless coverage for a touchdown. Another Black and Brown kick-off. Two more sloppy Crimson plays. Another punt, but better coverage. The Black and Brown finally had the ball. Gus assembled the team at the line and called the pass play. Tackle back right. Jacob Rourke on the wing. Gus received the ball from the center and made the five-yard sideways sprint. The lead tackle blocked the corner as he rushed in to contain the play. Eddie ran the curl route. The defensive back moved toward him. With the corner out of the way, Rourke was wide open. Gus made a chest pass. Rourke trapped the ball against his body and tucked it in the crook of his arm. He turned downfield, a linebacker closing in on him. Eddie blocked his man long enough for Rourke to get by. He raced down the sideline with the linebacker on his heels. Just inside the twenty, the linebacker tackled Rourke with a dive at back of his legs.

The Black and Brown supporters loudly cheered the run. Then all of the spectators surrounding the field broke into applause. Tom and Eddie jogged side-by-side to the new line of scrimmage.

"Why's everyone clapping?" Eddie said.

"I think they've been waiting to see a forward pass," Tom said.

"Sounds like they like it."

"A thirty yard gain. I like it, too."

The referee placed the ball where the Rourke was tackled, about six feet in from the sideline. The Black and Brown lined up with an unbalanced formation. Billy was at wingback. Tom was the only lineman to the right of the center. The vast width of the field lay to the left. Gus called the on-side kick. The center passed the ball back. Tom's man rose out of his stance and nudged against him. He was taking a breather on this down. With the ball so close to the sideline, he knew the play would be run to the opposite side. Tom obliged him by nudging back. No sense wasting energy. Tom watched the play develop. He heard the thump of the punt; saw it barely clear the heads of the linemen; watched it fly in the direction of the far sideline. The punt surprised the corner. He made an awkward leap at the low kick as Billy ran by him. The end should also have been running for the ball, but he must've been held up at the line. From his deep position, the Crimson defensive back made a sprint for the loose ball. The punt struck the turf and bounded end over end toward the sideline for about fifteen yards. Billy and defensive back converged on the ball in an all-out foot race. Billy won by a few yards. He dove on the ball and wrapped his body around it.

A twelve yard gain. First and goal to go. Maybe these new rules weren't so bad after all, Tom thought. Gus went back to the run. In two plays, the Black and Brown pounded the ball past the goal line.

The Black and Brown attempted five more passes in their next series of possessions. The Crimson reacted better. When the corner and defensive back saw Gus carry the ball to the outside, they quickly closed down on the wingback and end. A linebacker hustled into the area where the pass might be thrown. All five attempts were incomplete. Twice the Black and Brown lost possession because the ball did not touch a player from either team before it hit the ground. The Crimson also recovered the Black and Brown's second on-side kick attempt. With ten minutes left, Jesse ended the experiment with the new rules. He sent in the six players waiting on the bench in a mass substitution.

The subs ran onto the field calling out the names of the players they were replacing. Tom was ready to wrap up the game. He listened expectantly for his name. He heard someone call for Eddie.

No one called for him. He resigned himself to remaining in. Gus was staying in, too.

The new players were giddy as they lined up, eager to score against a hapless opponent. Tom had to dig deep to find some energy to match theirs. Fortunately, his opponent was not putting up any resistance. Gus stuck with the running attack. Between plays, the new ends and backs pleaded for another pass attempt. Finally Gus gave in.

Tackle back left. Gus and his blockers sprinted to the left. The Crimson defense reacted quickly. They covered all three pass catchers. Their rushers were breaking through. Gus looked to his right and saw Turner, the replacement halfback, standing alone in the backfield. Gus side-armed a lateral to him. Turner caught the ball, sliced through a gap in the line, and galloped down the field on fresh legs. Crossing the goal line, he took a knee and touched the ball to the ground. Tad's kick after goal was good. The Black and Brown now led 51 to 0.

The subs were satisfied. They heard the supporters sing the fight song for them. They eased up on the Crimson. After a few more minutes of half-hearted play by both teams, the referee signaled that time had run out.

Chapter Eleven
Wednesday Morning, September 18, 1974

"What does it mean?"
"How should I know?" Elena replied. "You're investigator."
Clint was at Elena's house, trying to make sense of something that resembled a poem. On Tuesday evening, he had returned to his apartment and checked his answering machine. The first message was from Terry McCann. Clint was surprised to hear from him so quickly. He figured it would take Terry a few days to find a relative who knew something about Patrick's football team. The next message was from Elena. It surprised him even more. "Call me," she said. Her Russian accent was soft, her voice urgent. "I have something. It may interest you." Clint dialed her number immediately.
"Some thoughts came to me about your case," Elena said. "I wrote them down."
"Can you read them over the phone?"
Elena obliged. Clint tried to copy as she read. The thoughts were longer than he expected and cryptic, and he couldn't understand some of the words due to her accent. Clint didn't want to ask her to read it again. So he arranged a time in the morning to pay a visit.
At 9:00 AM Clint was back in Squirrel Hill. Elena's green eyes met him at the door. She brought him into her church-like front room. Clint smelled her exotic perfume. It relaxed him, made him feel a little light-headed. Then he noticed the tallow aroma of a burning votive candle. She handed him a sheet of composition paper.
"Yesterday, I had some thoughts," Elena said. "At first they perplexed me, they were so strange. Then I realized they were about your case. I kept thinking I should write them down, so I wouldn't forget. I found paper and pen. Suddenly, all of these words came to me. I wrote them so quickly. There was a little more, but those thoughts escaped me before I could write them." She pointed her open palm towards the paper in Clint's hand. "That is original, exactly as it came to me. I did not rewrite anything."

Clint looked at the sheet. The handwriting was hasty but neat, easy to read. There were no cross-outs or corrections. He read it quickly, too quickly to gain anything but the most rudimentary comprehension. Then he read it again slowly.

From the anthem city they rode anew.
A talisman's power their armor bore.
With quick death the new behemoths they slew,
inspiring devotion unseen before.

Each campaign ends in the ultimate test.
Lucky the foes the thoroughbred vanquish,
in future campaigns they will be well blessed.
But two foes reap Pyrrhic wins, years of anguish.

Fortune reverses for the prince untrue.
His fate is to thrice feel humbling defeat,
and to stoke the fires of sorrow anew.
Then his own glory would but once repeat.

Those whose retribution comes each tomorrow,
to the devoted, they must make amends.
This act alone will lift the cloud of sorrow:
Pay homage to wearers of the talisman.

"I don't know what this has to do with my case," Clint said. He almost asked if maybe she had given him a message intended for someone else. He bit his tongue. The question was too sarcastic.

"I think you must interpret," Elena said.

"Is this the kind of information you give the police? Do they have to interpret it?" He pictured a team of detectives with Styrofoam cups of coffee and shoulder holsters crowded around a desk, working together on what amounted to a poetry appreciation exercise, looking for clues amid the symbolism.

"No. Usually it is more, how you say...specific."

"You said there was more. Do you remember any of it?"

"No. This is all. I will call you if there is anything else." Elena sounded impatient. She moved toward the door. The meeting was over. Clint thanked her and left.

Clint walked briskly to his car, the soles of his shoes tapping on the sidewalk. He mentally raked over fragments of the poem - the anthem city, the talisman, Pyrrhic wins, the prince untrue - looking for a connection to his case. The door to a blue Chevy Nova opened in front of him. A man got out. He was brawny, about Clint's age, with jaw-length dark blond hair parted down the middle and a bushy mustache. He wore a gray T-shirt, jeans, and mirror sunglasses. He rested his forearms along the top of the door and watched Clint approach.

"Good morning, Mr. Ronson," the man said. "What brings you to Madame Ivanova's? Business or pleasure?"

Clint quickly glanced over his shoulder, making sure the blonde guy didn't have any accomplices sneaking up from behind. Whoever this guy is, Clint thought, he must've followed me to Squirrel Hill.

"You don't seem like the kind who believes in psychics, so it must be pleasure," the blonde guy said. "I don't blame you. Elena's still a hot number. A little weird, but hot. I'd do her."

Clint suddenly felt protective about Elena. The "weird" comment irked him more than this jerk saying he'd do her. "You're not her type," he said.

"How do you know who's type I am?"

"Spying from a parked car? Women call that creepy."

"I'm just doing my job. You're lucky I didn't have my telephoto. Know what I mean? I'm sure you had to investigate a few cases of improper fraternization. The general getting it on with his female driver, things like that."

So this guy's another private investigator, Clint thought. Getting the goods against a cheating spouse, that's a staple of the trade. Did he really think Clint was having an affair with Elena? Was he trying to get some compromising pictures? If so, why tell Clint?

"I've staked out my share of no-tell motels," the guy said. "Sleazy stuff."

Clint had enough. "What do you want?" he said.

"I work for Thomas DeAngelo, attorney for City Councilman Steve Harris. Does that ring a bell? Mr. DeAngelo wants to know why you didn't return his call. Are you going to keep him informed on your progress, like he asked?"

What did Walsh say about DeAngelo? That he'll play rough if he needs to? Maybe this guy really was trying to get some photos. Clint pictured the meeting: "Cooperate with us, Mr. Ronson, or we'll show these photos to..." To who? Even if they got a snapshot of him and Elena in an embrace and a deep kiss, so what? Clint was unmarried, unattached, immune to that kind of extortion.

"Why does DeAngelo want to be informed about my progress?"

"Mine is not to wonder why, my friend."

This guy was all show with his mirror sunglasses and know-it-all sarcasm. He wasn't looking for a confrontation. He was staying safely behind the car door, using it like a shield against Clint. He was just a message boy, and a snoop.

"Stay out of my business," Clint said. "I'll report my findings, not my progress."

"Have it your way," the blonde guy said. "If you won't keep DeAngelo updated, I will." He nodded toward Elena's house. "Like you visited a psychic. Don't you think that'll make your findings a little suspect? Maybe even your credibility?" The blonde guy turned to get into the car.

"Hey," Clint called. The guy looked back at him. "The next time you plan to tail me, leave a note on my windshield. I'll drive slow for you, to make it fair."

The blonde guy spat on the ground.

"Real funny, man," he said. "We'll see who gets the last laugh when this is over."

Chapter Twelve
Wednesday Afternoon, September 18, 1974

Exactly twenty-four hours after his first visit, Clint returned to McCann's Bar and Grill. Terry the bartender was there. The heavy guy with the mustache and carefully combed hair sat at the bar talking to him. The guy with the bullet-shaped head and sideburns was next to him. The old man was the only person missing. Like yesterday, no one else was in the bar.

"Clint, pull up a seat," Terry said. "We asked around last night. We found some interesting information for you. Before we get to that, let me introduce you to two old family friends. This is Jimmy." The heavy guy reached down the bar and shook hands with Clint. "And this is Simon." Simon leaned forward to look around Jimmy. He gave Clint a perfunctory nod.

"Simon's better known as Psycho," Terry said. "He's been on his best behavior lately, so you don't need to worry."

Clint wasn't worried. Bullet-head probably got tagged with Psycho for no other reason than it sounded like Simon. Then again, Psycho was the kind of nickname kids outgrew when they aged out of their teens. For some reason the name stuck with him. Maybe it was his appearance. Maybe he tried to live up to it. Worried, no. Watchful, yes.

"Here's what we found out," Terry said. He glanced at Jimmy. Jimmy placed his forearms on the bar, folded his hands and cleared his throat, like he was going to make an announcement.

"The tournament you're asking about was played in 1906," Jimmy said. Clint noticed that all three men were looking at him, trying to read his reaction to Jimmy's information.

"A Pittsburgh newspaper sponsored it and offered prize money."

Clint gave a slight, acknowledging nod.

"Terry's grandfather entered his team. They made it to the tournament championship." Again, Clint nodded slightly.

"In fact, McCann's won that game," Jimmy said. "They won the tournament."

"Who'd they beat?" Clint asked. "What was the score?"

"We don't know the details of the game," Terry said. "Some of my aunts and uncles remember hearing my grandfather complain that his football team won some sort of championship but never received the prize money."

Clint thought about what he had just heard. When Jimmy told him that McCann's played in the tournament and that the team never collected its prize money, he was feeding him information Clint had shared with Terry yesterday. On the other hand, they must have talked to someone who knew something about the tournament. Jimmy said it was played in 1906 and that a newspaper sponsored it. Clint had not told Terry those things.

"Do you have proof?" Clint said.

"Proof?" Terry said.

"You know, a newspaper article, an old letter. Something indisputable that says McCann's won."

"What more do you need?" Terry said. "We just told you what my aunts and uncles said."

"Put yourself in my position. You go to a magazine publisher and say, 'I wrote an article about one of the first football championships ever played. No one knows if the prize money was awarded. In fact, no one knows who won. Until now. Three guys in a bar told me their grandfather's team did. They said their relatives told them.'"

Terry dipped his face toward his cupped hands to light a cigarette. He leaned back, pulled the cigarette out of his mouth, and blew out some smoke. "I see your point," he said. He exchanged glances with Jimmy and Simon. Clint thought he saw Simon sneer.

"What if one of the men who played in the game tells you who won?" Terry said.

"Can you prove he played in the game?" Clint asked.

Jimmy looked downward, exhaled loudly, and shook his head in frustration. Clint sensed this was turning out to be harder than they expected.

"He might be able to prove it," Terry said.

A lot of non-verbal communication was going on between these three, Clint noted. Like they were trying to keep each other on the same script. As for the player, if his name was on the roster, that would be proof. But his testimony alone would still not be good enough. Memory can play tricks on a person, especially after sixty-eight years. Nonetheless, a former player might shed some new light on the case.

Jimmy raised his head toward Terry.

"Okay," Terry said. "We'll let you know."

"You've got my number."

"And I've got a question for you," Jimmy said. "What do you, a magazine writer, have to do with awarding the prize money?"

"I would give my findings to the lawyer who has custody over the account," Clint said.

"I see... Who's this lawyer?"

"That's confidential."

"You know his name. You just don't want to tell us."

"That's what confidential means."

"I see," Jimmy said again.

Awkward silence. None of them were looking at Clint now. Jimmy was looking down into his lap like he was deep in thought. Terry and Simon were staring off into space. Terry was smoking his cigarette. Clint felt like he had worn out his welcome. He slid off the bar stool.

"Let me know when I can meet this player," he said.

"One more thing," Jimmy said slowly. From the tone of his voice, Clint expected some sort of warning or ultimatum. Of the three, Jimmy seemed to be the one in charge. This was a McCann family matter, but Jimmy had the main speaking role. He must be a very close friend, Clint thought. Someone as trusted as a blood relative.

"We really appreciate the work you're putting into this," Jimmy said. "We thought this game was all but forgotten. In fact, to show you how much we appreciate it, when we get the prize money, we're going to share it with you. I think maybe seven percent. It would be a little gratuity, our way of saying thank you for your effort."

FROM THE ANTHEM CITY

Terry was nodding in approval. Simon was still staring into space. Clint was surprised by the offer, and by Jimmy's apparent sincerity. He didn't know what to say. Turn it down? Cite conflict of interest? The meeting had already been uneasy. Rejecting their gesture wouldn't help. Clint decided to play along, just not too enthusiastically.

"Cool," he said.

Chapter Thirteen
Thursday Evening, September 19, 1974

"*I called the Waylan Coalcrackers and guess what? They said they won the 1906 tournament.*"

Clint nearly dropped the phone. Alarms went off inside him. The last thing he needed was Vince Gleason making phone calls related to the investigation.

"Tell me again who you called?" Clint said.

"The Waylan Coalcrackers. They're a semipro team."

"Why did you call them?"

"I wanted to find out if they were related to the Waylan Athletic Club, the one that played in the tournament. Personal curiosity, that's all."

"Why did you ask them if they won?"

"It just sort of came up," Vince said.

"What do you mean, it just came up?"

"Look, all I did was ask the guy if the present-day Coalcrackers were related to the Waylan Athletic Club that played in a tournament in 1906. He said they were the same club. He said they've been in continuous operation since the 1890s, and that they won the tournament. He said he was surprised that I even knew about it."

"Vince, I don't need you making phone calls related to the investigation. Too many people asking too many questions is a recipe for disaster. More than one is too many."

Clint knew that successfully managing an investigation meant knowing who to question, when to question them, what to ask and how to ask it. Indiscriminate questions meant too much information out on the street. Anybody could the piece things together and fill in the blanks. In a criminal case, suspects could work up an alibi. In a case like Clint's, someone itching for a big payday could concoct a credible-sounding story. Clint would end up wasting time checking it out.

"Hey man, I didn't mean to make you angry," Vince said. "I wasn't even thinking about your investigation. As soon as I saw that

FROM THE ANTHEM CITY

one of the 1906 teams was from Waylan, I had to find out if there was a connection. That kind of stuff fascinates me. I'm sorry if I screwed things up for you."

"When I wrap this up, I'll give you the file. You can call anybody you want. In the meantime, knock it off."

"Okay," Vince said. He sounded both contrite and impatient, like a schoolboy facing a reprimand and wanting to get it over.

"Besides, whoever told you Waylan won the tournament didn't know what they were talking about. The *Pittsburgh Sentry* reported that Monessen beat Waylan in the semifinal. Coming from a third party source like a newspaper, I take it to be fact."

"Why would the guy make up something like that?"

"I don't know," Clint said. "By the way, the reason I called you, I need your knowledge of football history to help me decipher something. How soon can you get over here?"

"Right away!" Vince said.

Thirty minutes later, Clint's doorbell rang. Vince Gleason stood in the breezeway entrance with the wide-eyed look of a kid on Christmas morning. Was he excited to be invited over? Clint guessed he didn't receive many invitations, business or social. He was probably happy to get a pardon for his transgression, too. And as always, he was pleased to be recognized for his football history expertise.

"C'mon in," Clint said. "Make yourself at home."

Vince paused inside the doorway to look at Clint's apartment. A long, rectangular room had a living area by the entrance and a dining area behind it. Clint had put a weight bench back there instead of a table and chairs. He used the space for his work-outs. A counter separated the work-out area from the kitchen. Cabinets hung above the counter. To the right, a hallway ran past the kitchen to the bathroom and bedroom. To the left, in the living area, was a sliding glass door. Clint had a sofa, two chairs, a coffee table, two end tables and TV in the living area. The eggshell walls were bare.

"Nice place," Vince said.

"Nothing beats....what did you call your place?"

"Cava Vincente. Hell yeah, it beats it. You got more room and your own kitchen."
"Right. Can I get you a beer?"
"Sure," Vince said. He sat down.
Clint took two Iron City cans out of the refrigerator and gave one to Vince. Then he handed him the paper from Elena and took a seat.
"What's this?"
"Somebody gave it to me," Clint said. "It's supposed to have clues about the 1906 tournament."
Vince put his beer on the end table and settled back in the chair to read the paper. Suddenly he sat up. His lips moved quickly and silently, his attention fully absorbed by the words. Then he turned his big head toward Clint.
"Wow! This is really cool! It reminds me of Nostradamus, the way it's written in sets of four verses. They're called quatrains. I read his book once. Some people believe it's prophetic. The only problem is that it's taken hindsight to realize a quatrain might be describing a future event."
"So Nostradamus hasn't been very useful in predicting the future."
"No. But some of his quatrains sound awfully similar to things that happened after they were written, so it makes you think…"
"Well, Nostradamus didn't write this."
"Who did?"
"Never mind who did."
Vince turned his attention back to the paper.
"This could be about a band of warriors in a mythical kingdom," he said. "Coming from a legendary city-state where they were bred to be fighters, defeating monsters in battle, inflicting curses on enemies who defeat them, a treacherous prince, achieving redemption by paying homage. Its got everything. This would make a great novel."
Vince looked at it again.
"But there's not one word about football. You sure it's about the tournament?"

"That's what I was told," Clint said. "It's written metaphorically. It's supposed to contain clues. The clues should lead me to evidence revealing the team that won. I need you to help me decipher those clues."

"Who did you get this from?"

"Don't worry about where it came from," Clint said firmly.

"Okay, I won't ask anymore. But that could be your first clue. Where do we start?"

"How about at the beginning, then go line by line." Clint opened his notebook to a blank page.

"'From the anthem city they rode anew'," Vince read aloud. "From the anthem city…"

"What exactly is an anthem?"

"A national song?"

"The writer probably chose the key words for their precise meaning," Clint said. "It might help if we had exact definitions." He left the room and returned a few seconds later with a dictionary. He leafed through the pages.

"An anthem is a song or hymn of praise or loyalty," Clint summarized. "You're from Pittsburgh. As far as you know, are either Monessen or Homestead known for a song of praise or loyalty?"

Vince settled back again, resting his head on the top of the chair. He gazed at the ceiling. A long minute passed. If he has to ponder every line like this, Clint thought, we'll be here all night. More time passed. Then Vince picked his head up.

"In high school we took a field trip to Homestead. You know they had a famous strike there," he said.

"I heard of it."

"The museum had this pamphlet with a song that praised the strikers. I remember it 'cause we tried to sing it."

"So that could make Homestead the anthem city," Clint said. "Do you know anything about Monessen? Does it have its own claim to an anthem?"

"I can't think of anything." Clint was ready to move on to the next verse, then Vince said, "You know what our test was for that lesson? We had to make protest posters showing our support for the strikers. That's all. No questions. No essays. I drew a guy with a hard hat firing a rifle and wrote 'Feel Our Steel.' I got an 'A' for it."

"Some history class."

"The teacher was one of those radicals who believed all of history was the struggle of the exploited against their exploiters."

"We go overseas to fight Commies and then we let them teach our kids at home. Is this a great county, or what?" Clint said.

"You know what else…"

"Tell me later, Vince. What's the next verse."

"We're still on the first verse. The rest of it is 'They rode anew'."

Clint looked up 'anew' and told Vince it meant 'again'.

"It could refer to a team that was disbanded and then brought back into existence," Clint said.

"Maybe it just means a team that's back to play another season."

"Sounds like it rules out any team that played for the first time in 1906."

Clint made a note to find out when McCann's and the Monessen Terrors first played. Where could he find that information, he wondered.

"Now the next verse," Clint said.

"'A talisman's power their armor bore.'."

Clint quickly turned pages in the dictionary. "A talisman is an object believed to confer on its bearer supernatural powers or protection," he said.

"A good luck charm."

"I saw a photograph of a Fighting Irish player. His jersey had a harp logo sewn on the front."

"Where'd you find that photo?" Vince said. "I'd love to see it."

"I'll tell you after I finish the investigation. But here's something unusual - the guy in the photo was over sixty years old. His grandson said he was a player as well as the owner. He was also a Civil War veteran. He served in some all-Irish unit."

"That would have been the Irish Brigade," Vince said. "The Fighting Irish. The guy used his army unit's nickname for his team."

"So you were right. McCann's wasn't copying Notre Dame."

"Of course I was right."

"You're just a font of trivia, aren't you?" Clint said.

"Football and the Civil War, those're my specialties."

"There was something written under the photograph." Clint found where he had copied 'Faugh a ballagh' in his notebook and showed it to Vince. "Have you ever seen that before?"

"No. Maybe it's an Irish saying."

"I figured that much. How's your knowledge of symbols? Have you ever heard of a harp being a symbol of good luck?"

Vince shook his head. "I guess it could be an Irish tradition. What about Monessen's uniforms? What did they look like?"

"I haven't seen a picture yet. What do say we go on to the third verse?"

"'With quick death the new behemoths they slew'." Once again Vince laid his head back. He whispered "quick death" to himself several times. Then he lit up with inspiration. "Quick death - they scored fast, they scored often."

"That makes sense. What about 'new behemoths'."

"Look up behemoth."

Clint was already turning the pages. "A huge animal, or something enormous in size."

"Look up terrors."

"Anything that instills fear, a terrifying object or occurrence."

"Well, this is a stretch," Vince said, "but a huge animal could instill fear. Behemoths may refer to the Terrors."

"I'm thinking behemoths could be a general reference to powerful teams. But what's the reason for the adjective 'new'?"

Silence.

Suddenly Vince smacked the paper with the back of his hand.

"I got it! How does a team score fast and often? Through passing. This line refers to 1906, to the new game the rule changes created."

"Good thinking."

"The 'new behemoths' are the teams that turned into winners because they adapted to passing. That means the team these quatrains are about were the best of the passing teams. Do any of those newspapers mention the Irish or Terrors scoring through the air?"

"I don't recall. I'll reread them and check…Go on."

"Okay. Fourth line: 'inspiring devotion unseen before'. That's easy, the fans loved them."

"Just like today," Clint said, "everybody loves a winner."

"The next quatrain," Vince said. "First line: 'Each campaign ends in the ultimate test'. Again, that's easy. A campaign is a football season. The ultimate test is the championship."

"Or a campaign could be a tournament," Clint said.

"Either way, a campaign is a series of games ending in a championship match."

"Agreed."

"We have to analyze the next two lines together because it's one thought," Vince said. "'Lucky the foes the thoroughbred vanquish. In future campaigns they will be well-blessed'." He thought for a moment. "This phrase doesn't need much interpretation either - the teams that lose championship games to our team will get lucky in future seasons."

"Losing to them is a blessing in disguise."

"Right," Vince said. "Well-blessed - that could mean the team has winning seasons, or they win championships."

"Thoroughbred, Clint said. That's another one of those key words." He paged through the dictionary.

"Bred of pure stock; purebred; unmixed."

"If the Fighting Irish were all of Irish descent, that would make them thoroughbred by the definition," Vince said.

Clint opened the folder with the newspaper copies to the roster of McCann's.

"They all look like Irish names."

"What about Monessen?"

Clint found the Terrors' roster. "Some Irish, some German-sounding names, some Slavic..."

Vince looked up from the paper. "Man. It's looking more and more like these quatrains are about Homestead."

"Don't jump to conclusions," Clint said. A conclusion was the farthest thing from Clint's mind. He needed facts to draw a conclusion. So far all he had from these verses were assumptions and speculation. Nothing objective. Not even a lead that might produce a fact. "What's the next verse?"

"'But two reap *Pie-rik* wins, years of anguish'. Vince looked at Clint quizzically. "Pie-rik?"

"It's Peer-ik. A Pyrrhic victory is where you win, but the cost of winning doesn't make it worthwhile."

"So two teams must've beat the Irish in championship games. They ended up with streaks of bad luck."

"'Years of anguish'," Clint said. "Years of disappointment in some way."

"Losing seasons," Vince said.

"Or maybe they had good teams that couldn't win the championship. You know, high hopes that weren't fulfilled. That would be anguish."

"To see if this clue fits, you would need to know the results of the Irish in their championship games and the subsequent won-loss records of their opponents."

"Don't forget the Terrors. I haven't ruled them out yet," Clint said. "Where would I get information like that?"

"I don't know. Remember, I never heard of these two teams before."

"How long you been researching football?"

"About three years."

"How much research have you done?"

"At one time I was in a library somewhere almost every day, looking through old newspapers," Vince said. "I've slowed down lately. I sort of exhausted all the resources."

"All that research and you missed this tournament?"

"I wasn't very systematic about it. I'd find something interesting and I'd look up all I could about it. Then something else would catch my attention and I'd research that. After awhile I was crossing my own tracks."

Three years of research, Clint thought. Vince's method was random, but his effort was remarkable. Yet in all those archive visits, he hadn't run across any information about these two teams. What chance did Clint have of finding it? And what if he did? What if he lucked upon a trove of information that showed the verses described either Homestead or Monessen? Without the result of this tournament championship, he would still have no answer for the only question that mattered - who won? Clint felt like he was running in a circle with these verses. He felt like he was running in a circle with the whole case.

"Alright," he said, "Let's get this done. Read the next quatrain."

Vince held out his beer can and waggled it. "I'm out of inspiration." Clint went to the refrigerator and got two more Iron Citys. The phone rang. He handed a beer to Vince and answered the call.

"When?" Clint said. "Where?...I'll be there."

"I got to go," Clint said to Vince. "That was one of my interviews. Says he's got something important to show me."

"About the tournament?"

"No. Another case I'm working on."

"How many investigations you got going on?"

"As many as I can handle. Copy down those last two sets of verses. Think about them. We'll analyze them later."

Clint went into the bathroom to brush his teeth and gargle. When he came back into the living area, Vince was still copying.

"You write slow."

"I'm copying the whole thing."

"Why?"

"I think it's cool," he said. Then he gave Clint his "how about that" look.

Chapter Fourteen
Monday, September 17, 1906

The steam whistle wailed long and shrill. Another shift at the mill was over. Tom and Eddie met at the gate. "No time to waste, Eddie-boy," Tom said. They walked briskly along the stone-paved road toward the creek that separated the mill from the town center. Crossing the iron truss bridge, Eddie looked back.

"They're taking their time," he said.

"Good. We'll get there first."

They walked up a street of row buildings, passed a few shops, then turned into Patrick's Saloon.

Sam put two mugs of beer on the bar. "Why you two breathing so hard?" he said.

"We walked here fast to beat the crowd," Eddie said.

"What's your rush? I'm not gonna run out of beer."

"We didn't want to wait in line," Tom said.

"You in a hurry to get to practice?"

"Jesse gave us a break today. We just played two games in two days."

"I heard you won both of 'em. That's all I know. Don't know the scores or who you played or anything. I thought someone would of filled me in by now."

"Your brother didn't tell you anything?" Eddie said. "He was there."

"Who? Him? You ever see him around here? You'ld never know he's part owner. Always with that woman."

"Well, that's why we were in such a hurry," Tom said. "We knew you couldn't wait to hear the whole story."

Sam rested his elbows on the bar and stuck his head in close to Tom and Eddie, like the three of them were sharing a secret. "So what happened," he said. "And don't spare any details."

"There were eleven teams," Tom said.

"Instead of sixteen like the organizers wanted," Sam said. "None of them are well-known. You told me that before you left. You think I don't remember things?"

"You just said 'don't spare any details.'"

"Details about things you haven't told me already."

"First round was Saturday. Did I tell you that?"

"Go on."

"There were five games on Saturday. Ten of the teams were matched up through a drawing. The eleventh drew a bye."

"They didn't draw it, they were given it" Eddie said. "The organizers think they're the best team in the tournament."

"That gave them an advantage on Sunday," Sam said. "Not having to play on Saturday."

"Yeah. But it didn't affect us, so we didn't worry about it."

"We won our first game 51 to 0," Tom said.

"Fifty-one to nothing! Whoa! I want to hear about this."

The door swung open. A wave of mill workers poured in. They were soot-covered, sweaty and loud, exulting in their freedom from a long shift of making steel.

"Let me take care of this crowd," Sam said. "Hold the story until I get back."

Fifteen minutes later Sam returned, wiping his hands on a towel. "How did you score fifty-one points?" he said.

Tom and Eddie told him about Billy Pallister running for three touchdowns from scrimmage and returning a punt for another, about Gus Webb carrying for a touchdown, about Tad Crowell missing a kick after goal but making a field goal and running for a touchdown. They talked about Jacob Rourke catching the first forward pass and adding a big gain, about Pallister recovering their first on-side kick try, about Turner catching a lateral pass and scoring a touchdown, and about Tom's touchdown.

"You scored, Tom?" Sam said.

"I tackled their runner and he dropped the ball. I scooped it up and carried it over."

"Tom's being modest, Sam. Let me tell you what he really did. He caught that runner in the backfield, picked him up, spun around, and threw him on the ground. Hitting the ground knocked the ball loose."

"Good for you, Tom." Sam said. "And Pallister scored three touchdowns."

"He had four," Eddie said.

"He's unbelievable. I bet the other teams were worried hearing about your big win."

"They weren't worried a bit," Eddie said. "Everyone knew the Crimson was thrown together for the tournament."

"The *Sentry* wrote them up like an all-star team," Tom said. "Jesse talked to their coach after the game. He said he had some fellows who played for other teams, and he had some who never played before. They didn't practice much. We were their first game."

"They were in it for the money," Eddie said.

"What are you in it for?" Sam said.

"The glory, of course."

"Sunday was round two," Tom said. "The five winners from Saturday and the team that got the bye advanced. So did the two teams that lost by the closest scores. The organizers needed eight teams in the quarterfinals. They gave those two losing teams a second chance. They ranked the teams and set it up so the top-ranked team played the lowest ranked team, the second-ranked team played the seventh-ranked team, and so forth."

"We were the second-ranked team because we won by the most points," Eddie said. "Another team scored more points than us but they gave up some points, so we had the biggest win. We played the seventh-ranked team."

"One of the teams that got beat on Saturday?" Sam said.

"The one that lost by the smallest margin," Tom said.

"They were arrogant bastards for a second chance team," Eddie said. "Tom and me, we went to a tavern Saturday night…"

"To drink the one beer Jesse let us have," Tom said.

"A bunch of them were in there. They said they deserved to advance because they were robbed. Then they started bragging about how they were going to whip us."

"They said that to you?" Sam said.

"They didn't know who we were. We were in a corner by ourselves. They were at the bar."

"They were having more than one beer," Tom said. "Quite a few more."

"They said they wouldn't let us stand in the way of eight thousand dollars. Then they said they could whip us even if no money was at stake."

Tom said, "Someone yelled across the tavern, 'Didn't you hear they won fifty-one to nothing today?' I was thinking maybe they didn't know how big our win was. Maybe now they'll change their tune."

"They said we didn't play a real team; that a bunch of schoolgirls could of beat the team we played. That got under my skin. I wanted to go at 'em."

"You should of seen how fired up Eddie was," Tom said. "I had to settle him down. I told him their kind of arrogance was one of the seven deadly sins. I told him humility is a virtue. They would pay the price in the end."

"I told Tom I didn't want to wait for Judgment Day."

"I said he wouldn't have to. The reckoning comes tomorrow."

"Did you give 'em religion?" Sam said.

"They gave us a devil of a fight at first," Tom said. "They tried to live up to their talk."

"For most of the first half, we punted back and forth," Eddie said. "Toward the end, we had a few good runs. Then Billy scored."

"They came right back," Tom said. "They drove against us and scored their own touchdown. It was tied six apiece at halftime."

Another group of millworkers pressed against the bar. Sam called his daughter. Lorena appeared in the doorway to a side room where she had been rinsing mugs and beer pails. She was young, maybe in her late teens. She had Sam's small, dark eyes and round face. Like Sam she wore a white blouse with a black bowtie. She filled the blouse out nicely. Her dark brown hair was pulled up in a bun. Eddie smiled at her. Lorena didn't seem to notice. Sam motioned to the group of men.

"Take care of these gentlemen," he told her.

Eddie watched her pull beers for the millworkers. She was serious and quiet, oblivious to their attempts at flirting.

Sam turned back to Tom and Eddie. "So the game was tied at halftime," he said.

"Six to six," Tom said. "Before I tell you about the second half, I have to tell you about our forward pass play. Seeing it in action against the Crimson, Jesse came up with a few ideas to improve it." Tom dug into his pocket for some coins to depict the play. Sam came in close to see.

"We used to have the end run a five-yard curl downfield and the wingback run a three-yard curl toward the sideline. Jesse changed it so the wingback ran downfield and the end ran to the sideline. Now the pass catchers were running criss-crossing routes. See? Jesse thought that would confuse the defenders."

"I like the criss-crossing," Sam said. "I bet that worked nicely."

Lorena finished serving beer and went back into the side room. Eddie returned to the conversation. "Tell him about the run option and the pass option," he said.

"The first time we used the pass play, Gus was supposed to run the ball instead of throw it. He had the two backs blocking for him, sort of like a mass run. After that, he could pass or run, depending on how the defense reacted."

"Jesse said he wanted to create a dilemma for the safety, corner and linebacker," Eddie said. "That's what he called it - a dilemma. Jesse likes to use those educated words."

"The dilemma is, do they play the run and let the pass catchers go, or do they cover the pass catchers and give the quarterback room to run?"

"Sometimes Jesse amazes me with the ideas he comes up with," Eddie said.

"It's hard to believe there are so many tactics in this game," Sam said. "Watching it, all it looks like is pushing and piling on and once in awhile a runner breaks free. How did these ideas work?"

"After all the planning, Jesse was reluctant to try it," Eddie said. "We didn't run the pass play at all in the first half."

"Why?"

"Passing's a risk and Jesse's not a gambler."

"In the first game, Gus threw seven or eight passes. Only two were caught, and one of those was a lateral," Tom said.

"And if a forward pass hits the ground without being touched by a member of either team, the offense loses possession," Eddie said. "That happened to us twice against the Crimson."

"At halftime, Jesse said we needed to break the stalemate. He was ready to take some risks."

"Jake Rourke ran the kick-off out to the forty, so we started the second half in a good position."

"First play, Gus used the run option," Tom said. "The corner tried to box the play inside. He didn't even notice Eddie running his pass route. We lined up and Gus called another pass to the right. The corner played the run again. Eddie was open. Gus lobbed the ball to him. The wingback blocked the safety. Eddie-boy here took off running with a linebacker on his tail. He could of scored our first touchdown from a forward pass, but the linebacker caught him at the twenty yard line."

"With your long legs, you couldn't outrun a linebacker," Sam said.

"Lugging that football throws my stride off. It's like carrying a watermelon."

"That was the turning point in the game," Tom said. "Might've been the first forward pass they ever saw. It put us near the goal line and threw them into confusion. From there, we ran off-tackle to the left and right until we got near the goal line. Then Billy plunged over."

"Tad missed the kick after goal, so it was 11 to 6," Eddie said.

"I thought Tad was a good kicker," Sam said.

"He's a powerful kicker. Not always so accurate."

"Tad was so mad about missing the point that he boomed the kick-off way down the field," Tom said. "They punted the ball right back to us."

"Gus called a quarterback on-side kick," Eddie said. "Billy recovered the ball on the twenty-five yard line. Another nice gain."

102

"Gus called the pass play again. We saw what Jesse meant about creating a dilemma. Their corner hesitated. He wasn't sure if he should play the run or cover Eddie."

"He remembered getting surprised by the forward pass," Eddie said.

"Eddie had another surprise for him. He decked him with a hard block."

"We had lots of good blocking on that play. The wingback blocked the safety and the backs took care of the linebacker and end. Gus had an easy run for a touchdown."

"This time Tad made the kick after goal," Tom said. "Just like that, we were leading 17 to 6. On their next possession, they tried their own forward pass. It was complete confusion."

"They looked like we did when we first practiced it," Eddie said. "Pass catchers running all over the place, the quarterback not knowing where they were."

"I almost had him," Tom said. "He panicked, threw the ball away. Nobody touched it. We took possession."

"So now we had the ball in their half of the field. That's when things got nasty."

"They knew if we scored again, the game would be out of reach. They did everything to stop us - punching, piling on, hitting after the whistle."

"They were fighting for the money," Sam said.

"We were fighting right back," Eddie said. "The referees had to separate players. Tempers were burning a short fuse. I expected things to explode at any moment."

"Third and a long way to go, maybe eight yards," Tom said. "Too far for a field goal try. Most times we would have punted. But with the lead and the field position, Gus gambled for a first down. He called for a forward pass to the left. He didn't have a chance to throw. They were hitting our pass catchers downfield. Just before a linebacker got to him, Gus tossed a short lateral to Rourke."

"Jake made a nice run after the catch. He got tackled out of bounds inside the five yard line."

"We could choose to have the ball placed five yards in from the sideline or fifteen yards in. Gus told the referees to put it down five yards in. The other team expected a run or pass to the wide side of the field. Their linebackers and safety shifted toward our left. Gus called a cross-buck to the right."

"What's a cross-buck?" Sam said.

"You said not to tell you anything I already told you," Tom said.

"I can't remember all those plays. Tell me again."

Tom diagrammed the play with the coins. "We run it from our regular formation, the one that looks like a "T." On this play, we had an unbalanced line because the ball was so close to the sideline."

"I moved to the left side," Eddie said.

"In a cross-buck to the right, the fullback runs into the line on the left side of the center," Tom said. "The quarterback fakes a hand-off to him to get the defense to react. The left halfback crosses behind the fullback, running from the quarterback's left rear into the line on the right side of the center. The quarterback hands the ball to him. The right halfback leads the ball carrier into the line."

"Brute force complemented by deception," Sam said.

"For this play, Gus told Billy and Tad to switch positions. Billy was now the fullback," Eddie said. "The defense had their sights on him throughout the game, so they went for the fake. Tad was the left halfback. They reacted too slowly to him. He found a hole and crossed the goal line untouched."

"That score took the fight out of them," Tom said.

"We didn't have much fight left in us, either. Sunday was just as hot as Saturday, and we had been playing at a furious pace."

"As we lined up for the kick-off, we shouted to Jesse to bring in the reserves. He told us we needed to score more to earn a higher bracket."

"We scored one more touchdown after a long, slow drive. All running plays. No big gains. Steady five or six yards on each run. The final score was 29 to 6."

"And now we're in the semifinal round," Tom said.

"Eleven teams started," Eddie said. "Four are still standing."

"When's your next game?" Sam said.

FROM THE ANTHEM CITY

"Next weekend," Tom said. "At the Westmoreland County Fair. Football players, cattle and hogs will be the main attractions."

Chapter Fifteen
Friday, September 20, 1974

Happy Hour. McCann's was busier than during Clint's previous two visits. Drab-looking patrons lined the bar, silently smoking and sipping their beers and double shots. They stared at the TV suspended high in the corner. Terry was behind the bar, a towel draped over one shoulder, monitoring the progress of the drinkers. Most of the tables in the dining area were full. There was even a waitress on duty.

Jimmy and Simon were at one of the tables. They sat on either side of a very old man, a pitcher of beer and several glasses in front of them. Jimmy waved Clint over.

"I'm starting to feel like a regular here," Clint said.

"We like regulars," Jimmy said. "We can trust 'em...Clint, this is Charlie Rooney. As far as we know, he's the last surviving member of the McCann's team that played in the tournament."

Clint sat down. "Rooney, huh? You related to the Chief?" He reached across the table and shook Charlie's hand.

Charlie looked confused. "Who?" he asked in a raspy voice.

"The Chief. The owner of the Steelers."

Charlie turned his head. "I don't know those guys."

Clint had the roster of the Fighting Irish in his pocket. He didn't need to check it. He remembered it listed a Charles Rooney. Charlie certainly looked old enough. Clint wanted to be sure. If Charlie was the right age to be playing football in 1906, Clint might be on to something.

"Charlie, do you have some ID? Something with your birth date on it?"

"What's a matter? Don't I look old enough to be in a bar?" He glanced at Jimmy and Simon, checking their reaction to his joke. They chuckled mildly.

"Were you old enough in 1906?"

Charlie shrugged. Slowly, stiffly, he pulled out his wallet. With trembling fingers, he leafed through the contents. Jimmy poured a

FROM THE ANTHEM CITY

glass of beer and pushed it across the table. Charlie found his driver's license and handed it to Clint.

"That thing's obsolete, but I don't drive no more anyhow."

"It expired two years ago," Clint noted. "So, you were nineteen in 1906."

"That was the first year I played. I weighed two hundred twenty back then." Charlie raised two bone-thin arms covered with blotchy, shriveled skin. "You'ld never know it to look at me now. Doctor says I weigh about one-sixty. Bad heart and everything. Let me tell you, getting old is hell."

"What position did you play?"

"I was a lineman. We played both ways in those days. None of this running on and off the field every time one team or the other gets the ball. We thought it was an insult to be taken out of the game. Let me tell you, you had to be tough to play back then."

Clint noticed someone at the bar keeping an eye on their table - a hollow-cheeked, gray-haired man with glasses and a mean look. He was the same guy who had been sitting with Jimmy and Psycho during Clint's first visit. At the table, Simon was keeping an eye on Clint, too; watching everything, saying nothing.

"What do you remember about the tournament?" Clint asked.

"Aw hell, I remember it like it was yesterday. We were looking for games to play. Someone saw this ad in a newspaper about a football tournament. It said it was for the world championship. We thought you had to qualify or something to get in. Turns out they were taking all comers. Whoever heard of that? All you gotta do to play for the world championship is sign up."

Clint jotted notes as Charlie talked.

"We played the first weekend at a county fair. We played the next weekend at a different county fair."

"What do you remember about the games?"

Charlie shook his head. "I don't remember the details. Just that we won."

"You don't remember who you played? The scores?"

"Nah."

"Why do you remember the tournament but not the games?" Clint asked.

"Like I said, it was supposed to be a world championship tournament but anyone could enter. That was odd. It stands out in my mind. The games..." Charlie gave a dismissive backhand wave. "I played in lots of games. They all run together after awhile."

"You don't remember anything about the final game. By winning it, McCann's was declared the world champion. That doesn't stand out in your mind?"

Charlie gave Jimmy an annoyed glance. He turned back to Clint. "I don't think we ever believed it was for the world championship, so it was just another game. What's all this about anyway? I thought this tournament was a forgotten deal."

"You could be in for some money, Charlie," Jimmy said. "They never paid the prize money. Clint's writing a magazine story about it. Maybe the survivors will get their winnings. You, being the only survivor, should get it all."

Charlie broke into a grin. "You don't say," he replied.

"So when does Charlie get his money?" Jimmy asked.

"That's not my call," Clint said. "My job is to uncover the facts and write an article. Speaking of facts, I need to confirm Charlie's story. Do my fact-checking."

Clint was pleased with himself for slipping in the phrase 'fact-checking'. It made him sound more like a journalist.

"What's there to confirm?" Jimmy said. "You got a guy who played in the tournament sitting right in front of you and he's telling you who won. You saying he's lying?"

"I can sell the story if I can prove it's true. If I can't sell it, nobody gets any money."

"Yeah."

"So I need proof beyond a reasonable doubt. A newspaper story or a letter or diary from 1906 would work. So would a corroborating statement from a witness."

"Who's holding this money?"

"It's rumored to be in a bank, in an account held by a law firm."

"That's right. The one you said was confidential." Jimmy shook his head. "A law firm. No wonder." He looked at Clint. "Where you gonna find a witness to something that happened sixty-eight years ago?"

"You hit the nail on the head, Jimmy." Clint handed Charlie a card. "Here's my number. If you remember anything else, or find anything to back up your story, call me."

Chapter Sixteen
Saturday, September 21, 1974

Clint opened his notebook. He looked at what he wrote on Thursday when he and Vince tried to make sense of Elena's verses. There was nothing useful - no hard clues about where to look or who to talk with to solve this case. All of his notes sounded like something from high school English class; kids trying to interpret symbolism in a poem they didn't understand. He was surprised he didn't get a phone call first thing Friday morning from Vince. Clint could picture him poring over the verses all night, trying to tease out some hidden meaning. Vince seemed like the kind of guy who would do that.

Might as well finish the job. He called Vince.

Clint: You get a chance to think about those last two sets of verses?
Vince: The last two quatrains? Yeah. You want me to come over?
Clint: No. Let's do it over the phone.
Vince: Don't you think it would be better if we brainstormed it face-to-face?
Clint: I don't have the time. You ready?
Vince: Let me get the paper.
Vince (back on the phone): I'm back.
Clint: Here we go. Third quatrain. Is that what you call them?
Vince: Yeah. A quatrain is a group of four verses.
Clint: Okay. Third quatrain: 'Fortune reverses for the prince untrue. His fate is to thrice feel humbling defeat, and to stoke the fires of sorrow anew. Then his own glory would but once repeat'. What do you think?
Vince: Obviously someone betrays the team in some way and gets cursed. It must be a player or a coach because their curse is to face three defeats before they experience victory.
Clint: Must be a star player if he's referred to as 'the prince'. How do you betray your team?
Vince: Jump to another team. Take a dive.

110

Clint: Maybe he was a hot prospect who didn't live up to expectations. You know, he didn't turn out to be the real thing.
Vince: That could be a reason for calling someone untrue. But I like betrayal better.
Clint: Those defeats, they must've been especially painful because they're called 'humbling'.
Vince: His team probably got beat in three big games. Maybe ones they were favored to win.
Clint: Maybe he made mistakes that cost them the games. That's another way of being untrue. He didn't play up to his potential when it counted.
Vince: Three times?
Clint: He's a choker. What could be more humbling?
Vince: Bummer.
Clint: Then he must go on to win two championships because it says he experiences glory and it repeats.
Vince: (whispering): 'Stoke the fires of sorrow anew...Stoke the fires of sorrow...'
Clint: What?
Vince: Whoever wrote this is a genius. The fires of sorrow, that's a funeral pyre. It's a word play with Pyrrhic win. It refers to the two teams that defeated our team in the championship. The prince untrue adds to their misery by beating them in key games.
Clint: Or maybe he ends up playing for them and hurting them in key games.
Vince: Either way, same result. So if we can figure out who the prince untrue is, we'll know who the winning team is.

Clint thought about that for a moment. How many possible interpretations had they come up with for 'prince untrue'? Maybe he was a traitor. Maybe he didn't live up to his potential. Maybe he choked. Maybe he beat the Pyrrhic victors. Maybe he played for them and cost them games. Who were the Pyrrhic victors anyway? What exactly did 'years of anguish' or 'fires of sorrow' mean? In order to figure out what those verses meant, if they meant anything, Clint would need an exhaustive knowledge of early 1900's football -

the teams, their year-by-year schedules and results, the players, all the teams they played for, and how they performed, and on and on. If he knew all that he couldn't help but know who won the tournament. He wouldn't need even Elena's verses.

Clint: Hold on, Vince. If I figure out who the prince untrue was, how does that help me know who won the tournament?
Vince: That quatrain wouldn't be there if the player it's about didn't have a connection to the winning team.
Clint: How do you know?
Vince (after a pause): It wouldn't make any sense...
Clint: It's *not* making any sense. None of this is making any sense, especially to my investigation.
Vince: I think you're wrong. I think the quatrains solve your case.
Clint: How?
Vince: All the clues point to McCann's - the anthem city, the talisman, purebred players. And it's got to be referring to the new passing game of 1906 with a phrase like 'quick death'.
Clint: Clues are facts. All we've got are interpretations. How useful did you say Nostradumus' stuff was for predicting the future?
Vince: Not very useful.
Clint: Not very? You mean not useful at all.
Vince: Okay. Not useful at all. But things have happened that when you go back...
Clint (cutting Vince off in mid-sentence): Well, this isn't useful to me for solving this case.
Vince: (after another pause): One thing's for sure. Whatever team this thing's about, the Irish or the Terrors, whoever pisses them off gets cursed, whether it's a player who let them down or an opponent that beats them in a championship.
Clint: Let's wrap this up. What about the last quatrain?
Vince: You just said this wasn't useful to you.
Clint: I've gotten this far. Let's get it over with. Read the last verse.
Vince: 'Those whose retribution comes each tomorrow, to the devoted, they must make amends. This act alone will lift the cloud of sorrow: Pay homage to wearers of the talisman'....It's obviously

about the Pyrrhic victors. Retribution is the payback they suffer for beating our team in the championship. 'Each tomorrow' is a metaphor for each new season."
Clint: Not one new hint about the identity of the teams.
Vince (pause): I wonder if those two teams knew what they had to do?
Clint: Pay homage?
Vince: Yes. It would lift the curse, and it's self-serving. It would make their victory even more impressive. Think how it would look if their coach or captain talked about how good a team they beat. But how would they have known to do it?
Clint: I don't know.
Vince: When were these quatrains written? Recently or long ago?
Clint: Recently.
Vince: Interesting. Look how the quatrains are written. The first one is in the past tense. The second and third foretell future events. The last one's about something that still needs to be done.
Clint: Why's that interesting?
Vince: That means the teams with the tainted victories must still exist. If the quatrains were written recently and the teams no longer existed, why talk about something they need to do to change their fortunes?
Clint: What are you saying?
Vince: Start by finding one of those teams.
Clint: I'm not going to look for a team based on verb tense.
Vince: What if one of the Pyrrhic victories was the tournament championship? What if the team these quatrains are about was the loser?
Clint: Another interpretation?
Vince: It fits.
Clint: That's the problem. If any interpretation can be valid, then no interpretation can be valid.
Vince: You have to figure out which one is correct.
Clint: This thing is supposed to be an aid to my investigation, not the purpose of it.
Vince: You sure it's not useful?

Clint: What do you think?
Vince (another pause): Well, I'm going to prove you wrong.
Clint: Just don't make any phone calls related to the case.
Vince: I'm not. I'm going to figure out what these quatrains mean. When you solve your case, I'm going to show you the answer was right in front of you the whole time.
Clint (feeling like he's heard enough): I got to go, Vince. Thanks for your help. It's always interesting talking to you.

 Clint hung up. He looked over his notes. Then he clipped his pen onto the pages and tossed the notebook onto the countertop. Almost two weeks into the investigation and he only had one piece of solid evidence - the newspaper account that said McCann's and Monessen won their semifinals. And he had Charlie Rooney's unsubstantiated story. He had been skeptical about Elena's verses but felt he needed to give them a shot. At best he got some possible references to Homestead in the first two sets. The last two sets were really nebulous. Maybe he needed to run with the Homestead references; go there and dig around in the library. That museum Vince mentioned might have something.
 Or maybe this was one of the nine times out of ten that Madame Ivanova misfired.

Chapter Seventeen
Monday Afternoon, September 23, 1974

Clint picked up Olivia for another lunch. She wore a navy blue pullover shirt, khaki slacks and a shiny black belt with a holstered pistol, her PPD badge displayed in front of the weapon. Today she had short-cropped, blond hair and wore minimal make-up. She was prettier in a natural way, even sexier, than the last time he saw her. He would rather take this version of Olivia to bed, if he had the chance, than her undercover red-headed hooker persona. Of course, the desperate slut look sold better on the street.

Olivia settled into the passenger seat. "Where do you normally eat lunch?" she said.

"At home or at hamburger joints," Clint said.

"Tragic."

"What's wrong with where I eat?"

"This city has so many great delis and you eat at hamburger joints?"

"I ate at a deli once where they put the french fries on the sandwich. That was pretty good. Let's go there."

"Primanti Brothers. They're closed for renovation. Supposed to reopen next year. Today we start your education in eating well in Pittsburgh. DeLuca's will be your first lesson."

Clint drove to Penn Avenue in the Strip District. DeLuca's was a small storefront café in row of partially gentrified buildings. Inside, pale green wooden booths lined one wall. A lunch counter and stools ran along the other. Clint and Olivia sat in one of the booths.

Clint looked at the menu. "What do you recommend?"

"I think you'll like "The 'Burg". It's a Pittsburgh version of a cheese steak sub. I'm going to have the ham and egg club."

The "'Burg" sounded good. Clint sat his menu aside.

"Did you watch the Steelers yesterday?" Olivia said.

"No. I heard it was a tie. They played Denver, didn't they?"

"First regular season overtime game in NFL history," she said proudly. "Should have been exciting, but the overtime was a letdown."

"Because it ended in a tie?"

"Well, yeah. The Steelers fell way behind. They battled back into the lead, then Denver tied it at the end. That was disappointing enough, to see that big comeback go for naught. When the announcer said the game was going into overtime, I thought, okay, cool. The Steelers have the momentum. Extra time works in their favor. The overtime turned out to be all defense."

"Denver's got the Steelers' number. I remember they beat 'em last year."

"I know, and they're not that good of a team," Olivia said. "I don't know why we struggle against them."

"How did you get to be such a football fan?"

"I grew up with it. I was the only girl in a family of boys. When I got older, I found out it gave me an edge with guys. Nothing amazes you'uns like a girl who understands football. It's like I speak your secret language."

"Is that how you became so athletic? Playing football with your brothers?"

"Probably," Olivia said. "So how's life as a private eye?"

"I'm marking time," Clint said, "trying to decide what to do next."

"What do you mean?"

"I'm trying to decide if I should go back."

"Back where?"

"In the army."

"How long were you in for?"

"Nine years."

"You were almost halfway to retirement. Why did you get out?"

"So I could finish my degree and become an FBI agent."

"How did you end up training to be a cop?"

"I traded my dreams for love, or maybe it was lust."

"Must've been lust. That sounds like something a soldier would do."

"It was definitely lust."

"Now I remember. You two broke up and that's when you left training," Olivia said. "Why do you want to go back in?"

"I said I'm trying to decide."

"Okay. Why are you thinking about going back in?"

"Going from the CID to the FBI, I'm just trading a uniform for a suit."

"Not really. The scope of the FBI's mission is much greater."

"I didn't feel limited in what I was doing."

"You must've been satisfied about something. You stayed for nine years."

"Truthfully, I miss it."

"Doesn't sound like you have anything left to decide."

"What's left is letting go of the dream. That's hard to do. The FBI has been my light in the distance. I've been driving toward it since I was a teenager."

"Things have changed since you left. It's a volunteer army now."

"I heard they call it VOLAR or something. My friends tell me the lower enlisted get more privileges. They get treated more like adults."

"Makes sense. They're volunteers. They're not draftees who don't want to be there," Olivia said. "How's your football case going?"

"Stalled. The only newspaper covering the tournament went out of business before they announced the winner. I can't find any other contemporary accounts. It's almost like the final game was never played."

That was a possibility Clint hadn't considered. What if there were no reports about the championship game because there was no game? What if the paper shut its doors before the game was played?

"Anything else?"

Clint hastily regrouped his thoughts. "There's a city councilman who, for some reason, is interested in the outcome of the investigation. In fact, he's so interested his lawyer hired a PI to follow me."

"How did Madame Ivanova work out?"

"She gave me something I could work with. She suggested I check out a tavern. Turns out it's owned by the McCann family, the same family that sponsored the Fighting Irish. That's one of the two teams that might've won the tournament."

"Really?"

"Yeah. The people there knew details that I didn't expect them to know - the year it was played, the fact that it was organized by a newspaper. Then they introduce me to an old man, Charlie Rooney, who says he played in the tournament for the Irish. He's the right age, and his name matches a name on their roster. He tells me the Irish won."

"You need corroboration."

"I know. He could be lying, his memory could be bad…"

"What's next?"

"I thought that when a psychic helps the police, she tells them something like 'look in such and such lake.' They drag the lake and the divers go in and they find a body or the murder weapon or something."

"And it's case closed," Olivia said.

"Instead, she gives me this cryptic set of verses, a poem or prophecy of some sort. What's interesting is that it can be interpreted to about the Fighting Irish in 1906. Part of it, anyway."

"How so?"

"Well, it mentions a talisman on their armor. The Irish had a harp logo on the front of their jerseys. It says the team came from the anthem city. Homestead, where the Irish were from, has an anthem written about the big strike. It says they slew a behemoth with quick death. We figured 'quick death' refers to scoring fast by throwing the ball. In 1906 the rules for football changed to allow passing."

"Who's we?"

"Remember the football historian I told you about?"

"He's your expert witness?" Olivia said.

"You could say that."

"What's the behemoth?"

"A metaphor for a powerful opponent." Clint saw the look in her eyes, an equal mix of bewilderment and skepticism.

"I know what you're thinking," he said. "This interpretation isn't sufficient to corroborate Rooney's story. It's not irrefutable on its own merits. But it's consistent with Ivanova's suggestion about visiting the tavern. Maybe that tavern will be the lake."

"Keep diving and dragging until you find something."

Clint shrugged.

"Slow down, diver boy," Olivia said. "In Ireland, a picture of a harp is not a talisman. It's not a good luck charm."

"What is it?"

"It's Brian Boru's harp. It's just a symbol of Ireland."

"Are you sure?"

Olivia leaned toward him with wide eyes, amazed at his apparent lack of perception.

"Clint, my last name is Foley. I'm half Irish."

Clint gazed into Olivia's big, emphatic eyes. He suddenly felt amateurish. Not so much about looking for clues in the verses, but about the way he did it. No methodology. No rigor. Just two guys throwing out ideas, once while drinking beer. He needed to apply some scrutiny to the interpretation before he revealed anything more. Time to change the subject.

"What do you know about Councilman Harris?" Clint said.

"If you're asking me why he would be interested in this case, I don't know."

"What's his reputation?"

"It's clean," Olivia said, "or he does an excellent job of covering his tracks. His father was a whole 'nother story. He was up to his armpits, alleged to be up to his armpits, in corruption - bribery, kickbacks, shady campaign contributions, under the table deals, obstruction of justice, not to mention an active extramarital life."

"He ever get convicted?"

"He never got tried. He had too much dirt on too many people. They protected him."

"I guess the moral of the story is, if you're going to go, go big. What's he doing now?"

"He's retired somewhere in Florida. Said to be living off a private account he funded with his graft. No, Steve Harris is not a chip off the old block. He's part of the post-Watergate breed of politician. You know, more ethical."

Olivia took a sip from her iced tea.

"Being ethical has its drawbacks in politics," she said. "Harris is in a tough re-election fight. The newspaper says he's having trouble raising campaign money."

"Big donors contribute to get influence," Clint said. "They're not sure if they can trust a principled politician."

"Well said. So, what you gonna do next?"

"Go to Homestead and dig around. Maybe drive over to Monessen and start asking questions. See where it leads me."

"Asking ques-tions in Moe-nessen." Olivia smiled. "I like that. It's got a cadence to it."

Chapter Eighteen
Monday Evening, September 23, 1974

Back in his apartment, Clint had one phone message waiting. He immediately recognized Karen's girlish, smart-alecky voice.

"Good evening, Mr. McQueen. How are things in Tinseltown? They must be pretty good 'cause we haven't seen you in awhile. Mr. Walsh asks that you be available at your Hollywood mansion to receive his call around nine tomorrow morning. Or you can please your fan club by paying a visit to the office. You remember where that is, don't you? Good niiiight."

A few hours later, another phone call. Clint answered it, "Ronson here." As soon as he heard the raspy voice he knew the caller was Charlie Rooney. Clint felt a rush. He hoped this call was the breakthrough he needed. Why else would Charlie call unless he had information that he didn't remember, or wasn't prepared to share, during the interview? Generally when Clint got a callback the person was talkative - eager to set the record straight, willing to reveal additional information, anxious to purge guilty feelings. Sometimes the call was just an outpouring that added no value to the investigation. Sometimes there was a nugget of gold.

"Is this a bad time to call? I hope I didn't wake you up or something," Charlie said.

"No sir. I appreciate you calling me back." Clint was solicitous, wanting to put Charlie at ease.

Charlie started into the reason for his call. He spoke slowly and sounded like he had rehearsed what he was going to say.

"I'm eighty-seven years old. I've had a good life. I thank God for every additional day. But sooner or later I'm going to have to give an account of my life. One thing I don't want to say is I lied to you to get that prize money."

"Lied. What did you lie about?"

"About McCann's winning that tournament. We didn't win. We got beat fair and square."

"So Monessen won."

"Nah, it wasn't Monessen. I don't remember who they were. But I know it wasn't Monessen."

"Are you sure?"

"That's who we were expecting to play, Monessen. I remember we were really surprised when this other team showed up. It might've shook our confidence a little bit. We knew we could beat Monessen. We beat'em every time we played 'em. We never played this other team."

"Do you remember anything about the game? Do you remember the score?"

"I just remember it was a real close game. They won with kicking. There was a lot more kicking in the game back then - punting and place-kicking and the like. I guess that's why they called it football. Anyway, they had a better kicker."

A field goal. A long range strike for a score. Quick death, Clint thought. Why hadn't that occurred to him and Vince? Didn't Vince say a field goal was worth almost as much as a touchdown back then? And kicking was an established part of the game. Passing was in its infancy. It was probably more of a novelty than a threat.

"Is there anything else," Clint said.

"Nah. That's it. I apologize. I should've known better but I had a moment of weakness."

"Thank you for calling me," Clint said. "You're a good man for wanting to set the record straight."

"Well, I just had to get it off my chest," Charlie said. "I won't keep you any longer. Goodbye."

Clint heard a click on the other end, then the hum of the dial tone.

His mind went into overdrive. Which of Charlie's stories was correct? The one he told at McCann's? Or this one? If this was the true story, why did he first say the Fighting Irish had won? Did he have the tournament confused with another one? Did he intend to deceive? Or did he simply recall incorrectly? He said he lied, but that could have been a figure of speech - his way of saying he didn't speak accurately. Didn't he say he had a moment of weakness? Was that an admission of intent to deceive, or another figure of speech -

his recognition that his memory was playing tricks on him. If he really did lie at McCann's, why? Did someone put him up to it? He sounded contrite, but very elderly people almost always sounded contrite if they felt the fault was theirs.

Enough about Charlie's frame of mind, Clint thought. Assume he's now telling the truth. His statement that McCann's lost was a critical piece of information. Even more so was his assertion that the winner was not Monessen. That statement challenged one of the facts - that the Fighting Irish and Monessen played in the final. Clint pulled out the tournament bracket he had sketched. He wanted to see who played Monessen in the semifinal. Who might've beaten them to advance.

It was Waylan. He remembered Vince saying he called Waylan. Whoever he talked to said they had won the tournament. The newspaper said Monessen won, but the newspaper had given detailed reports of every game except that one. What if the latest report at press time had Monessen winning and the paper ran it? The *Pittsburgh Sentry* couldn't provide a full story because the game wasn't over. Maybe Waylan pulled it out. Or if Monessen did win, maybe something prevented them from playing in the final. Clint wondered if that could be one of the Pyrrhic wins mentioned in Elena's verses – Monessen won but couldn't advance. Then he wondered why his mind kept going back to the verses. Why did he keep thinking about his and Vince's interpretation of them?

Back to the facts. Four teams played in two semi-final games on Saturday, September 22, at the Westmoreland County Fair. The *Pittsburgh Sentry* reported McCann's Fighting Irish defeated the Ambridge Football Club by a score of 4 to 2, and Monessen defeated the Waylan Athletic Club. The Fighting Irish should have played the Terrors on Sunday in the tournament final. But Charlie Rooney just said the Irish did not play the Terrors. That would mean they played Waylan.

There was an outside chance that they played Ambridge again. Clint formulated a scenario: Monessen won but then couldn't play on Sunday. The opportunity to advance went to Waylan, but they were already on their way home. The organizers then turned to Ambridge and offered them a rematch against McCann's. The organizers had already set a precedent of offering losing teams a second chance. But Charlie would have remembered replaying them. It was remarkable to him and his teammates that they weren't playing their expected opponent. It would have been just as remarkable if they were playing the same team again. Especially so, since they had barely beaten Ambridge the day before. Furthermore, Charlie said they didn't know who their opponent was. He wouldn't have said that if it was Ambridge.

Clint considered one more possibility. What if Monessen couldn't advance and Ambridge and Waylan had both left town after losing their semifinal game? Could the organizers have brought in another team just to put on a championship show? He decided this scenario was far-fetched. It would have looked like the organizers were changing the rules to deny McCann's the prize money. The Fighting Irish would have raised holy hell. No doubt they would have reacted the same way if they had to play Ambridge again. Charlie would've remembered the protest.

Clint thought about his next move. Homestead definitely played in the final. If he went there, he might dig up information about the result. Success would equal case closed. For Monessen, he had the *Sentry* saying they won their semi-final game. Clint had to put more credence in that than in Charlie's revised story. If he went to Monessen, he might be able to confirm that they won the semi-final. If they did, he might learn the result of the final. Two steps to success.

As for Waylan, he had the *Sentry* saying they lost in the semi-final. He had an unconfirmed, second-hand conversation in which a Waylan supporter said they won the whole thing. He also had Charlie's new story from which he could infer that Waylan won the tournament. But those facts were contradictory and mostly unsubstantiated. Taken together, Clint didn't think the evidence for Waylan was as strong as the evidence for Monessen. Besides, if he went to Waylan, the sequence looked like Monessen's: Confirm or deny, if possible, that Waylan won the semi-final. If they advanced, find out, if possible, who won the final. Again, two steps to success.

FROM THE ANTHEM CITY

Homestead was the shortest path to success. Clint was going there first. If Homestead turned up dry, Monessen was next. Waylan was the last resort.

Chapter Nineteen
Tuesday, September 24, 1974

Clint waited in his apartment, drinking coffee, changing the channel from one network morning show to another. Promptly at nine the phone rang. This time Karen was the professional receptionist.

"Hello, Clint. Mr. Walsh wants to talk to you. Please hold." A few moments later Michael Walsh picked up.

"Clint, it's been two weeks since I gave you the Prentiss case. Where're you at with it?"

Clint felt mildly embarrassed. During those two weeks he had wrapped up a few other cases for Walsh and reported the status of a couple of others. He hadn't updated him on Prentiss. Clint gave Walsh a quick summary: One of three teams had probably won the tournament - McCann's Fighting Irish of Homestead, the Monessen Terrors, or the Waylan Athletic Club. The *Pittsburgh Sentry* reported the Irish and Terrors had won their semifinal games, but the paper ceased operation before publishing the result of the final game. The reason the paper shut down was the violent death of its publisher, the great uncle of City Councilman Steve Harris. Clint had interviewed a surviving member of the Irish who told him they won, but then the man changed his story. He now says that the Irish's opponent, which was not Monessen, had won. If his new story was true, then Waylan was the likely champion. Clint's plan was to go to Homestead, then Monessen, then Waylan. He was going to personally dig through every archive he could find, see if he could uncover any contemporary documents about the teams and tournament. Clint avoided mentioning Elena Ivanova and the cryptic verses.

"What a soap opera," Walsh said.

"That's why it's taking so long. It's more convoluted than I expected."

"I'll say...Why did the man change his story?"

"Could be a case of faulty memory. The guy is eighty-seven years old. He played football before they used helmets."

"How did Harris' great uncle die?"

"Gunshot to the head. His body was found along the riverbank."

"Murder or suicide?"

"I don't know at this time."

"That's got to be why Harris is interested in this case," Walsh said. "He knows, or suspects, how his uncle died. He wants to control how the story gets out."

"Maybe he knows why he died and doesn't want us to find out."

"Speaking of Harris, his lawyer's been in touch with me. How much of what you just told me can I share with him?"

"I don't want you to share anything," Clint said. "If he thinks he knows something relevant, or knows someone who knows something, tell me. Otherwise, I don't like outside people looking over my shoulder during an investigation."

"Fair enough. I'll pass that on to him and let him know you'll provide a full report when you're finished."

"One more thing," Clint said. "He's got his own PI tailing me. I'd appreciate it if you told him to knock it off."

"I'll see what I can do," Walsh said. "By the way, pick up the pace on this one. I'm tired of DeAngelo pestering me about it."

Twenty minutes later the phone rang again. The caller was DeAngelo's investigator. His voice was relaxed but business-like.

"Clint, I'm calling to see if I can get an update on the Prentiss case for Thomas DeAngelo. Councilman Harris has been asking about it. Kind of makes us look bad when we don't know anything."

"Give him a list of the places I checked out," Clint said. "I'm sure Ivanova's home wasn't the only place you tailed me to."

"I wouldn't follow you if you would keep us informed."

"I'll give my final report to Michael Walsh. If his client agrees to give it to DeAngelo, that's his call."

"C'mon, Clint. Update me on what's going on. Consider it a professional courtesy. I'd do the same for you."

"I don't report to Michael Walsh every time I learn something new. I'm not going to report to you or Thomas DeAngelo."

The PI's voice quickly changed from pleasant to irritated. "You're awfully independent for someone who came up doing things by the book."

Clint didn't respond.

"So, you're not going to work with me?"

"You got my answer."

"You're not going to make this easy for yourself," the PI growled. "Have it your way."

Clint heard the clunk of the hang-up. Obviously Walsh had called DeAngelo right after talking to Clint. Then DeAngelo immediately called the PI. Clint could picture DeAngelo chewing out the PI for not getting some cooperation. DeAngelo was probably taking heat from Harris for the lack of updates. That old adage from the army - shit flows downhill - applied to the civilian world as well. Clint had a moment of wicked satisfaction thinking about the discomfort his stubbornness had caused DeAngelo and his PI. It wouldn't have hurt to have thrown the PI a bone, except that he'd be back looking for another one. If he gave the PI something, he might get a little cooperation in return. He might glean an insight into Harris' interest in the case. Did he really need more insight than what Walsh had just provided? Besides, it was more fun injecting stress into the lives of DeAngelo and his PI.

Another phone call. Clint was starting to feel popular.

"Hey, this is Terry McCann. Charlie Rooney asked me to call to find out when he's getting his prize money."

Did he? Clint thought.

"If the money exists, all surviving members from the winning team will share it," Clint said. "Before I start looking for more survivors, I need to prove I found the winning team."

"Prove it to who?" Terry said.

"To the law firm that's holding the money."

"Well, you heard it right from Charlie himself. McCann's won."

"I'm still investigating."

"Why?" Terry asked. "Is something wrong?"

"Like I said before, I need to do fact-checking. I need to confirm the story."

"What Charlie told you, that was good, wasn't it?"

"I still need something to back it up. Would you want to be convicted on one man's testimony?"

"We're not talking about a conviction," Terry said. "We're talking about prize money."

"No one's going to award it based on the word of one man. Besides, there's something else I need to look into." Clint cringed as soon as the words came out. Bad slip. Terry didn't need to know that.

"Something else?"

"Routine stuff. Might support Charlie's story." His second one, Clint thought.

"Good," Terry said unenthusiastically. "As far as any other survivors, I don't think there are any."

"I'll need to be sure."

Terry was quiet for a few moments. Then he said, "Are you positive this money exists?"

"The evidence looks pretty strong."

"What bank's the money in? What law firm has it?"

"That's confidential. Remember?"

"How do I know you didn't make up a story about this money?"

"Why would I do that?"

"To get us to cooperate with your magazine article."

"I guess you have to trust me."

Terry was quiet again. Then he said, "It could take awhile to look for survivors, couldn't it?"

"It's been sixty-eight years," Clint said. "What's a few more weeks?"

"Charlie's not going to live forever," Terry said. Another moment of quiet, followed by, "OK, I'll tell him you're trying to find something to back up his story."

"Right," Clint said. Either one of them.

Chapter Twenty
Wednesday, September 25, 1974

Two days earlier Karen had left a message suggesting that Clint should pay a visit to the office. She said, "You remember where that is, don't you?" - making it sound like he had been out of contact for awhile. The truth was, he called or stopped by every day. He checked in to see if he had any phone messages or mail, to get an assignment, or to brief a lawyer or a client on a case. Otherwise, he didn't need to be in the office. All of his work - interviews, research, surveillance - required him to be out in the field. Clint preferred it that way. Offices made him feel restless. He liked to be moving, doing something. The only desk work his job required besides telephone interviews was doing write-ups on his cases. Clint did his reports at home in the evening with the radio on, the TV was too distracting, and a cold one nearby. Or he wrote them during lunch between bites of hamburger. He brought them in for Karen to type.

"As if I don't have enough to do," she always said, rolling her eyes.

Today he decided to linger at the office to make sure everybody saw him. He sat at an open desk, writing up a case he had just finished.

Karen found him and said to pick up line two. He had a call waiting.

"I was hoping I'd catch you there," Olivia said. Clint was delighted to hear from her. Talking to her was a better way to pass time than writing a report. He was in the mood to chat, to flirt a little. She wasn't interested. She got right to the point.

"That old football player you interviewed, what did you say his name was?"

"Charlie Rooney."

"He was found dead in his apartment this morning. Possible heart attack. It may have occurred during a struggle. He has bruises on his forearms, like someone grabbed them. Bruises on his knees, too.

Maybe someone pushed him down from behind. The phone was knocked on the floor."

"Was it a robbery?"

"Nothing seems to have been taken."

"He called me two days ago and changed his story. He told me the Irish got beat and the team that beat them wasn't Monessen."

"That's a real twist to your investigation."

"A guy from the tavern called me, too. One of the guys who set up my meeting with Rooney. He said Rooney wanted to know when he was getting his prize money, but he was fishing for something else."

"Like what?"

"He sounded suspicious. Maybe he wanted to find out if Rooney had talked to me."

"You didn't tell him, did you?"

"Of course not," Clint said.

What about the verbal slip? Clint quickly evaluated what he had told Terry. He said there was something else he needed to check out. Then he covered it over by saying it was routine stuff, something that might back up Rooney's story. He didn't flat out tell Terry that Rooney had changed his story. All he really told him was that he was continuing to investigate. Nothing wrong with that. Clint said the same thing during their meeting in the tavern. The case was still open. But the way he said it, that there was 'something else,' could have fed Terry's suspicion.

"Rooney might have," Clint said. "He sounded like it really weighed on him to have lied about winning. Maybe he came clean to the guys at the tavern."

"If they didn't think he talked to you yet, maybe they were trying to get to him before he did."

"That's a possibility."

"Look, I got to go. I got a call on the other line," Olivia said.

"Okay. Talk to you later."

Clint smacked the receiver in his hand a few times before hanging up. Poor Charlie Rooney. He said sooner or later he'd have to give an account of his life. Maybe that wasn't just the sentiment of an old man facing his mortality. Maybe he realized the trouble he found himself in. His death may have been unintentional, but the guys at the tavern had to be behind it. Maybe not Terry, but Jimmy or that goon Simon. They want the prize money. Clint remembered that they had even dangled a percentage in front of him. They called it a gratuity. Clint knew it was a bribe.

How did they know so much about the tournament? Maybe Paddy McCann talked about it years ago. Maybe his stories had become part of the family story - the world championship they lost, the glory that could have been, the prize money that got away.

Is there a connection between McCann's and Harris, Clint wondered? Something got Harris' attention in a big enough way that he hired his own PI. His interest wasn't simply altruistic. That talk about looking out for the family of a friend of his long-deceased great uncle didn't ring true from the beginning. The tournament and the unpaid prize money could be part of the Harris family story as well. Conveniently enough, the money surfaces at a time when he's desperate for campaign cash. Maybe he knew enough about the tournament to know the trail would lead to the tavern. If Terry and his friends could convince Clint that the Irish had won, then Walsh would award the prize money to Rooney. Rooney and the tavern trio would keep a percentage and pass the balance to Harris.

That scenario explains why DeAngelo wants updates and why he put a PI on Clint. He wants to make sure Clint was moving toward their desired finding. Their PI would probably help him stay on the scent if Clint had been willing to cooperate. Good thing he stuck to his "no interference" policy. It also explains why Terry was in a hurry to get the money. Harris needs to spend it now if it's going to do his campaign any good.

Another light went on in Clint's head. What about Ivanova? Had they gotten to her? Was that why she told him to check out the tavern? She had called him back right after his first visit. Maybe DeAngelo's PI had followed him there, just like he did on his second visit. Come to think of it, maybe he didn't follow Clint on the second visit. What if Ivanova had tipped him off?

What about her cryptic verses? One stanza mentioned campaigns. Could it literally refer to political campaigns? Clint pulled out the verses and reread them. This time he saw a politician who was benevolent to opponents he defeated and vengeful toward those who beat him, unless they granted him favors. What other messages were hidden in those verses? Was Elena trying to give Clint a warning about his investigation? Would it turn out to be a Pyrrhic victory for him if he learned the winner of the tournament and it wasn't McCann's Fighting Irish?

Clint sank back into his chair. Okay, he thought to himself, you've just formulated a theory. It's built on some facts and at least an equal number of assumptions. It perfectly explains the actions of every party in this investigation. Still, it's just a theory. It doesn't directly impact the question you're trying to answer. But the theory gives an idea about the motives of the parties; it gives an appreciation of the environment of this investigation.

And that environment is dangerous. Just ask Charlie Rooney.

Clint needed to flip the priorities he had worked out. Homestead and Monessen could wait. It was time to look into Waylan.

Clint called Vince at the motor vehicle office. He asked for the number to the Waylan Athletic Club. Vince said he didn't have it on him. It was at home. Clint asked him when he would get home. Vince said around five-thirty. Then he asked why he wanted it. Clint said he'd tell him later.

At five-thirty he called Vince at home.

"You thinking the guy I talked to down there was right?" Vince said.

"Just give me the number."

The person who answered gave the phone handed it to someone named Joe Walczak.

"I'm researching the 1906 football tournament that was sponsored by the *Pittsburgh Sentry*," Clint said.

"You're the second fellow to call here about that tournament," Joe said. "We won it. We were the world champions back in 1906. Why all the interest all of a sudden?"

"Do you have any documentation to back up your claim?"

"Documentation?"

"A newspaper article or something?"

"Hell, yes. We got a bunch of old programs and newspapers here."

Clint felt a rush of excitement. "When can we meet?" he asked.

Chapter Twenty-One
Saturday Evening, September 22, 1906

Jesse found Tom and Eddie sitting at a table in the hotel dining room.
"What's this?" he said. "Drinking before the big game?"
Tom couldn't tell if he was kidding or irritated. They weren't breaking any of his rules. Last weekend, Jesse said they could have one beer on nights before games. Maybe he hoped they would abstain altogether.
"We're just having a beer," Eddie said. "Helps us relax before we hit the sack."
"I heard the other team is having a party," Tom said. "They're celebrating the win they got today and the one they expect to get tomorrow."
"Where they staying?" Jesse said. "I want to send them some whiskey, a whole barrel. Compliments of the Black and Brown."
"Have a seat," Tom said. "A beer will do you good."
"What about him?" Jesse nodded toward a corner table. There was no mistaking his irritation now. Tom saw Billy alone at the table, a liquor bottle in front of him.
"I don't see anything unusual," Eddie said.
Jesse stared across the room at Billy, trying to decide what to do. Tom pulled out a chair. "Best you leave him alone," he said. Jesse slowly sat down, still looking at Billy, his irritation simmering. Eddie poured him a beer.
"Doesn't he know we're playing the championship tomorrow?" Jesse said.
"Right now, probably not," Eddie said.
Tom had noticed the locals coming in to the front desk to place telephone calls and pick up messages. Phones were popular but few homes were connected to the line. The hotel was making extra money by offering the use of its instrument to the public. One man caught Tom's attention. He was rotund and well-dressed in a gray suit. He had a bushy mustache, a cigar, and an air of self-importance.

The man talked to the clerk. The clerk leaned across the desk, peered into the dining room, and pointed at Jesse. The man strode toward them, leaving a wake of cigar smoke behind him. He stopped at the table next to Eddie.

"I'm looking for Jesse Mitchell," he said.

"You found him," Jesse said.

"My name is George Stonebridge. I'm the tournament director."

"What can I do for you?"

"A formal protest has been lodged about the outcome of your game today."

"A protest?" Jesse glanced at Tom and Eddie, his irritation replaced by confusion. He looked up at Stonebridge. "What's under protest?"

"The forward pass that put your team in position to score the winning touchdown. The protest is that the pass did not cross the line five yards out from the center as required by the new rules."

"Are the Maroons protesting? Their captain didn't complain to the referees after the play. Their coach didn't say anything at the end of the game."

"The Maroons are not protesting."

"Then who is?"

Stonebridge took a long drag on his cigar. He slowly exhaled the smoke. "Officially, the *Pittsburgh Sentry*," he said.

"The *Pittsburgh Sentry*! That's the tournament sponsor."

"As the sponsor, they need to ensure the result of every game is indisputable. They're responsible to safeguard the integrity of the tournament."

"I never heard of such a thing." Jesse's irritation was back in full bloom.

"They're not just the sponsor," Tom said. "They're the organizer. They're running the tournament. If the organizer is protesting a game, then who's going to rule on the protest?"

"How can the *Pittsburgh Sentry* be impartial about its own protest?" Eddie said.

"How did this protest come about?" Jesse said. "Did someone see something they thought was illegal? And if they did, why didn't they complain immediately? How can you investigate a pass play now? The game's been over for hours."

"I'm going to question the referees," Stonebridge said. "They're on their way over here now. If there's any uncertainty on their part, I'll question the players and any witnesses who come forward."

"There was no uncertainty when the play ended," Tom said. "This whole thing sounds crooked."

"How can the *Pittsburgh Sentry* be impartial about its own protest?" Eddie said again.

"As reporters of the news, we have a duty to be impartial," Stonebridge said, looking down at Eddie. "Otherwise, how could we maintain the public's trust?"

"What do you mean by 'we'?" Tom said. "Are you with the newspaper?"

"I'm the editor of the sporting news." Stonebridge took another drag and exhaled. "I'm also a lawyer. I'm well-equipped to handle this kind of inquiry."

"Let me get this straight," Jesse said. "You work for the *Sentry*. The *Sentry* is protesting the game. And you're going to conduct the inquiry?"

"I'll be serving in my role as the tournament director. The *Sentry* expects me to function independently to uphold the integrity of the event."

"Well, this is how I want to uphold integrity." Jesse rapped his knuckles on the table. "I want your inquiry to take place right here. I want witnesses. I want people to hear what's being said."

"Very well," Stonebridge said. "I'll be back with the referees."

Four and a half hours earlier, Tom and the team had taken the field against the Maroons. The Black and Brown received the opening kickoff and returned it to the thirty-one. First down: punt. Gus was taking no chances, Tom thought. Get the ball out of our end of the field. If we recover it downfield, it would be a big gain, a huge turn in our favor. Tad put some range on the kick. The ball bounced and rolled. A Maroon player fell on it at the fifteen. The Maroons punted right back on their first down. Both quarterbacks were following the conventional game strategy.

The Black and Brown took over at midfield. Gus called two run plays: Billy into the line for no gain, Billy off-tackle for a one-yard loss. Billy's hesitant, Tom noticed. Stutter-stepping when he should be driving, looking for a hole instead of making his own. He must be hung-over. Last night he was celebrating in the hotel bar like it was New Year's Eve, offering to buy drinks for anyone who passed by. "Take it easy, Billy," one of his teammates told him. "Don't spend your prize money before you win it."

Third down: Tad punted to the Maroon fifteen. The Maroons punted right back. First down at the Maroon forty-five. After an exchange of four punts between the teams, the Black and Brown had improved their field position by twenty-five yards. Their tactical kicking game was working.

Gus started using his other backs or ran the ball himself. The Black and Brown gained two first downs. The ball was inside the twenty-five. Two more runs. Third and four inside the twenty. Tad kicked a field goal. The Black and Brown led 4 to 0.

The Maroons counterattacked with a series of perfectly-executed run plays. They drove against the Black and Brown, moving the ball in relentless five to seven yard bursts. From two yards out, their fullback plunged across the goal line. With the kick after goal, they led 6 to 4.

The Maroons were good, Tom thought. They were easily better than the two previous teams the Black and Brown had played - the hapless Crimson and that other bunch that was big talk and little play. The Maroon players had sharper skills. They were bigger and quicker. They were aggressive on defense and disciplined on offense. Tom still felt the Black and Brown was the stronger team. He felt they were equal to the Maroons in all those areas, and they were tougher. That edge in toughness would compound through the game - wearing the Maroons down physically, shaking off their best shots, eroding their will to win, little advantages piling up play by play - until the Black and Brown took control of the game. The key was for every man to give his all on offense and defense.

There was the problem. Billy Pallister was playing badly. As linebacker, he normally made quick reads and delivered low, bone-jarring shoulder tackles. Billy always dominated his half of the line. Today he was as hesitant at linebacker as he was at halfback. He was using his arms to tackle, trying to wrap them around the runner's waist or legs as he went by. On the Maroon scoring drive, Billy was the weak spot. They ran most of their plays toward his side.

"Billy, I'm replacing you with Turner," Jesse said at halftime.

"It took me awhile to get started, but I'm ready now," Billy said.

"Get started? The game's half over."

"The second half's gonna be different."

"I can't take that chance."

Billy put his hand on Jesse's shoulder. He looked him in the eye.

"Leave me in, coach," he said. "I won't let you down."

At the outset of the second half, the old Billy was back. He was a wildman at linebacker, wrecking two Maroon run plays and forcing them to punt. Next he blasted into the line with two leg-churning runs that scattered players like bowling pins. Then it was over. The hesitant, soft Billy reemerged.

Maybe he's trying to hide an injury, Tom thought. He could show his old form for a few plays, but now the pain's flaring up. He might be too proud to take himself out, but he's hurting the team. It's like playing with ten men against eleven.

Jesse thought so, too. After the Black and Brown punted, he called time out and sent Turner in. Billy jogged off the field with his head down. Getting carried off the field injured was a badge of honor. Getting replaced when the team had a large lead was understandable. But being replaced for poor play- that was the ultimate indignity.

Tom glanced at the table in the corner of the room. Billy sat there, drunk, bawling, holding his face in his hands, a whiskey bottle in front of him.

"I let you boys down," he wailed at passing team mates. "I let everyone down."

"Take it easy," they would reply in a mix of pity and disgust. "You can make it up to us tomorrow."

Tom needed to talk to Billy when he sobered up; try to find out what was going on. Billy was always a hard one to talk to. He kept his teammates at arm's length. He put up an arrogant front if you tried to get close. But that was when he was playing well. Now that he had been humiliated, maybe he would open up.

The game had been a stalemate since the Maroon touchdown, a grinding struggle of meager runs and punts. Gus tried to spark the Black and Brown offense with pass plays. The first attempt was a turnover. The throw hit the ground untouched. The next two bounced incomplete off the intended pass catchers.

Suddenly Jesse was yelling from the sideline. He was holding his stopwatch and shouting that the game was down to the final minutes. The Maroons still led by two points. The Black and Brown regained possession, probably for the last time.

These were the moments that Tom loved, the ones that got his blood up - the impending finality, the clarity of purpose, the urgency. Block out pain and distractions. Wring out the last drops of strength. Beat the clock. Do whatever it takes to get the score. Tom sensed the whole team was infused with the same fierce determination.

On the first play Turner gained two yards off-tackle. Then Gus pitched the ball to Jake Rourke around the end. Rourke swerved through defenders for twenty-five yards. The Black and Brown rapidly lined up. The Maroon defense was slow to get set. A quick pass from center. Tad plunged through the line for five. The Maroons were losing their composure. The Black and Brown struck with two more runs. The Maroons were reeling. Gus called a pass. He sprinted to his right, saw Eddie facing him wide open, and side-armed the ball to him. The throw was high. Eddie leaped, stretched his arms overhead and snared the ball between his fingers. He pulled it to his chest as he fell backwards at the two. The next play was a mass run around the left end. Rourke touched the ball down across the goal line. Black and Brown 9, Maroons 6.

Stonebridge returned to the table with the three referees in a file behind him. They looked tense; unsure about what they were going to face. Tom recognized the head referee, a bantam man with a neat mustache, black hair and darting brown eyes under a high forehead. Tom normally didn't remember much about referees unless they blew a call. He remembered this one because he did a good job. He took charge on the field, made quick decisions, and kept the game moving.

"Have a seat, gentlemen. I have a few questions to ask you." Stonebridge pulled a chair away from the table and sat down near Eddie. The referees sat across from him. Stonebridge slouched in his chair, tilted his head to the right and narrowed his eyes at the referees. He already looked skeptical about anything they might say.

"What's all this about?" the head referee said. Tom remembered his sharp, nasal-toned voice and feisty manner from the game. He was amusing at first - a little emperor strutting around and making calls on the field. Then it became obvious that he knew what he was doing.

Stonebridge examined his cigar as he spoke, turning it between his thumb and forefinger. "A spectator at today's second game informed our office that he saw an illegal play which affected the result of the game."

"If you think you're going to intimidate us into changing our decision, you're mistaken."

"I'm not going to ask you to change any calls you made on the field, just to explain them. The *Pittsburgh Sentry* will make any decisions about the outcome of the game."

The head referee looked up at the players standing around the table. He glanced over his left shoulder, then his right shoulder, at the ones behind him. Turning back to Stonebridge he said, "Why can't we do this in private with representatives from both teams?"

"One team has requested an open hearing. And the other team has already left."

"Then who's protesting the game?"

Jesse said, "The *Pittsburgh Sentry*. Isn't that unbelievable?"

Stonebridge glared at him. This is my inquiry," he growled. "You may witness the proceedings, but you may not ask questions or make comments."

"The sponsor is questioning the outcome of the game?" the head referee said.

"The *Sentry* simply wants to make sure the result is indisputable. I think that's understandable given the stakes of this tournament and the new rules that are in effect."

"Then the sponsor is questioning our competence as referees."

"The *Sentry* wants to investigate the report of a spectator."

"But you said the *Sentry* would make decisions about the outcome of the game, which means they think the result is not final."

More Black and Brown players surrounded the table. The small crowd and tense atmosphere caught the attention of a few of the locals coming in to use the telephone service. Tom watched them cautiously creep into the dining room. They listened for several minutes before going back to the lobby.

"Let me restate my purpose for calling you here," Stonebridge said. He shifted in his chair, acting like he was making a special effort to remain patient. "A spectator complained to the office of the *Pittsburgh Sentry* about an important call made during one of today's games. Since a spectator can't protest a game, the *Sentry* formally filed the protest. As the appointed tournament director, I am responsible to investigate the protest. If it has merit, the newspaper may have to reconsider the outcome of the game. I apologize for not making this clear from the outset."

This didn't sound good, Tom thought. Stonebridge had claimed he functioned independently as the tournament director. Now he was saying the newspaper had the final word on game results.

"This is ridiculous," the head referee said. "Spectators always complain about referees, especially spectators who support the losing team. If we gave their complaints credence, there would be no end to them, and the outcome of every game played would be in limbo. That's why only the competing teams can file protests."

"This is a special situation," Stonebridge said. "The spectator who made this complaint is uniquely credible."

A special situation? Was that a fancy way of saying someone who had special pull with the newspaper? This didn't sound good at all, Tom thought.

"How big is their wager?" Eddie said.

"You hit the nail on the head, Eddie. That's what this is all about," Jesse said.

Stonebridge slowly rolled his head back until he was staring at the ceiling. He inhaled deeply. "Are you finished?" he said. No answer. He lowered his gaze toward the head referee.

"Are you ready to answer my questions?"

"Ask your questions, sir. Now I'm glad to be answering them in front of all these people. I think the *Pittsburgh Sentry* has already decided what outcome it wants. I want everyone to hear that we are capable referees and that we called the game correctly. I don't want our reputations sullied by backroom deals."

"Very well. For the record, state your names and your assignments for the second game."

"My name is William Loomis. I was the referee."

"I'm Bill Luehring," the next one said. "I was the umpire."

The third said, "Fred Jones. Head linesman."

Stonebridge reached inside his jacket for some notes.

"The play in question occurred about five minutes before the end of the game," he said. "The team in black jerseys was losing 6 to 4. They had possession of the ball about ten yards away from the goal line. It was second down. The black team needed to gain three yards for a first down. They completed a forward pass for eight. The complaint is that the forward pass crossed the line of scrimmage within five yards of the center. As you know, the new forward pass rules prescribe that the pass must cross the line of scrimmage more than five yards out from the center."

"That was your catch," Tom whispered to Eddie.

"I distinctly remember that play," Loomis said. "I can assure you the pass was legal."

"What makes you so sure?"

"As referee, I position myself behind the offensive backs, aligned with the center. When plays are run to the outside, I remain in that position until the ball is carried more than five yards along the line of scrimmage. Then I follow the ball to maintain a good perspective."

"How can you be sure the ball is more than five yards out from the center when it's thrown?"

"I use the gridlines that run the length of the field as a reference. They're five yards apart."

"With the gridlines, you can be sure of the location of the passer when he throws the ball," Stonebridge said, "but how can you be sure the pass crossed the line of scrimmage at least five yards out? That's the rule."

"If the passer is more than five yards out, the pass will cross the line of scrimmage at least five yards out, unless he drops deep and throws the pass toward the center of the formation. In that case, I would note the position of the pass catcher in relation to me and make the decision. If I have any doubt about the play, I would confer with the umpire."

Tom was impressed with Loomis. The referee had some fight in him. He knew the rules and he had a system to find order in the chaos of a play. He was standing up to Stonebridge, taking charge here just like he did on the field. Now it was the umpire's turn.

"I also keep a close eye on pass plays," Luehring said. "Like the referee, I align myself with the center, but on the defensive side of the ball. The forward pass rule states that a pass cannot be caught in a rectangle that extends five yards out from the center and runs the length of the field. It's my job to enforce that rule. Using the gridlines, I can easily see if the pass catcher was in the rectangle."

Loomis said, "To address the play in question, I was positioned about one yard to the right of a grid line. The quarterback was more than two yards past the next grid line when he threw. He was clearly more than five yards from the center. He threw the ball to the outside. There is no possibility that it crossed the line less than five yards out."

"And the player who caught it was well outside the prohibited rectangle," Luehring said.

Stonebridge turned his attention to the third referee. "What did you see?"

"I'm the head linesman," Jones said. "I stand on the line of scrimmage. For any forward pass, my job is to make sure the quarterback is behind the line when he throws the ball and the pass catcher is beyond it. That was true for all the passes attempted in this game."

"I see." Stonebridge took a pull on his cigar and gazed into the distance as he slowly blew out the smoke. Then he said, "How can all of you be sure you're remembering the play in question? Both teams ran dozens of plays."

"The Maroons did not try any forward passes," Loomis said. "The Black and Brown tried four. They only completed one. As soon as I saw the catch, I double-checked my position and that of the quarterback. That play was an important and singular event in the game. How could anyone who paid attention to it not remember the details?"

"All of you are certain the pass was legal."

"Yes," Luehring said. Jones nodded.

"Absolutely," Loomis said. "And the fact that the other team did not argue the play at the moment is further proof."

Good work, Tom thought. Loomis had shot down any possible doubt about that "important and singular event," whatever that meant.

"Does anyone else have a question for these gentlemen," Stonebridge said.

"None of us had a question to begin with," Tom said.

"I have a question for you, sir," Loomis said to Stonebridge. "What did this spectator claim he saw?"

"All I know about his complaint is what I told you."

"If the only information he provided was speculation that the pass was not legal, if he could provide no other facts to support his allegation, then you've both wasted our time and insulted us," Loomis said.

Very good, Tom thought. Turn the table. Expose the absurdity of this inquiry.

"I'm just performing my duties," Stonebridge said. "To bring this to a close, I want you to write down exactly what happened and sign it. In the meantime, I'm going to place a telephone call to the *Sentry* and report what you've told me."

"Make me a copy, too," Jesse said to the referees.

"Then someone needs to get us some paper," Loomis said.

Jesse asked Eddie to see if the desk had paper. Then he said to Stonebridge, "I take it this protest has no merit. When are we going to hear from the *Sentry*?"

"That's the *Sentry's* decision."

"And if they change the outcome, then what?" Tom said. "The other team already went home."

"That will be the *Sentry*'s concern," Stonebridge said. He stood up and walked away.

The onlookers dispersed, mumbling between themselves as they left. A player approached the table.

"Coach, we still got a game tomorrow?"

"We won today, didn't we?" Jesse said.

"I was just wondering," the player said.

Jesse said, "We better have a game tomorrow, or I'll go to every newspaper I can find. I'll show them the referees' statements and tell them what a rigged deal this tournament was. They might not want to report on it now, but they will when they find out everything wasn't on the level."

Eddie came back with paper and pencils.

"What are you going to write, Will?" Luehring said to Loomis.

"I'm going to sketch the play. Draw the gridlines and show where I was positioned."

Eddie sat down next to Tom. On the other side of Tom, Jesse was quietly seething. Stonebridge's cigar smoke hung over the table. Eddie placed his hands around his empty beer glass and started turning it between his fingers.

"I knew something like this was going to happen," Eddie said to Tom. "The spectators aren't familiar with the new rules. The players aren't. The coaches aren't, except for Jesse. Lucky for us, our referees knew the rules."

"Whoever's behind this came up with a clever way to throw a game," Tom said. "Challenge a play that's covered by new, complicated rules. Most times, the referees won't remember enough to explain their call."

"They'll say, 'Take our word. We got it right.'"

"Their word would only be as good as their explanation."

"Not this time," Eddie said.

"Whoever's behind this didn't expect these refs to be so sure of themselves," Tom said.

"If we win, someone loses a big payday. That's what this is all about."

Tom shook his head. "I never heard of a game getting thrown like this," he said. "I always figured a player would take a dive or a referee would do the dirty work. I never thought the organizers themselves would be part of it."

"You think they put someone up to lie about what they saw?"

"Maybe. Who was this spectator, anyway?"

"How do we know he was even at the game?" Eddie said.

"He knew about you catching the forward pass."

Eddie sat quietly, the glass turning between his fingers, his mind turning. Then he said, "What if the spectator was Stonebridge?"

More silence. More thinking. Then Jesse said, "I just feel sorry for you boys. This tournament cost you a lot of money - travel, food, lodging. And everyone worked so hard to get ready. To have it all taken away like this. It's terrible. It's unbelievable."

"What do you expect's going to happen, Tom," Eddie said.

"I expect we'll play tomorrow. It's going to be hard to dispute what these referees said. Even if Stonebridge was behind it."

"I hope you're right," Eddie said.

"And I hope we have these refs. This Loomis is the first referee I ever took a liking to."

Chapter Twenty-Two
Thursday, September 26, 1974

Time on the road gave Clint time to think. CID or FBI? Clint was going to be careful about making this decision. His last life-changing decision turned out badly. Fortunately, Gina broke things off during the engagement. Things would've been a lot more complicated if they divorced after he became a police officer. As it was, he quit training only a few weeks in and picked up the trail of his ambition where he got off. He had mapped out this trail, through the army and college, to get him to the FBI. Problem was, he was no longer sure he wanted to be an FBI agent. The army suddenly looked very appealing. He had been comfortable there. He had success. The army would no doubt take him back into CID. He wouldn't go back if they wanted to assign him to a different specialty. Or would he? Maybe he was just longing for something familiar and steady. He had experienced a lot of turbulence in his life lately. Clint liked being a private investigator, too. He liked operating independently. But he didn't see a reason to stay in Pittsburgh. Maybe he should do his twenty in the army, then start his own investigation service. Like Olivia said, he was almost halfway to retirement in the army. He'd have his pension plus his earnings from the business. That sounded like a plan.

What about Olivia? Clint felt a tug in the middle of his chest just thinking of her name. She could complicate the decision. Not by anything she did, just by her presence in his life. Clint liked this spunky blonde. He liked her self-confidence, her lively energy, her teasing banter. He liked how she could be strong but girlie at the same time. He liked how she was good-looking in a simple, natural way. Clint liked her a lot.

Was he getting carried away over her? After all, they only had two casual lunches together and talked on the phone a few times. They rarely discussed anything personal. They had never gone out on a real date. Was he wrapped up in the excitement of meeting someone new? Was he rebounding from Gina? Why had he called her in the first place?

CID or FBI? Or was it stay or go? Maybe he had a reason to stay in Pittsburgh after all.

Waylan was not a convenient place to get to. Clint drove from the interstate to a state road to a well-traveled county road to a narrow and winding county road before finally reaching the only road that led into town. He steered through two sharp switchbacks as the road wound down the mountain, a rock wall on one side of the car, a railing and a drop on the other. Clint wondered why anyone would choose to live in such an isolated place.

Waylan was a typical Allegheny industrial town. It was pinched into a valley at the junction of a creek and a river. The heart of the town consisted of narrow two and three-story buildings made of brick, stone or hardboard. They were lined up in tight rows along the main street and a few adjoining side streets. An iron truss bridge crossed the creek and connected the center of town with a steel mill, a rail yard and an enormous brick building that appeared to be some sort of railcar repair shop. Several dozen white wood-frame houses overlooked the town from scattered locations on the flanking mountainsides.

Clint parked and walked along the main street until he found the address. A sign on the door read "Waylan Athletic Club, Home of the Coalcrackers." He opened the door. A small bell attached to the inside top edge tinkled. Clint smelled cigarette smoke and stale beer. His eyes adjusted to the darkness. He had expected an establishment that called itself an athletic club to be a gym. This was a bar; an unpretentious place where a blue collar guy could feel at home - dim lighting, paneled walls, two pinball machines side-by-side, a jukebox, a few tables and chairs, a television mounted overhead in a corner.

It was also a shrine to the club's semi-pro football team. Framed photographs hung on the walls - teams, game action, and individual players. Clint guessed the oldest player photos were from the fifties and early sixties. They showed Coalcrackers in vintage uniforms and outdated hairstyles posed in exaggerated action stances - a running back imitating the Heisman trophy, a receiver stretching for an invisible ball, a growling blocker. More memorabilia was displayed amid the liquor bottles on the shelves behind the bar - four black helmets, including a leather one and a plastic one without a face mask, a half dozen footballs, and a square-toed kicking shoe. The oldest balls were fat and round with crudely stitched laces. The newer ones were shaped like sleek missiles.

Clint quickly surveyed the clientele. A man banged away at one of the pinball machines. Two others, oblivious to the ringing and jangling, carried on a conversation at a nearby table. The three men sitting at the bar and the bartender were transfixed by a TV show.

Clint took a seat at the bar. The bartender looked him up and down, then asked what he was having.

"I'm looking for Joe Walczak," Clint said.

"That would be me. You the one doing the research?" Joe was stocky and broad-shouldered with a bulldog face, pale blue eyes, and close-cut brown hair.

"Yeah. You said you have some newspaper clippings."

"Hey, everybody!" Joe suddenly announced. "This is the guy I was telling you about, the guy who's researching our team." The patrons interrupted what they were doing and eyed Clint for moment. Most of them quickly went back to their TV watching or beer drinking or pinball playing. A few gazes curiously lingered on Joe and Clint.

"Whatcha doing research for?" Joe asked.

"I'm writing an article about that tournament I told you about. Nobody knows who won. The newspaper accounts end with the semifinal games. Even the result of one of those games is in doubt. I'm trying to solve the mystery."

"I can show you who won," Joe said. He went to the wall, removed a framed photo and placed it on the bar. "These guys here."

A black and white photo oxidized to shades of brown and yellow showed a team of about twenty men. The players seemed to have gathered quickly for the picture, like someone had unexpectedly called for a team photo after a game or practice. They wore football uniforms, but the uniforms were hardly identical - thick turtleneck sweaters, jerseys with padded shoulders, jerseys with striped sleeves. A man with a rakish mustache stood in the middle wearing a jacket, tie and bowler. Clint thought he might be the coach. Onlookers in the distant background indicated the photo was taken outdoors. Someone had written "1906 World Champions" above the heads of the players.

"May I take it out of the frame?" Clint asked. Joe nodded.

Clint used his penknife to carefully pry the fasteners and remove the cardboard backing. On the reverse side someone had written the names of the players.

"I had no idea there was anything written on the back," Joe said, almost in awe at the discovery.

Clint checked the names against the roster printed by the *Pittsburgh Sentry*. Almost all of them matched.

"You said you have some newspaper articles," Clint said.

"We have a storage room upstairs where we keep all the historical stuff - schedules, photographs, newspapers, programs, game film, what have you. Now, 1906 is going back quite a ways. I looked through the boxes but I didn't find anything. Turns out the only thing we have is that photo."

Clint looked up at the artifacts behind the bar. His eyes moved from the helmets to the footballs to the kicking shoe.

"You've got some museum pieces back there," he said.

"We're proud of our team," Joe said. "It's been in continuous operation since the 1890s. It's probably one of the oldest semi-pro teams in the country."

"How do you know Waylan won the tournament, other than the handwriting on the picture?"

"It's just common knowledge here. You ask any sports fan when his favorite team won championships and he can rattle off the years."

"There's usually a record book that backs up those claims."

"When I was younger, I used to hear the old-timers talk about winning that tournament. The Coalcrackers've won a lot of league championships, but nineteen-owe-six is the only time we won the world championship."

Clint decided not to tell Joe that "world championship" was an inflated claim for the 1906 *Pittsburgh Sentry* tournament.

"Do you remember what the old-timers said about the tournament?"

"Just that they won," Joe said, "and they didn't get the recognition for it?"

"Recognition?"

"I guess they felt that as time went on, nobody believed they were world champions."

"Are any of those guys still around?"

"I haven't seen 'em in years."

The bell on the door tinkled. Clint glanced at the entrance. A man wearing a dingy white T-shirt slunk in. He glanced around the room warily. Then he turned a chair away from an empty table and perched himself on the front edge, poised like he was ready to make a hasty exit if necessary.

Clint began reassembling the picture frame. "I need a newspaper report to back this up," he said.

"The picture's not good enough, with all the names and the inscription?" Joe said.

"I don't know who wrote it," Clint said, "or when, or if it even refers to the *Pittsburgh Sentry* tournament. How do I know they didn't win a different tournament in 1906 that also claimed to be a world championship? I need something to authenticate it."

"Alright," Joe said. "I'll look through the boxes again. I'll spread the word around town, too. Let 'em know what you're looking for. Somebody might have something from 1906."

"Good idea," Clint said.

Coming out of the dark bar, Clint was nearly overwhelmed by the bright sunshine. He squinted tightly as he walked to his car. He pulled in deep breaths to clear the cigarette smoke out of his lungs. Quick footsteps approached from behind. He turned suddenly. The pursuer stopped a few feet from him.

"That game you're looking into…before you tell them what you find, I need you to tell me," the man said.

This out-of-breath man in a soiled, limp T-shirt was a poor excuse for a PI, Clint thought. He seemed anxious. He lacked the cool detachment needed in this profession. Maybe they weren't as sophisticated here in the backwoods.

"Look, man. It's important."

"You working for DeAngelo?" Clint said. "Or is someone else paying you?"

"DeAngelo?" The man had a quizzical look. Clint thought if he doesn't know DeAngelo, then DeAngelo's PI must've hired him.

"They already got my answer," Clint said.

The man's voice rose. "You already talked to them!" He reached toward Clint.

In a blink of an eye, Clint grabbed the man's wrist, twisted his arm behind his back, spun him around, and shoved him chest-first onto the hood of a parked car.

"What are you doing?!" the man protested.

Clint lowered his mouth near the man's ear. Quietly and firmly he said, "Tell whoever you're working for that nobody interferes in my investigation."

"What the freak you talking about?"

Clint pushed himself away from the man. He started walking away backwards to keep an eye on him. The man rolled over and supported himself on the car, even more out of breath.

"You better watch yourself down here," he shouted to Clint. "This is personal now."

What an amateur, Clint thought as he drove away. Never let a case get personal, no matter how physical it becomes. That was one of the cardinal rules for any investigator. Clint remembered seeing the man come into the club. He looked uneasy. Clint never would've guessed he was doing PI work. How did he know Clint was there? Did the guy tail him? More likely, he was a watchdog. Someone gave him Clint's photo and told him to keep an eye on the club. Why did he confront Clint? Why didn't he just report back to whoever contracted him? Maybe he knew they wanted information from Clint. If he could get it, he could bargain for a bigger payment. Then again, maybe Clint was right the first time. Maybe he was just an amateur.

Chapter Twenty-Three
Friday, September 27, 1974

Olivia got into the Javelin.
"You said you liked DeLuca's, right? I picked out another place I think you'll like. It's called The White Eagle. A Polish couple owns it. It's over in the Strip District, a few blocks from DeLuca's."
"How did you become such a connoisseur of delicatessens?"
"Pittsburgh has dozens of ethnic delis. They're casual, inexpensive, and good. What's not to like?"
"You're getting me hooked," Clint said. Did he mean on delis or Olivia? He was sure he could even get excited about hot dog stands if eating at them meant seeing this pert young detective.
"The Steelers play the Raiders on Sunday. That's the hot rivalry ever since the Immaculate Reception."
"The Raiders got their revenge in the play-offs last year," Clint said, his eyes on the rearview mirror.
"It wouldn't be a rivalry if it was one-sided. You going to watch the game?"
"It'll probably be blacked out."
"I don't need to worry about that. I'm going."
"How'd you get tickets?"
"I'm going with a guy. He got the tickets."
"You know him well?" Clint said, feeling jealous but trying to be cool.
"Casually."
"Was he amazed that you understood football."
"You bet."
The White Eagle was on Smallman near the ramp to the 31st Street Bridge, in the western side of the Strip District. Gentrification had not taken hold here yet. It was more of a working section of town - machine shops and industrial supply and repair businesses.
"How did you find this place?" Clint said.
"Word of mouth."

Inside, they placed their orders over a display case full of cold cuts, sausages and cheeses. Too many choices for Clint. The lady behind the counter suggested traditional Polish ham with cheese. That sounded fine.

"Do you want everything?" the lady asked. "Tomato, lettuce, green pepper, onion, mayonnaise, mustard?"

Clint said he did. Olivia ordered the same thing. They sat at a small table against the front window. Clint looked at the occasional passing car or pedestrian on Smallman.

"Have you made a decision about the army yet?" Olivia said.

"I have. I'm going to call warrant officer management. See if they'll take me back in."

"They'll welcome you with open arms." Olivia sounded dead certain, as if she had some kind of special insight about warrants re-entering the army. Then Clint saw her momentary reaction - a flash of disappointment followed instantly by a brave face. He had seen that reaction before as a young troop. He was sitting in a snack bar in Ray Barracks with his soldier girlfriend. He told her he had come down on orders for CID school. He had illusions about keeping in touch through letters and phone calls and seeing each other during leave. She instinctively knew their relationship was doomed. It was too new, too shallow, to survive the separation and demands of duty. Getting upset wouldn't change anything. They were soldiers. What could she do other than accept it, suck it up, and drive on? Olivia knew the drill. She reacted the same way. Clint changed the subject.

"I drove down to Waylan, to the Waylan Athletic Club."

"What happened to 'asking questions in Moe-nessen'?"

"When Charlie changed his story, Waylan looked more like the champion. Plus, I got tipped off that they claim they won."

"Did they know prize money's involved?"

"No. They made the claim voluntarily, without knowledge of my investigation."

"Find anything worthwhile?"

"A team photo with an inscription saying they were the 1906 world champions. The team roster is written on the back. Most of the names match the list in the newspaper."

"That's good, but is it good enough?"

"The guy I talked to, his name is Joe, said they have boxes of memorabilia in a storage room. I asked him to look for anything from 1906."

"Hopefully he can find a newspaper story about the tournament."

"Something else. There was another PI down there keeping tabs on me. He must've been a local guy. He was pretty raw for a PI."

"Maybe investigations are a sideline for him."

"Either DeAngelo hired him or DeAngelo's investigator did. Either way, it goes back to Harris. Something about this case interests him enough to track my every move."

"How did he know you were going down there?"

"I don't know. Maybe someone knew the trail might lead to Waylan. Maybe they gave this guy my description and told him to keep an eye out for me."

Clint watched Olivia lean forward to take a bite of her sandwich; an unguarded moment. He took in her delicate features and sporty hairstyle with the bangs swept across her forehead. Man, he was going to miss this girl. From the reaction he got a minute ago, she was going to miss him, too. Was she enough to make him change his mind? No. He wasn't going down that path again. He wasn't going to change his plans over a girl again. Her eyes rose up to meet his.

"What?" she said.

"Nothing," Clint said with a quick shake of his head and a tight smile. "Anything new on Charlie Rooney?"

"Nothing. Nobody heard anything. Nobody saw anybody going to or coming from his home. No useable fingerprints."

Olivia wiped her lips with a napkin.

"By the way, I pulled the file on the Harris case, out of curiosity," she said.

"Did you have trouble finding it?"

"Yeah. It was deep in the vault."

"What'd it say?"

"The police report said a night switchman was sitting in a shed at the end of the Monongahela River Bridge."

"Where's that?"

"It's the railroad bridge next to the Liberty Bridge. Everyone calls it the Panhandle Bridge."

"I can picture it."

"He heard a shot and a splash about three o'clock in the morning. He waited a few minutes before going out to investigate. He said he didn't see anyone on or near the bridge, but it was too dark to be sure."

"The same story that was in the newspaper," Clint said.

"He notified police when he got off work at seven AM. In the meantime, someone found the body along the riverbank at daybreak. Harris had been shot in the right temple at close range."

"Sounds like a suicide. Was any blood or tissue found on the bridge?"

"No."

"Suicide note?"

"Didn't say anything about it."

"Did they check for residue on his right hand."

"They didn't do that back then."

"It still sounds like a suicide. The guy's business is failing. The pressure may have gotten to him. He probably knew the drop into the river wouldn't kill him, so he climbed over the railing and shot himself."

"If he was a proud person, or if he wanted to spare his family the anguish, he might've hoped his body would float down the river."

"Never to be found," Clint said.

"There's an argument to be made for homicide," Olivia said. "Some bad guys abduct him. They want him to cooperate, so they take him out on the bridge and dangle him over the side. Maybe one of them threatens him with a gun to the head. The gun goes off accidentally, or Harris refuses to cooperate and they execute him. The body and the evidence drop into the river."

"That's plausible," Clint said. "Harris might've borrowed money from some shady characters to keep the newspaper afloat."

"And if he was overdue on the payments..."

"But there had to be noise. Harris terrified, pleading for his life. The abductors shouting demands over his yelling. The switchman didn't say he heard anything like that."

"Maybe the switchman wasn't telling everything he knew," Olivia said.

"So, it could've been a suicide or a murder. Almost seventy years ago. Why would it matter to Councilman Harris?"

"It's a potential public relations problem in the heat of an election campaign. The press would love this; the dark side of a powerful, well-known family. Think of the headline - 'Publisher's Death Still a Mystery.' If it's a suicide, then a skeleton just walked out of the Harris family closet. If it's an execution, then all the old stories about Harris family corruption resurface. Bad news for someone who has styled himself as a post-Watergate politician."

"It would blow over in a week."

"Clint, this is late September," Olivia said. "The election is in the first week of November. Spending a week dealing with an issue like this could be fatal to his campaign."

"I'll tell you what could be fatal - running out of money. You said Harris' campaign was having problems getting donations?"

"Yeah."

"Then this investigation is a potential godsend, not a PR problem. Assume Harris knows about the 1906 tournament and that McCann's played in the final. He knows there's no record of who won. He knows the prize money was never paid. Maybe he suspected Prentiss still had it. Sure enough, he did, and it's part of his estate. Harris gets the McCanns to cooperate so he can persuade Prentiss' lawyer that the Fighting Irish won the tournament. The McCanns get the prize money. They keep a share and hand the rest under the table to Harris' campaign."

"Who's the link between Harris and the McCanns?"

"DeAngelo's PI. He's the go-between."

"Do you have proof?"

"Not yet."

Olivia leaned back in her chair. "Wow...That's a helluva theory."

"It explains everything that's happened so far. It explains why Harris is interested in this case. He wants updates. He has PIs following me to make sure I don't go out of bounds in my investigation. It explains why someone confronted Charlie when he changed his story. They thought he was their ace in the hole, a surviving participant from the championship game. If he said McCann's won, they thought that would be enough to award the money to them."

"How does Harris know so much about the 1906 tournament?"

"It's one of those family stories that gets handed down from generation to generation."

"What about Ivanova?"

"I think they got to her. She's the one who told me about McCanns."

"What about those cryptic verses?"

"They're a distraction. Something to blow smoke over what's really going on."

"To conceal the conspiracy?"

"Yeah."

"Do you think Elena wrote them?"

"I doubt it."

"Then who did?"

"I don't know."

"Clint," Olivia said slowly. "Remember Occam's Razor: the simplest explanation is usually the correct one. Harris is trying to protect his image. The McCanns are trying to get their hands on some unclaimed money. You happen to be in the middle. From your perspective, coincidence looks like conspiracy."

Something across the street across the street caught Olivia's attention. She stared out the window.

"What you looking at?"

"See those two guys? Remember I told you about a loan shark who was beating his delinquent customers half to death with baseball bats?"

"Yeah."

"We think they're the ones doing the beatings."

Clint followed her gaze. At the other end, two men stood beside a parked car. One was a bald with thick sideburns. The other was a round-faced with a mustache, double chin and perfectly combed hair. They exchanged conversation intermittently, like they were making small talk while waiting for something.

"That's Jimmy and Psycho."

"You know them?"

"They're connected to McCanns. Family friends or something. They were with Charlie the night I met him."

Clint glanced at Olivia. She looked back at him wordlessly.

"Wanna know what I suspect?" Clint said.

"What?"

"You're looking at Charlie's killers."

Chapter Twenty-Four
Sunday, September 29, 1974

Elena called him on Saturday. She said she had something important to show him. He told her he would be right over.

Clint dutifully made the drive to Squirrel Hill. He was uncertain about Elena. On the plus side, she had suggested he check out McCann's Bar and Grill, which led him to Charlie Rooney. Thanks to Charlie's phone call confession, Clint was pretty sure the Fighting Irish had not won the tournament. With the circumstances of Charlie's death, Waylan moved to the top of Clint's list. He intended to remain focused on that club until he could eliminate them or until the evidence was inconclusive.

On the negative side, Clint thought Harris' PI was using Elena to get to him. She calls, he comes running. She passes some information to him that she got from Harris' people. Was she a willing participant, or were they forcing her in some way? Those cryptic verses - what purpose did they serve except to obscure and distract?

Clint wondered if he was going to meet Harris' PI on this trip. That would be a friendly encounter, given that Clint had blown off his attempt to build cooperation. He checked his rearview mirror for following cars as he drove along the quiet streets of the neighborhood. Walking from his car to Elena's house, he looked for the blue Chevy Nova, or any parked cars with occupants.

Elena was waiting at the door. She brought him into her front room.

"There's another private investigator who's interested in this case," Clint said. "Has he talked to you?" Clint didn't expect her to admit it. He wanted to see her reaction. He wanted to let her know what he suspected.

"No. No one has talked to me."

A straightforward answer. Not a hint of dishonesty on her face. She's good, Clint thought, or she's telling the truth. Might as well bring up the next thing that was bothering him.

"Elena, I have to tell you, those verses you gave me haven't been any help. They're too vague."

"That is why I called you. Maybe this will help." She handed him a slip of paper. "The talisman," she said. She seemed pleased with herself, like she had come up with something that Clint would find very valuable.

At first glance, the figure on the paper resembled the letter "U". The bottom was bulb-shaped, with the curve skewed to the left side. On the right side, the line turned straight up, then doubled back on itself. On the left side, the line curved up and inward from the bottom, then suddenly turned out, creating a small lip at the top. At second glance, the figure could have been a hastily scrawled number "2" without the loop on the bottom, a doubled line running up and down from the right side of the base.

"What is it?" Clint asked.

"The talisman," she said again. "You know, in the verses I gave you."

"What's it supposed to be?"

Elena shrugged. "You are investigator," she said. "That is for you to find out."

"How did you get it?"

"Remember I told you there was another verse? I was trying to recall it, to give it to you. This figure came into my mind."

The doubts came into Clint's mind.

"Elena, I feel like you're playing a game with me. Feeding me clues. Waiting to see if I can figure them out."

Now Clint got a reaction from her. She stiffened. Her face went blank. Clint saw the fire of emotions -surprise, hurt, indignation - in her green eyes.

"Mr. Ronson, it was you who asked for my help, and so I am helping. If you think I am playing game, perhaps you should not come back."

Back in the car, Clint looked at the slip of paper again. An accurate depiction of the talisman might unlock the meaning of the verses, if there was any meaning. Instead of an accurate depiction, Clint had just received a cryptic symbol. It was as open to subjective interpretation as the verses themselves. Maybe Elena was right. Maybe there was no point in him coming back.

"'Faugh a ballagh' means clear the way," Vince said over the phone.

"How did you find that out?" Clint said.

"I did some research for you. Don't lose your cool. I didn't call any semipro teams. I went to the library, looked up the Irish Brigade, the 69th New York. 'Faugh a ballagh' was their battle cry."

"McCann's Fighting Irish must've adopted it as their motto."

"It's a perfect fit. An all-Irish team, and the way they played football back then, massed blockers at the point of attack. Who was the guy you told me served in the 69th?"

"Paddy McCann."

"If he was in for the duration of the war, then he saw some action. They were in all the big battles - Antietam, Fredericksburg, Chancellorsville, Gettysburg."

"I don't know how long he served."

"Odds are he didn't serve through the whole war. He probably wouldn't have survived. The Irish Brigade took some huge casualties. They were almost wiped out a few times... Hey. There's a bar called Magarac's. They got a special antenna so they can pick up Steeler games when they're blacked out. What do you say we get together and watch the game?"

Clint wasn't one to sit around watching sports on TV. When he put a game on, he usually did something else at the same time. He'd turn his attention to the TV whenever he heard the announcers get excited so he could catch the replay. But he felt he owed something to Vince for his help with the case, and he wanted to hear what he thought about the talisman sketch Elena gave him.

As big as Vince was, it was easy for Clint to spot him in the bar. He was sitting alone at a small table. looking like the lord of the manor presiding over a feast. He had two burgers and a huge pile of fries, a pitcher of beer, and a clear line of sight to the TV. Life couldn't get any better. Vince beckoned Clint with a welcoming wave. The broadcast was already underway. Magarac's special antenna worked pretty well. The audio was clear; the picture just barely fuzzy.

"These are two hard-nosed teams," Vince said, "and they hate each other." He poured Clint a beer. "This is going to be a helluva game."

Clint watched the crowd on TV cheer and swing Terrible Towels over their heads as the stadium announcer introduced the Steeler starters. Olivia was somewhere in there. He pictured her lithe figure in tight jeans and a sweater, her face lit up from the excitement surrounding her. He felt a stab of jealousy. No doubt she would enjoy the game and the riotous atmosphere of Three Rivers. Clint hoped she wouldn't enjoy her date's company too much.

First quarter. The Raiders' quarterback Stabler scored on a one-yard run. The Magarac crowd groaned. Blanda kicked the extra point.

"Jeez," Vince said. "Another slow start. The Steelers've started slow every game this year. They were only beating Baltimore three to nothing at the end of the first quarter. They were losing to Denver twenty-one to seven. Noll's gotta get'em to start stronger."

"It's early. They came from behind against Denver," Clint said, remembering Olivia's summary of last week's game.

"That was Denver. This is Oakland."

Second quarter. Stabler threw a touchdown pass. More groans from the Magarac crowd. Vince turned his head and growled in disgust. Blanda kicked a field goal. More disgust.

"How old is Blanda now?" Clint said.

"Forty-six or forty-seven."

"This must be his twenty-fifth season. That's unbelievable."

"Born and raised in Pittsburgh. They bring 'em up tough here."

Halftime. The TV showed highlights from other games. Clint got another pitcher of beer and poured glasses for Vince and himself.

Second half. Vince was riveted to the broadcast. "C'mon, Steelers. Get something going," he muttered every time Pittsburgh got the ball.

The Steel Curtain finally got a handle on the Raiders' attack, but Pittsburgh's offense continued to sputter. Gilliam threw eight completions, twenty-one incompletions and two interceptions. Bradshaw came in at the end and threw a completion and another interception. Raiders 17, Steelers 0.

Vince slouched his big frame in the chair. He looked spent from three hours of intense football watching.

"Well, in three games, we beat a weak team, tied a middle-of-the-road team and got thoroughly beat by a good team," he said. "If that's any indication, it doesn't look good for the rest of the season."

"They need to get Bradshaw back in the line-up," Clint said, "or maybe Hanratty."

Vince went to the restroom. When he got back, Clint slid the paper across the table to him.

"I got this from the same person who gave me the verses. It's supposed to be the talisman. What do you make of it?"

"I thought the verses were useless to you."

"They wouldn't be if I could get something worthwhile out of them."

Vince turned the paper sideways, then upside down. Clint reached over and turned it the way he received it from Elena.

"I think it's supposed to be oriented like that."

"I think we need to look at it from all angles."

"Fair enough," Clint said, but he thought Vince was making it more complicated than it needed to be.

After looking at it from different perspectives, Vince turned the paper the way Clint showed him. He settled back in his chair and sipped a beer as he studied the symbol.

"Check this out," Vince said. He sat up at the table and painstakingly drew an exact copy of the symbol on a napkin. Then he added an arc across the open top that blended in with the bulb-shaped curve. He turned the symbol upside down and filled the middle with a series of lines drawn parallel to the doubled line. He showed the napkin to Clint.

"What's this look like?"

"A harp," Clint replied. Vince tilted his head back and gave Clint his "how about that" look.

These guys were playing a clever game, Clint thought. Getting Elena to direct him to McCann's. Giving him a set of verses that could be interpreted to be about the Fighting Irish. And now, when he started showing interest in Waylan, giving him another clue that indicated the Fighting Irish. Who was behind it? Who was coming up with all of this? Terry, Simon and Jimmy didn't seem creative enough. It didn't matter. Clint wasn't buying it.

"You're probably right, Vince. It's probably a harp."

"So that means I was right about the verses," Vince said.

"You probably were."

"So what are you gonna do?"

Clint got out of his chair. "I'm gonna call Waylan," he said.

"Whoa!" Vince said. "Wait a minute! Two weeks ago you were sure Waylan didn't win."

"Two weeks ago I might've been wrong." Clint walked away. Vince spun around in his chair after him.

"What changed your mind?" he asked loudly, but Clint was already out of earshot.

Clint stopped at the pay phone in the hallway leading to the rest rooms. He pulled out his notebook and found the number for the Waylan Athletic Club. Clint dropped some coins into the slot and listened to them tumble into the phone. He dialed the number. In a few moments he had Joe Walczak on the line. Clint asked him if anyone had come forward with information about the tournament. Joe said no. Then he said he had done everything he could think of to get the word out. Clint told him about the man who confronted him outside the athletic club. He asked Joe if he knew who he was. Clint got an unexpected answer.

Back at the table, Vince again asked, "What changed your mind about Waylan?"

"Never mind," Clint said. "I just heard something interesting."

"What?"

"When I left the Waylan Athletic Club, a man confronted me. He wanted me to tell him what I knew about the tournament."

"When did you go to Waylan?"

"A few days ago. The athletic club is really a bar. You'd love it. It's full of photos and old football stuff."

"Take me along next time you go."

"If you behave yourself."

"How did this guy know you were researching the tournament?"

"Everybody down there knew," Clint said. "The guy who runs the club, a named guy Joe, told them I was coming."

"I think that's who I talked to," Vince said. He thought for a moment. "Joe...Yeah, I think that was his name."

"Anyway, I asked him if he knew this guy. You know what he told me?"

"What?"

"The man's grandfather played for Waylan in the tournament. His teammates accused him of taking a bribe to throw a game. The accusation was such an insult to the family, it was such an affront to their sense of honor, that they're still touchy about it."

Vince's face lit up. "He's the prince untrue!" He tapped the tabletop twice with his index finger for emphasis.

The prince untrue? Clint was still coming to grips with the idea that the guy in Waylan wasn't some sort of PI. No wonder he acted confused when Clint asked him who he worked for. Clint had completely misread the situation. It turns out the guy was related to one of the players and had a story to tell. Clint had missed a chance to talk to him; maybe learn something worthwhile. The last thing he would've thought of was a connection to Elena's verses.

"Hold on," Clint said. "If the talisman is a harp, then the team in the verses would have to be the Fighting Irish. So how could the prince untrue be on Waylan's team?"

Vince pulled his copy of the verses out of a pocket and laid it on the table.

"That quatrain doesn't say the prince played for the talisman team. It says his fate was to torment the teams that upset the talisman team. In fact, the quatrains don't give any hint at all about who actually won the tournament. I think they're just clues about who played in the final game."

Vince waited impatiently for a response from Clint. Clint took the paper and silently re-read the verses. Vince could wait no longer.

"The Fighting Irish played Waylan in the final," he said. He looked closely at Clint. "You already knew that, didn't you?"

Clint's mind was racing. Twenty minutes ago he was sure the verses were either a fabrication to keep him focused on McCann's or a distraction from a conspiracy. Vince's new take made sense to him. What's more, it lined up perfectly with Charlie Rooney's phone call.

Chapter Twenty-Five
Monday, September 30, 1974

Clint crunched out two hundred sit-ups to finish his work-out. Putting a weight bench and barbells in his apartment was one of the best ideas he ever had. He could lift whenever he pleased. All he had to do was click on the radio or TV and get started. One drawback to a solitary work-out was not having a spotter. He couldn't push himself to muscle failure in exercises like the bench press. He would risk getting pinned under the barbell. Clint liked the reactions of visitors when they saw the weight set in the dining area - their surprise at the incongruity of it, their puzzlement at what it said about him. Above all he liked the smug feeling he got when male visitors realized what it said: that he was fit enough to kick their ass.

Clint had *Monday Night Football* on the TV, the Redskins versus the Broncos. After the sit-ups, he grabbed a glass of water and sat down to watch. The game offered no suspense, no excitement. The Redskins established their superiority with an early touchdown. Then they methodically wore the Broncos down. Clint got bored. He leafed through a pile of old magazines. A *Sports Illustrated* from the summer of 1972 caught his attention. The cover photo was a close-up of Johnny Unitas in home blue dropping back to pass. Unitas clutched the ball in front of him with both hands, partially obscuring the famed number nineteen on his jersey. His right shoulder was slightly dipped. He looked over his left shoulder, his intense gaze scanning the secondary over the two-bar face mask. The blue horseshoe logo was prominent on the white helmet. The caption read "The Old Master and His Art."

Seventy-two turned out to be the last year that Unitas wore the classic, understated uniform of the Colts. The team struggled. He was benched, and then shipped off to the Chargers before the next season. The trade was shocking. The photos of Unitas in the cartoon superhero uniform of the Chargers, with its pastels and lightening bolts, was startling. The old master still possessed his art, but inept San Diego was not fertile ground for it to flourish. After one win in four brutal starts, it was over. Clint recalled hearing that the Steelers, with a pair of injured quarterbacks, were interested in Unitas. The idea was enticing. Unitas playing for a contender, back in his hometown, back with the team that drafted him. The Steelers making amends for cutting him in 1955. It could have been a fascinating complete-the-circle story. But it was more sportswriter rumor-mongering than a serious personnel consideration. Unitas stayed with the Chargers. At the end of the 1973 season, he retired.

The inglorious end did not diminish the accomplishments of his seventeen years with the Colts. The team won a lot of games in those years - often by stunningly large margins, sometimes with thrilling comebacks - thanks to a bold offensive attack. Unitas was the brilliance behind that attack. He personified the Colts with the ruthless efficiency of his play and his no-nonsense demeanor. Clint remembered that his little brother identified Unitas so closely with the Colts that he thought the horseshoe helmet logo was actually a monogrammed "U".

Those times were an entirely different era for the Colts. They were days of promise and optimism and excitement. Their present reality was grim by any comparison. While Unitas closed out his career on the West Coast, the Colts fell to their second straight losing season. The current season was shaping up to be a continuation of that trend. The Colts had lost their first three games...

Something clicked in Clint's mind. Elena had given him a sketch of something that looked like a "U". Clint opened his notebook and found the drawing. The left side, with the bulb-shaped bottom and lip at the top, resembled the left side of the Colts horseshoe logo. She said the sketch was the talisman, a clue to the identity of the team in the cryptic verses. Clint turned to the page where he had copied the verses.

From the anthem city they rode anew.

What city had a better claim to being called the anthem city than Baltimore with Fort McHenry and Francis Scott Key and the "Star Spangled Banner" having been written there? And weren't the current Colts the second incarnation of the team? Clint remembered the story about how the Colt marching band continued to perform in the years when the city had no team, a halftime show in exile. It was a display of loyalty and stubbornness and faith that would have generated eye-rolling anywhere else. In Baltimore it was a point of pride.

A talisman's power their armor bore.

The Colt helmet, the most obvious piece of football protective gear, displayed a horseshoe, the most well-known good luck symbol.

With quick death the new behemoths they slew,

Clint remembered looking up the word in the dictionary. A behemoth was defined as a huge animal, or something enormous in size. So a behemoth was a giant. In this case a new giant, a New York Giant. "Quick death" was obviously a synonym for "sudden death," which was shorthand for the NFL's rule governing overtime play. The first "sudden death" game was the 1958 championship, when the Colts defeated the Giants.

Inspiring devotion unseen before.

On a January day in 1952 the citizens of Baltimore experienced the heady rush, the affirming thrill, of being selected for "the team." Except in this case, they were selected to receive a team - a new franchise in the National Football League. Collectively, the city of Baltimore offered their new team a warm, enthusiastic, and almost naively trusting embrace. To its delight, the team returned the embrace. The team's personality could've been shaped by a few glamorous, All-American college boys who might've looked down on the unpretentious town of rowhouses, factories, wharves and industrial odors. Instead, the Colts turned out to be regular guys, hard-working average Joes, many with ethnic names like most Baltimoreans, who happened to be remarkable athletes. They moved into the neighborhoods, hung out at the bars, and made the city their home. The followers of pro teams in other cities might be described as fanatic or passionate. In Baltimore, the tenor of the relationship was different. Deeper emotions were involved. The followers of the Colts were devoted, truly and deeply, to their team.

Clint raced ahead to the next stanza, the one that mentioned Pyrrhic wins in the ultimate test. Who were the teams that had defeated the Colts in championship games? The Browns did, in the mid-sixties. The Jets did of course, in Super Bowl III. Clint remembered both games because they were huge upsets. How had the Browns and Jets fared since those wins? Clint was not enough of a sports fan to recite the list of champions from seasons past, that was Vince's specialty. But he couldn't recall the Browns or Jets winning the big one recently. The Colts also had other post-season defeats. There was that overtime play-off game against the Packers; the one in which the game-tying field goal was outside the uprights but the referee called it good for Green Bay anyway. Then there was that conference championship thumping a few years ago by Miami. The Packers and Dolphins had certainly gone on to win championships. There was nothing Pyrrhic about their victories over the Colts. Wait a minute, Clint thought. Play-offs and conference championship games were not the "ultimate tests." That was the Super Bowl, and the league championship in the days before the Super Bowl. The verse only applied to those games.

The pieces were fitting together. The reference to thoroughbreds clearly meant race horses, the inspiration for the Colt name. The pieces were fitting together nicely. Clint couldn't wait to see Vince's expression when he heard this new interpretation.

Who was the "prince untrue?" Shula, for jumping to the Dolphins? The old owner, for selling the franchise? The new owner? Things had sure fallen apart under his stewardship. If stoking "the fires of sorrow" meant inflicting key defeats on the Pyrrhic victors, as Vince suggested, then the prince had to be a player or a coach. An owner was too far removed from the action to get credit for beating another team. Then there was the reference to three defeats and once repeated glory. Clint paused on that one. No ideas came to mind.

That stanza would require more thought and analysis. On to the next set of verses.

These lines said the Pyrrhic victors would pay the price year after year until they made amends to the Colt devoted, which they could do by paying homage to their team. Why? What was so special about the Colts? Why did the teams that beat them in championship games need to pay homage before they won another title?

So the verses weren't about the 1906 tournament. Clint had been right all along. They really were useless to his investigation. Why would Elena give him something about the Colts?

Hold on …This interpretation was valid only if Clint was right about the talisman. He needed to have Elena say yes, the symbol she drew was indeed a horseshoe. Then he could dismiss the cryptic verses as a red herring. He needed to call her first thing tomorrow.

And she would be glad to talk to him again, wouldn't she? How did their last meeting end? Clint had told her he felt like she was playing a game with him. Elena got indignant and told him perhaps he shouldn't come back. Tomorrow's phone call would be uncomfortable. Oh, well. No guts. No glory.

Chapter Twenty-Six
Tuesday, October 1, 1974

Clint called Elena at nine in the morning. He hoped she wasn't a late sleeper. He told her he wanted to show her a picture, find out if it was the talisman.

"Aren't you the one who says I'm playing games?" she said.

Clint started his reply with humility. He apologized. He said he had been irritated by his lack of progress with the case. Then he added a note of graciousness. He thanked her for her help. He said her idea to check out McCann's was the best lead he had so far. Elena's attitude softened, but she sounded mildly impatient. "I am getting ready to go out of town today," she said. "If you come by at noon, I can see you for a few minutes. After that, no more visits. I have done all I can for you."

Clint assumed she forgot that two of his three visits had been at her beckoning. He was tempted to save her this intrusion by asking over the phone if the figure was a horseshoe. Specifically, was it the horseshoe logo of the Colts? But he suspected she wasn't familiar with the Colts and their logo. She didn't seem like a pro football fan. Moreover, he wanted an irrefutable confirmation form her. He could only get that by having her look at a photo of the logo and state that it was or was not the figure she had drawn. If he got the answer he expected, he wouldn't need to bother her anymore.

Thirty minutes later the phone rang.

"Man, I got something you gotta see," Vince gushed. "This is it. It's the smoking gun. It's case closed."

"What is it?"

"I'll be right over to show you."

Clint estimated it would take Vince thirty minutes to drive over. An hour passed and he had not shown up. Then two hours. Clint couldn't wait any longer. He needed to leave to make his noontime appointment with Elena.

As he unlocked his car door, he saw a grinning Vince loping toward him from across the parking lot, hailing him with a sweeping wave over his head.

"What took you so long?" Clint said.

"I got stuck in a meeting."

"Why didn't you call me?"

"I was in a meeting. I couldn't just get up and make a phone call."

"Whatcha got?"

"I found a newspaper article that says Waylan won the 1906 championship." Vince held up a copy of the article.

Clint glanced at his watch. "I'm running late for an appointment," he said. "Jump in. You can read it to me on the way." Clint got in. He reached across to unlock the passenger door. Vince settled into his seat.

"A Javelin," Vince said, looking around the interior. "What year is it?"

"Seventy-one."

"Nice car. I never rode in one of these before."

"First time for everything," Clint said. He turned the key. The engine rumbled to life. "Tell me about this article."

"I've been digging through the university archives, seeing what I could find on Waylan. I came across a bunch of articles, but nothing helpful. Then I struck gold. This is from 1954."

Vince read the article aloud. It reported that the Waylan Coalcrackers had won their semipro league championship for the third consecutive time with their second consecutive undefeated season. The article called the Coalcrackers "The Monsters of the Monongahela," then listed their past accomplishments.

"In 1906," Vince read, "the Coalcrackers won a tournament that gave them bragging rights as the world champions of football." With his peripheral vision, Clint saw Vince giving his "how about that" look.

"How do you know it's the *Pittsburgh Sentry* tournament?"

"Clint, in all my research I never heard of any tournament in western P. A. in 1906 until I heard about this one."

"Maybe you missed one. You missed this one."

Clint stopped in front of Elena's house.
"Who lives here?" Vince said.
"The person who gave me the verses."
"Who is he?"
"It's a she."
"A woman wrote those verses?"
"I didn't say she wrote them. I said she gave them to me."
"Can I meet her?"
Clint planned to have Vince wait in the car while he talked to Elena. He changed his mind. How could it hurt if he met her? Besides, the meeting should be short, and he could keep an eye on Vince.

In the house, Vince's eyes darted from icon to icon, pausing in between on the dark, heavy furniture. Clint introduced him to Elena. She gave him a disapproving glance.
"Is he investigator, too?" she asked in her soft, pleasantly accented voice. Clint enjoyed listening to her talk. He inhaled deeply, hoping to catch the scent of her exotic cologne that made his head swim. He wondered if it was a European brand.
"No. He's an expert who's helping me."
"He doesn't look like investigator. What's he expert in?"
"The history of football in western Pennsylvania," Vince said.
"Oh," Elena said, unimpressed.
Clint held up the sketch of the "U".
"You said this is the talisman that's mentioned in the verses." Elena's brow furrowed. She nodded cautiously.
"Yes."
Clint showed her the *Sports Illustrated* cover. He pointed to the horseshoe logo.
"Is this the talisman?"
Elena nodded. "Yes, that is exactly it."
"Those verses are about the Colts?" Vince said. Clint shot him a stern look to shut him up. He turned back to Elena.

"Why didn't you draw it to look more like a horseshoe?" Clint said. "Then it would've been obvious to me."

"That is how it came to me," she said. She smiled at Clint, but her green eyes narrowed. "You like things to be obvious, don't you, Mr. Ronson? Makes your job easier. That's why you came to me, huh?"

Clint didn't know what to say. He was surprised by her change in tone, and he didn't like it when someone could read him so well.

"You think too much about form," Elena said. "Not enough about meaning."

Because my job is to find facts, Clint wanted to say. Tangible, irrefutable, hard evidence. Instead, he calmly said:

"Elena, I thought the verses were supposed to help me solve my case." He held up the magazine. "This team didn't even exist when the tournament took place."

Elena shrugged nonchalantly. "There must've been something in my presence with a connection to the team." She took the magazine and studied the cover for a few moments. She handed it back.

"Are you a follower of this team?"

"Yes."

Elena held out her hand, palm upward, toward Clint.

"There, you have it."

"What do these verses have to do with my case?"

"I don't know. Maybe nothing."

Clint had the answer he was looking for. He had been right about the verses. They had no bearing on the investigation. Intentionally or not, they had been a distraction. Clint was ready to close the door on them. Vince was not. To Clint's surprise, Vince opened his wallet and took out his handwritten copy.

"You wrote these verses?" Vince said.

"I wrote words on paper, yes. But I didn't think them up," Elena said.

"Did you copy them from somewhere?"

"No. They came into my mind."

"How's that? How did they come into your mind but you didn't think them up?"

Elena looked at Vince for a moment like she didn't know how to answer his question. She glanced at Clint for help. You brought this guy here, her look seemed to say, you explain it to him.

"Elena has psychic abilities," Clint said. "Sometimes she uses them to help with investigations."

Vince's eyes widened. "Wow," he said. "I've always been fascinated with psychic phenomenon."

"Please. I don't want attention for this," Elena said. "I don't want people lined up at my door wanting me to tell their fortunes."

"Your secret is safe with me. I just want to ask you a few questions."

"I don't think Elena wants to talk about it," Clint said.

"It's okay." Elena held her hand up toward Clint in a calming gesture. Then to Vince: "What are your questions?"

On the spot, Vince fumbled for words. Finally he said, "Well, for example, how do you have a psychic experience?"

Elena went to the bookcase and removed a slim volume.

"I have read many books, trying to understand my ability. This one gave me best explanation."

She handed it to Vince.

"*Synchronicity: An Acausal Connecting Principle.* By C.G. Jung." Vince read the cover aloud, pronouncing Jung with a hard "J."

"It's pronounced 'Yoong'," Elena said. "He's Swiss."

"It looks Chinese," Vince said.

Elena said, "This idea of synchronicity, Jung says it occurs when a person experiences a psychic state that coincides with a real event. He calls it 'meaningful coincidence' because the two events are connected by meaning. When I first read it, I became very excited. This synchronicity perfectly describes my ability. I have read it again and again to understand it better."

"What do you mean by a psychic state?"

"Jung says it's when an unconscious image moves into consciousness, maybe as a dream, or a thought, or a feeling."

"A premonition," Vince said.

"Yes, a premonition. Surely you have had an experience where for no reason you thought of someone you had not heard from in a long time. Out of the blue, as they say. Then, soon after, you receive a surprise letter or phone call from them, or you meet them."

"Y-e-a-h," Vince dragged out the word and nodded slowly. "That's happened to me."

"That is what Jung calls synchronicity. Everyone experiences it. I think some people experience it more often and more strongly than others."

"How does it happen?"

"The concept is quite abstract," Elena said, "and the book is dense. I confess I do not understand it very well. I will try my best to explain. I must also add that Jung says these are his thoughts on the subject, not a complete explanation. He says something called the collective unconscious is present in all humans. The archetypes organize the workings of the collective unconscious."

"What are the archetypes?"

"Archetypes. How can I explain," Elena said quietly, almost to herself. She thought for a moment. Then she said, "They are concepts of different types of persons or beings. These concepts are present in everyone's mind from birth. Concepts like the hero, the devil, and the wise man. Because the concept is present in everyone's mind, everyone recognizes them." Elena tilted her head toward Vince. "You understand?"

"Like stock characters."

"Something like that. So, in certain emotional states, the archetypes have a quality that allows the unconscious to move into consciousness. Within the unconscious is a form of *a priori* knowledge..."

"What kind of knowledge?"

"It is called *a priori* knowledge. It is an idea from philosophy, I think. Or maybe psychology. As Jung uses the phrase, it means to know something before you experience a reason for knowing it. Foreknowledge is another word for it."

"Or intuition," Vince said.

"Yes. He calls it that, too."

"These verses that came to you, they're the psychic event."
"Yes."
"And they contain foreknowledge of events yet to happen."
"Or events that have already happened that I shouldn't know about." Elena pointed to the magazine cover. "You see the talisman is a horseshoe. It could represent an archetype, the animal helper. The horse has been a powerful symbol all over the world throughout history."
"Is that why a horseshoe is considered lucky?" Vince said. "Because it represents an archetype that allows people to experience synchronicity?"
"Perhaps."
Elena thought for a moment. Then she said, "What is different about these verses, they describe a state or condition that lasts maybe a long time. Synchronicity almost always involves an individual event."
Vince looked over his shoulder at Clint. "Are you listening to this?"
"C'mon, Vince. We've taken up enough of Miss Ivanova's time."
Elena gave Clint the calming gesture again. "It's okay," she said. She seemed content to answer Vince's questions. This was probably a rare experience for her. Of all the people who asked for her help, Clint guessed only a few asked her how she did it. Probably even fewer showed as much interest in her answers as Vince.
Vince said, "The team on the magazine cover is called the Colts. You might've heard of them."
"No," Elena said, shaking her head quickly. "I do not follow your football."
"They won the championship..." Vince began counting on the fingers of his right hand with his thumb. Each time his thumb touched a finger, he whispered something to himself. "They won the championship three times. They lost two times, to teams they were heavily favored to beat."

Suddenly Clint recognized the inverse symmetry between the Colts' championship record and the fate of the "prince untrue." He kept the thought to himself.

"The fourth quatrain seems to say those two teams are punished by the will of the Colt fans," Vince said. "Like they've been cursed. Can that be true?"

"Let me see." Vince handed her the paper. She read the whole set of verses.

"When you say the teams are punished by the will of the fans, you mean there is cause and effect," Elena said. "These verses do not say that for sure. They simply foretell a series of events. You can infer that the victories are Pyrrhic as a result of the wrath of the fans. But how can you show that one causes the other? The same if the lifting of sorrow follows the paying of homage."

"One seems to control the other," Vince said.

"One follows the other. Coincidence. Both of them. I can see where they appear to be meaningful coincidences. Even so, I do not believe they are meaningful coincidence as Jung describes it."

"Okay. But one quatrain clearly says the fate of the prince untrue is determined, and they say the Pyrrhic victors' fates are, too."

Clint shook his head with disapproval. Vince's questions were drifting into the realm of fantasy.

"Dramatic language," Elena said.

"But that's what is says."

Elena read the verses again. "It says here 'devotion unseen before,'" she said. "So there was great love for this team?"

"Just like we love the Steelers," Vince said.

"And there was much bitterness when this team lost?"

"Yes," Clint said, happy to interject something. "A lot of bitterness and disappointment."

"Let me read you something." Elena held out her hand to get the book back from Vince. "Please." She opened the book and found the page.

"This is Jung quoting Albert the Great, who is discussing something Avicenna wrote." She glanced up from the book at Vince and Clint. "Avicenna was a Persian philosopher, in case you don't know."

Clint was happy to get the explanation. He was still stuck on Albert the Great. Elena read a few lines to them about the power that exists in the human soul, and how it can influence things as it pleases when the soul is excited by great passion. She closed the book.

"Something for you to ponder," she said. Clint saw a faint smile on her face.

"Wow," Vince said. "Some sort of psychic energy must be involved."

"Jung is quite clear that the transmission of energy is not involved."

"That's unbelievable!" Vince said.

"It is," Clint said. He glanced at his watch. "Vince, Miss Ivanova needs to get ready for her trip. I think we need to go."

"Why didn't you tell me the quatrains were about the Colts?" Vince said when they got into the car.

"I just made the connection last night. That's why I wanted to see Elena today, to see if I was right about the talisman."

Driving back to his apartment, Clint explained how he came to associate the sketch of the talisman and the horseshoe logo, and how the first eight verses described the Colts. This interpretation was direct and tidy. It required none of the contortions needed to make the verses fit the Fighting Irish or Waylan.

"That's brilliant," Vince said. "Everything fits, and that Russian woman confirmed your interpretation."

"She also confirmed the verses are irrelevant to the case."

"Man, this is bigger than your case. You've heard of curses on sports teams? The Curse of the Bambino? The Red Sox haven't won a World Series since 1918. The Curse of the Black Sox? The White Sox haven't won the Series since 1917? I could name others."

Clint barely suppressed a smile. The kid was fascinated by anything off-beat - Nostradumus, prehistoric football, sports team curses. Socially awkward people, the smarter ones anyway, always seemed to have that tendency. They staked out interests that were on the fringes of the mainstream. They became experts, sometimes fanatics. Whenever one of their favorite topics came up, the awkward person was in their element; unexpectedly knowledgeable and enthusiastic and comfortable with themselves. Yet at the same time, being an expert in an off-beat topic was odd in itself.

Vince went on: "The problem with most of the curses is that their origin doesn't seem significant enough to change the cosmic order of things. That might not be true with the Black Sox scandal. I mean, they were trying to throw the World Series, the biggest sporting event in America at the time. But a player getting angry when he finds out his team sold him, telling them they'll never win another championship without him. Does that sound like enough to curse a team for decades?"

"Sounds like a temper tantrum," Clint said. He wanted to ask Vince to explain "the cosmic order of things." Problem was, Vince would have an answer.

"Many times, there's no proof that the cause of the curse ever really happened," Vince said. "At least, not the way it's said to have happened. But think of this, if all the fans of a team, possibly millions of them, are bitter over a loss and wish revenge upon the other team. Well, that's a huge amount of psychic energy."

"Vince, the sting of a defeat, even the awareness of it, fades over time. New fans join the ranks every year that didn't experience the loss firsthand. Even if your idea made sense, wouldn't the intensity of this psychic energy diminish over a few years to the point that it couldn't affect another team?"

"I'm not talking about the fans renewing their revenge wish year after year. What I mean is the strong emotions that are unleashed right after a defeat send a burst of psychic energy through time to affect the other team. That's why the quatrain says they have to make amends to the devoted. They're the ones who experienced the bitter emotions. Those emotions need to be soothed to dissipate the energy."

"A burst of psychic energy through time?"

"Something like that."

"Didn't Elena say energy wasn't involved?"

"I'm just throwing out ideas. Maybe that horseshoe logo, if it represents an archetype, has something to do with it."

"Listen to what you're saying: a team can lose because of the negative thoughts of another team's fans from years earlier. Doesn't that sound crazy to you?"

"Crazy? You heard what the Russian woman read. Power exists in the human soul to influence things as it pleases, especially when great passions are involved. I'm just brainstorming on that idea."

Back in his apartment, Clint found a message from Karen on his answering machine.

"Good afternoon, Clint. See, I didn't call you Steve McQueen this time. Mr. Walsh wants you here at 10 AM tomorrow for a meeting with Tommy Dreamboat, I mean Thomas DeAngelo, the esteemed attorney. He said Mr. Dreamboat has something v-e-r-y important to tell you."

Clint rewound the cassette tape. He didn't know what Mike Walsh saw in Karen, other than she was young, attractive and generally entertaining to have around. Her casual phone manners were out of line for a law office. Steve McQueen. Tommy Dreamboat. Did Mike know how she was conducting business? Surely, she didn't talk like that to everyone. Even so, sooner or later she would say something flip to the wrong person. The office's image would take a hit. Mike didn't need that kind of embarrassment.

As for the substance of the message, what did DeAngelo have to say that was v-e-r-y important? Did he know who won the tournament? Probably not. More than likely it was a ploy to learn what Clint knew. Maybe his PI had dug up, or fabricated, something damaging to Clint. He could use that to apply pressure. Maybe DeAngelo was going to resort to his own temper tantrum. Whatever it was, Clint would find out at ten.

Chapter Twenty-Seven
Wednesday Morning, October 2, 1974

Michael Walsh slouched in the leather chair behind his desk. His right elbow rested on the chair arm. His head tilted onto his raised right hand, its fingers pressing into his cheek. He looked bored and annoyed, like he had something better to do. Thomas DeAngelo, stylishly dressed, immaculately coifed, and nicely scented, sat in front of the desk. From his demeanor, Clint expected Walsh to say "let's get his over with." Instead he said, "Clint, pull up a chair." DeAngelo wasted no time starting the discussion.

"I think I should come clean with you about why I wanted updates on your investigation," DeAngelo said.

It's about time, Clint thought.

"Councilman Harris' father used to say the only man he feared was Anthony Prentiss because he knew where the bodies were hidden. When the councilman saw Prentiss' obituary, he asked me to get in touch with the family and offer assistance. Frankly, he wanted to get someone trusted on the inside to head off any public relations problems. Tony Prentiss, the son, told me he was already working with Mike on the will. He said the only loose end was the awarding of prize money from some long ago football tournament. Councilman Harris was alarmed to hear that. His great uncle was brutally murdered at the time the tournament was played. There were rumors that organized crime killed him. As you probably heard, Councilman Harris is in a tough re-election fight. It's well-known that the councilman's father had some unsavory connections when he was in politics. The councilman's opponent is trying to tarnish his reputation by bringing up his father's misdeeds."

"Like father, like son," Clint said.

"That pretty well describes his opponent's campaign message. Anyway, it would be very difficult right now if his great-uncle's murder and all the old allegations resurfaced. It would give Councilman Harris' opponent more ammunition to attack his character."

So Olivia was right, Clint thought. Shrewd girl. With instincts like that, she had to be a good detective. But what was she right about? Their intentions? Or their latest cover story?

"Why didn't you tell me this when we first met?" Clint said.

"We hoped you wouldn't come across this information on your own, and we didn't want to give you a reason to look for it."

"Why was your investigator following me around town? The only place I could've learned about Harris' death was in a library archive. All he had to do was check the sign-in book."

DeAngelo shrugged. "My investigator was overzealous in the pursuit of his duties. What can I say?"

"I learned about William Harris' death within hours after we met."

"How?"

"It was in the newspaper."

Concern flashed across DeAngelo's face. "When?"

"It was in a newspaper in the archive."

DeAngelo's concern changed to relief. "What did you learn?"

"That he died brutally at the time the tournament was being played."

"That's all?"

"That's all."

"Did this information have any bearing on your investigation?"

"I don't discuss an investigation that's in progress."

"That's why I'm asking if it had any bearing on your investigation. Because if it didn't, you shouldn't feel reluctant to discuss it."

Walsh said, "Clint, I think a little professional courtesy is in order."

"As a professional, I don't discuss details of an investigation without my client's permission."

"Very well," DeAngelo said. "I'll respect that. With your concern about client confidentiality, Councilman Harris should have no worries about a leak. Mike, would you contact Mr. Prentiss and see if he'll authorize Clint to discuss his on-going investigation with me."

"Will do," Walsh said.

DeAngelo slapped the tops of his thighs and stood up. "My business is done here. Mike, I look forward to hearing from you. Clint, keep up the good work." DeAngelo started to leave, then stopped in the doorway and nodded toward Clint. "Mike, would you ever consider loaning him out?"

"Clint's a free agent. It's up to him."

"What do you think, Clint? I could use someone like you."

"Karen upfront has my cards. I'm sure she'll be delighted to give you one."

Walsh told Clint to close the door.

"Clint, he's just trying to find out if you know any details about William Harris's death. Did you see how he reacted when you said you read about it in the paper? He thought you meant a recent paper."

"I don't believe him. I think he's after something else, and I think you should advise Prentiss against allowing me to discuss anything."

"Why?"

"I have a theory that Councilman Harris is trying to get the prize money."

Walsh lowered his arm and folded his hands on his belly. "Explain your theory," he said.

"Remember I told you I interviewed a surviving member of the Fighting Irish?" Walsh nodded. "His name was Charlie Rooney. The owner of a bar and grill called McCann's introduced me to him. This McCann's is the same establishment that sponsored the Fighting Irish in 1906. It's also the hangout for a couple of foot soldiers who work for a local loan shark and bookie. After Charlie changed his story about who won, he had a fatal heart attack, probably during a confrontation in his home. I think the thugs paid him a visit and either threatened him or roughed him up over changing his story. The stress was too much for the old guy."

"So, McCann's is trying to get the prize money, or maybe the loan shark is. How's this connect to Harris?"

"I went to McCann's at the suggestion of a psychic."

"A psychic?"

"Yeah."

Walsh closed his eyes and slowly shook his head, saying, "Clint, there are some things I don't want to know."

"She's credible. The Pittsburgh detectives use her once in awhile. I visited her when I ran out of leads. A few days later she called and mentioned McCann's. The second time I visited her, DeAngelo's PI was waiting for me. I think he followed me there the first time and persuaded her to tell me to check out McCann's."

"What's your evidence?"

"Just the fact that he was outside her house the second time I visited."

"What's the Harris connection?"

"I think Harris knows all about the tournament and he knows the prize money was never paid. I think he also knows how and why his great-uncle died."

"What makes you think Harris knows all this stuff?"

"Because he got DeAngelo involved in our first meeting with Prentiss."

"Go on."

"Harris' campaign needs cash. When he heard about Prentiss' will, he worked out a deal with McCann's. If they could convince me the Fighting Irish won the tournament, they could keep a share of the prize money. Harris' campaign would get the rest. The go-between is DeAngelo's PI."

"Anything else?"

"That's it."

Clint expected Walsh to think about the theory for a moment or two. He figured he'd appreciate the sophistication of it more than Olivia did, how it tied everything together. He was ready for a little pat on the back.

He got an immediate rebuttal.

"Other than the part about the McCanns trying to get the money, it's all speculation. You've got no evidence. I could never go to trial with a story like that."

"It's a theory," Clint said, feeling like he was backpedaling. "If I can show that DeAngelo's PI is the connection, it would be a conspiracy."

"Keep it to yourself. If this theory gets out, Harris will discredit you, he will defame you, he will destroy you."

"Understand."

"I'm not paying you to find out if DeAngelo's PI is the connection. I'm paying you to find out who won the damn tournament. This case is dragging on longer than I expected. What are you doing to get it resolved?"

"Based on Charlie's revised story, a team from Waylan probably won the tournament," Clint said.

"Waylan? Where's that?"

"It's a little town south of here. I went down there. I found a team photo in a bar with an inscription that says they're the 1906 world champions. I also found a newspaper article that says the same thing. The only problem is neither one specifically says it was the *Pittsburgh Sentry's* tournament."

"How many world championship football tournaments were there in 1906?"

"Football had no governing bodies back then. Anyone could organize a tournament and bill it as the world championship. For that matter, any team could call themselves world champions."

"Okay. What else?"

"I got a guy down there who's on the lookout for anyone who has knowledge about the tournament."

"What if he doesn't find anyone?"

"I still need to check out whatever archives I can find in Homestead. In Monessen, too."

"You haven't done that yet?"

"I called up there. I haven't gone there to personally dig through the files."

"What's Monessen got to do with this?"

"They played Waylan in the semifinal. Maybe a local newspaper followed the tournament to its conclusion."

"What if that doesn't work?"

"I'll take the team rosters and try to track down survivors or relatives. See if they know anything."

"Why aren't you doing that now?"

"I thought I'd try quick and easy before long and hard."

"Clint, quick and easy isn't turning out to be very quick. You have to take these steps simultaneously, not sequentially. You'll cover more ground faster that way."

Walsh waited for a response. Clint had none. Walsh said, "Do what you need to do. Just get this case resolved so I can settle Prentiss' estate and get DeAngleo out of my hair."

Chapter Twenty-Eight
Wednesday Evening, October 2, 1974

"We don't have synchronicity," Vince said over the phone. *"But we have a prophecy. Actually, we have three."*

Clint didn't want to hear anything else about synchronicity or quatrains or bursts of psychic energy. Now Vince was talking about prophecies. Clint *really* didn't want to hear about that. He was tired of the verses. He felt duped about giving them as much consideration as he did. Elena had confirmed that they were about the Baltimore Colts and not about the 1906 tournament. Even as a Colt fan, he only found them momentarily interesting. To sift through them looking for some sort of metaphysical meaning, that seemed weird.

"What are you talking about?" he said.

"The quatrains do not fit the Colts yet. Well, they mostly do, but not entirely. Specifically, part of the second one doesn't fit. I think the third one is about the future. The fourth one is definitely about the future."

"Vince, you're wasting my time. Those quatrains, as you call them, are useless to my investigation."

"You're the one who figured out they were about the Colts. Just let me show you what I came up with and I'll never bother you about this again."

"If that's what it takes."

"I'll be right over."

Vince walked into Clint's apartment carrying some three-by-five cards wrapped in a rubber band. Clint was in the kitchen. Vince went into the dining area that was now a workout room. He took the band off and sat the small stack of cards on the countertop that separated the two rooms.

"When you explained your interpretation of the quatrains, about how they described the Colts, everything seemed to fit perfectly," Vince said. "I wondered if I could find something factual to back it up. I looked at the Colts' record in championship games, and then the championship results of the teams they played. Just like the quatrains predicted, the two teams that upset them in championship games, the Browns and the Jets, they've never won another championship. But the teams the Colts defeated, the Giants and the Cowboys, only the Cowboys have gone on to win a championship. The Cowboys lost to the Colts in Super Bowl V but won the Super Bowl the following year. Now the Giants, after losing to the Colts in 1958, they played in four championship games. They lost every one. They lost again to the Colts in 1959, to the Packers in 1961 and 1962, and the Bears in 1963."

"So what?"

"My first reaction was 'Clint's interpretation is wrong.' As neat as it sounds, it doesn't hold up when you bring in data."

"Data?"

"The records of the teams the Colts played in championships."

"Hmm," Clint grunted.

"Then I got to thinking, the fourth quatrain is obviously about something that hasn't happened yet. In the second quatrain, the data supports the interpretation for three of the four teams. What if the reason it doesn't support the fourth team is because that event will happen in the future?"

Clint, uninterested, turned around and opened the refrigerator. He said, "You want a beer?"

"Not right now."

Clint grabbed one and turned back to the countertop. He remembered this morning's meeting with Walsh. He pictured Mike sitting impatiently in his big desk chair as he listened to Clint's theory. Now Clint's role was reversed. He was the impatient one listening to a something like a theory.

"It's all speculation, Vince."

"Listen to this," Vince said. "Remember I noticed the verb tenses in the verses? Now I see a progression. The first quatrain is about things that have already happened, so it's easy to interpret. The second verse is mostly about things that have happened, but contains something yet to happen. The third verse is completely about something that *will* happen in the future. That's why it's so vague to us. The fourth verse is about something that *could* happen in the future. It's not pre-ordained like the third verse. For the fourth verse to happen, it requires the exercise of free will by specific parties. These quatrains are just like Nostradamus. They foretell the future. It's already unfolding before us, but it hasn't reached its conclusion."

"What's your point?"

"That is the point. The quatrains foretell the future. They're prophetic."

"Get real, Vince."

"I'm being real, Clint. I don't think the Russian lady…"

"Elena."

"I don't think Elena would have given the quatrains to you if they didn't contain the truth. Otherwise, what good would they be?"

"That's *my* point," Clint said. "What good are they?"

Vince wasn't listening. He was saying, "Remember we decided the phrase 'well-blessed' meant a team would win championships. If I changed it to mean a team that plays in a championship game but doesn't necessarily win, then it raises problems with the Pyrrhic win teams. The Browns lost to the Packers in the 1965 championship. That would make them as well-blessed as the Giants."

"Vince, your obsession with these quatrains is clouding your objectivity. You're trying to make the verses mean what you want them to mean."

"I realized that. So I came up with a guiding question, like I was doing an experiment." Vince picked up the three by five card on top of the stack and read it aloud: "Is there any team for which every opponent it defeated in a championship game subsequently won a championship and every opponent it lost to in a championship game has yet to win another championship?" Vince placed the card on the countertop. "That's the gist of the second quatrain."

"Hurry up, Vince. I'm losing interest."

"Bear with me. I'll be done in a few minutes." Vince spread the rest of the cards on the countertop. "To answer my question, I made a card for every team that played in a championship game in the NFL, the AFL and the All-American Football Conference. I started with the first NFL championship in 1933 and went right through to the Super Bowl for the 1973 season. You ever hear of the All-American Football Conference?"

"It was a pro league that played in the late 1940s."

"Why do you think I included their championship games?"

"What is this?" Clint said. "A test?"

"Some of their teams were absorbed into the NFL when the conference folded. That's why I included them."

"I knew that. I know a little football history."

"Let me explain how I defined a team," Vince said. "The quatrains emphasize the devotion of the fans to the team. If a franchise moved from one city to another, I counted them as separate teams. Most people won't remain fans of a franchise once it moves to another city. So I have cards for the Boston Redskins and the Washington Redskins, the Cleveland Rams and the Los Angeles Rams, and so forth."

"Got it."

"I interpreted the 'ultimate test' in the second quatrain to mean the highest championship a team could play in. So, for the NFL from 1933 until 1965 the highest championship was the league championship. Same for the AAFC from 1946 to 1949 and the AFL from 1960 until 1965. After the 1966 season, the first Super Bowl was played. From that point on, the Super Bowl has been the ultimate championship. On the left side of each team's card, I listed every opponent that team defeated in a championship game and the year. On the right side, I listed every opponent it lost to and the year. Whenever a team won a championship, I went back and highlighted that team on every other card that it appeared on."

Clint picked up the card with Vince's question and reread it: Is there any team for which every opponent it defeated in a championship game subsequently won a championship and every opponent it lost to in a championship game has yet to win another championship? He started looking at the team cards.

"In order to answer the question in the affirmative, every entry on the left side of the card needs to be highlighted and none of the entries on the right side can be highlighted," Vince said.

Clint held up a card. "What about this team? They lost the only championship game they played in. The team that beat them isn't highlighted."

"A team has to have both won and lost championship games, otherwise they don't meet the criteria of the question."

Vince had put some work into this, Clint thought. He had come up with an objective question. He devised a method to record and update the data. Then he examined each team's results against the question. Clint was impressed, although he wouldn't say that to the kid. He didn't want him to think he was interested. Then he'd never hear the end of it.

"How long did you work on this?" Clint said.

"All night. I got so wrapped up in it I couldn't go to sleep."

"You've been awake since yesterday morning?"

Vince shrugged as if it was no big deal. His bleary eyes told another story. Clint examined a few more of the team cards.

Vince said, "The only team that answers the question in the affirmative is the Cowboys, if that's what you're looking for. They defeated the Dolphins in the 1972 Super Bowl. The Dolphins won the next two Super Bowls. The Colts defeated them in the 1971 Super Bowl. The Colts haven't been back to the Super Bowl since."

Clint picked up the card for the Cowboys and looked at it for a moment.

"The problem with the Cowboys is they only lost one championship, so they don't fit the second quatrain." Clint couldn't believe he just said that. He was starting to sound like Vince.

"Righhhht." Vince said. "You're catching on."

Clint said, "As long as the NFL plays Super Bowls, this is a work in progress. The Cowboys might lose another one. The Giants might eventually win one. Or some other team might meet the criteria."

Vince said, "The quatrains are clearly about the Colts. No other team matches them so perfectly. When the Giants win a Super Bowl, we've got synchronicity. Until that happens, the quatrains are prophetic."

Clint was stumbling over the big, technical-sounding word. He didn't pay attention when Elena explained it. He didn't think it mattered to his investigation.

"Exactly what is synchronicity again?" Clint said.

"It's the coincidence between a psychic state and real events," Vince said. "When someone has thoughts about something and that something actually happens, that's synchronicity. The quatrains are the product of Elena's psychic state. The records of the Colts' championship opponents in subsequent seasons are the real events."

"What makes these quatrains prophetic?" Clint said. "To say a team will win a championship someday, that's not much of a prophecy. I thought a prophecy had to be more specific. Maybe talk about certain things happening that set the stage for a bigger event. The Four Horsemen of the Apocalypse coming before the end of the world, things like that."

"They do for the Pyrrhic victors and the prince."

The ringing phone interrupted the discussion. Clint sat the beer down and answered it. Joe Walczak was on the line.

"Clint," he said gravely, "I've got something here I think you should see."

"What is it?"

"There's a lady whose father played in 1906. She saw the announcement in her church bulletin. She brought in a box that contains her father's journal."

"I'll be there tomorrow. What time are you available?"

"I can get here by six after I get off from work," Joe said.

"I'll be there at six."

"Okay."

"One more thing."

"What's that?"

"Make sure you put that journal in a safe place."

"Don't worry, Clint. It'll be safe."

Clint hung up the phone. Vince let out a big yawn. He shook his head quickly and forced his eyes wide open, trying to hold off the drowsiness.

"That was the Waylan Athletic Club," Clint said. "A lady brought them an old journal. It might have entries about the tournament."

"You going there tomorrow?"

"Yeah."

"You mind if I tag along?"

"Why?"

"I want to see all the football memorabilia they have. You said I could go with you the next time."

"As long as I don't hear about quatrains or any of that stuff during the trip."

"You have my word." Vince started picking up his three by five cards.

"I have one more question about these verses," Clint said. "Let's assume everything you said about them is true, that they're prophetic and all that. What's so special about the Colts that the teams who beat them in championship games need to pay homage to win another title?"

"Both of those games were big upsets," Vince said.

"The Colts aren't the only team to ever lose in a big upset."

"Maybe because the Jets and Browns added insult to the upset. The Jets quarterback bad-mouthed the Colts and guaranteed a win. For the Browns, I remember hearing something about their quarterback trying to run up the score in the closing seconds of the game." Another yawn. "Maybe there's a need for these two teams to make amends to restore the balance of football karma."

"Restore the balance of football karma?" Clint said. "What the hell does that mean?"

Vince thought for a moment, a distant look in his eyes. "I don't know," he said. "Maybe I'm not thinking straight...no sleep and everything." He wrapped the rubber band around his cards. "I'm feeling tired. I need to go."

Clint said, "Other teams before and since the Browns and Jets have run up the score or talked trash about their opponents. Those teams have gone on to win additional championships. So back to my question: What's so special about the Colts?"

Vince's mind was turning. He absently plunked the rubber band a few times. Then he looked at Clint.
"Let me think about it."
Clint opened the refrigerator again. "You want one for the road?" he said.
"A beer would knock me out."
Clint handed Vince a cola.
"How about something to keep you awake?"

Chapter Twenty-Nine
Sunday, September 23, 1906

Tom thought Jesse was praying. He sat alone, eyes shut, head downcast, hands folded around a cup of coffee that he held close to his face.

"Good morning, coach," Tom said. Jesse looked at him with tired eyes.

"Good morning, my ass," Jesse said. "I couldn't get to sleep after what happened last night, I was so angry. I finally doze off and someone's knocking at the door at 4AM. It was Stonebridge. I could smell the cigar before I opened the door. I thought to myself, here comes the bad news."

"He was smoking a stogie at 4AM?"

"No. The man smells like a cigar. He must smoke them constantly."

"What'd he want?"

"He told me he just got a call from the *Pittsburgh Sentry*," Jesse said. "The protest was withdrawn. It was all a misunderstanding. He said our win stands unchallenged. I told him, 'We won fair and square. You bet it stands unchallenged.' Then I come down here and see this." Jesse pushed a folded newspaper to Tom. He ran his finger under a headline that said *Monessen Wins*.

Tom picked up the paper and read the single sentence. *In a third round game of the World Football Championship tournament, the Monessen Terrors defeated the Waylan Athletic Club.*

"You think they changed their mind?"

"You bet they changed their mind," Jesse said, "after the paper went to press. They were gonna strip us of the win. The bastards." He looked around the room. "Anyone seen Stonebridge? I wanna talk to him."

Two players came to the table.

"Coach, did you see the paper?"

"Yeah."

"What's going on?"

"I don't know."

"We playing today?"

"Damn right, we're playing today."

The two players turned and left. They brushed by Gus Webb, urgent concern on his face.

"Coach, Billy's missing."

Tom and Jesse glanced at the corner table where Billy had been drinking. Three players were sitting there eating breakfast.

"He didn't come up to the room last night. His bed is still made."

"He's probably sleeping it off in an alley somewhere," Tom said.

"You want us to search for him?" Gus said.

"The way he looked last night, what good's he gonna do us?" Jesse said.

"He was no help in yesterday's game," Tom said.

Jesse said, "If he doesn't show up on his own, we'll notify the constable. Is everybody else accounted for?"

"As far as I know," Gus said.

"I don't like what's going on," Jesse said. "In a few hours we play the biggest game ever for this team. Eight thousand dollars are at stake, along with someone's idea of a world championship. Right now, no one's mind is on football. Gus, after you eat breakfast, tell the boys the carriages will be in front of the hotel at noon. Tell them to be on time, and be ready to play. They can leave their bags in their rooms. The hotel is going to let us wash up after the game. Then we'll catch the train back to Waylan." Gus nodded and left.

"I don't like this one bit," Jesse said to Tom. "The newspaper says we lost and a player's missing. This is a helluva way to start the day."

On the field, Tom did his pre-game stretches. As he loosened up, he watched Tad Crowell practice punting. Tad's technique was so quick and smooth and effortless that it was easy to miss the intricate coordination of power and grace. Watching punt after punt, Tom began to see the components. Tad took two steps holding the ball in front of him with outstretched arms. With the second step, he built up power - his momentum increased, the step was longer, the plant leg was slightly bent at the knee, he leaned backwards. He dropped the football so the long axis was level with the field and parallel with the arc of his leg. The kicking leg was already in motion, perfectly straight, toe pointed downfield. He struck the ball on his shoe laces and followed through with a swing that ended with his leg almost straight up. How did he get so limber, Tom wondered? Was he born that way? The force of the kick lifted Tad about a foot off the ground and launched the ball on a high and long trajectory. Eddie and another player took turns fielding the punts and jogging the ball back to Tad. How did he perfect this technique? Was it natural ability?

Riding over on the carriage, Jesse had been anxious. Billy Pallister's absence was on his mind. He talked ceaselessly to Tom, repeating himself often, using words to vent his tension: "Playing a good team like McCann's without Billy means we'll have to win with tactical kicking and defense. Every exchange of punts that gives us positive yardage will be an advantage. If our defense gives up fewer yards than McCann's, we'll be in good shape. Eventually we'll get the ball in good field position. We'll be in range for a field goal attempt; maybe a short drive to the goal line. It's gonna be a close game, a low-scoring game. If we can complete a few passes, that would help. But it's going to come down to kicking and defense. We gotta do both better than McCann's."

If the game came down to kicking, Tom thought Waylan had the edge with a punter like Tad. But they would miss Billy as much at linebacker as they would at halfback. Well, they would miss him if he was the full-strength Billy. The player who showed up yesterday against the Maroons hurt the team more than helped it.

Tom stood with his legs spread like a wishbone and stretched with both hands reaching for his left foot. He switched the stretch to the right. He heard Jesse shout to Tad, "Don't wear your leg out before the game" and Tad say, "Last one, coach." He heard the thump of the punt. Still holding the stretch, he raised his eyes to look at the McCann's team. He saw seventeen players in shamrock green jerseys and brown pants warming up on the other half of the field. The jerseys had a harp sewn in the center of the chest. One player caught his attention.

Tom released the stretch and walked over to Eddie.
"You see that player over there?" Tom said.
"Which one?"
"The one with the gray hair. How old do you think he is?"
Eddie glanced over his shoulder. "About as old as my grandfather," he said.
"That's what I was thinking. I've never seen a football player that old."
"I'll bet he doesn't play. I'll bet he's the coach."
"Why's he in a uniform?"
"Ask him after the game."

The referees - Loomis, Luehring and Jones - showed up. They took off their bowlers, jackets and ties and placed them neatly on the ground away from the sideline. The bantam Loomis marched onto the field first with the other two in a column behind him.

"Team captains to the center of the field," Loomis announced in full stride.

"You can ask him now," Eddie said to Tom. "He's going for the coin flip."

Gus was on his way. Tom joined him. The old player arrived along with another Fighting Irish player. Tom got a close look at him. He had to be at least sixty, with fire in his eyes and a snarling temperament.

"You the coach?" Tom said.

The old man turned his head and spat on the ground. "If I was the coach, would I be out here?"

The old man's distinct Irish brogue surprised Tom. He pictured a leprechaun - a cranky, old leprechaun.

"I don't see a coach with your team," he said. "I thought maybe it was you."

"We coach ourselves. Who are you boys? The newspaper said Monessen won."

"Don't believe everything you read."

The old man said, "The newspaper got it wrong? The newspaper that's putting on this show?"

"The newspaper got it wrong," Loomis said. His nasal voice projected the authority that Tom liked. "I refereed the game. Waylan won. No question about it."

"No question from me," the old man said. "We'll beat whoever shows up."

Tom felt his anger spike. He didn't like this man, didn't like his attitude. Tom wanted to take a swing at the old grouch. Gus saw it. He leaned close to Tom and quietly said, "Save it for the game."

"Waylan, you're the visiting team," Loomis said. "Call it in the air, sir."

Back on the sideline, Jesse was walking back and forth and shouting things like "You gotta play hard from the opening whistle" and "The team that blocks and tackles best is gonna win." Tom guessed all coaches said stuff like that right before kick-off, as if the players had forgotten what it would take to win. Tom never paid attention. He knew what he needed to do.

Across the field, he watched McCann's huddle up, every player joining hands in the middle. They let loose with a mighty, deep-voiced cheer: "Faugh a ballagh!"

Standing on one side of Tom, Gus looked puzzled. "What did they say?"

Standing on the other side, Eddie replied, "I think they said 'fall on the ball.'"

Jesse shouted, "You gotta out-hustle them. You gotta beat them to loose balls."

Tom nodded. "Yeah. I think it was 'fall on the ball.'"

First down. McCann's Fighting Irish of Homestead and the Waylan Athletic Club faced off against each other in tight formations. Bright green jerseys and brown pants on one side; black jerseys and brown pants on the other. Five of the twenty-two players wore head protection. On both sides, seven linemen coiled themselves in low, four point stances. The halfbacks and fullback lined up in three point stances. The quarterback crouched about two feet behind the center, his arms outstretched toward the center's backside. The defensive backs behind the line stood with one foot in front of the other, knees bent, leaning forward, ready to charge toward the point of attack.

Tom was bigger than his opponent across the line. At first Tom thought he could overpower him. The Homestead player turned out to be surprisingly quick and strong. When Tom was on offense, he had his hands full trying to keep the player from darting past him. On defense, Tom's opponent delivered low, driving blocks. He couldn't push Tom out of the way to create a hole in the line, but he was tenacious enough to hold him up for the crucial opening seconds of a play.

The first half looked like intervals of close quarters combat interrupted by frequent punts. Tom was at the vortex - the center passing the ball back, opposing linemen launching out of squat stances into reckless crashes, bodies thudding against bodies, primal grunts, pushing, punching, hot blasts of breath from faces mashed against each other, cleated shoes clawing for traction, a shoulder ramming into the gut of the ball carrier, arms wrapping around his waist as a hard pumping knee hits a head, more players piling on, the referee whistling the play dead. Unpile. Quickly line up. Another pass back from center. Two run plays. Punt. Sprint down the field into a full speed collision. Change of possession. Quickly line up. Another pass back.

Between plays Tom tried to catch his breath. He rubbed sweat out of his eyes with a gritty hand. He felt the ache of bruises and the burning of abrasions. The respite passed in a flash. The time between the start of plays was about fifteen seconds. Five of those were the previous play. Both teams were trying to wear the other down with their rapid tempo of play. The players lined up immediately after the whistle. The quarterbacks called the plays at the line. Another pass back. Another play.

So far, Jesse was right. The game had been a contest of defense and kicking. Both defenses had stopped the opposing offense cold. Tad had given Waylan an edge in punting. The Black and Brown crept a few yards downfield with each exchange. Eventually, Tad launched a long, floating punt that McCann's fielded near the ten yard line. Backed up against their goal line, Tom knew McCann's had no option but to punt.

The Irish punter hurried the kick. His foot struck the ball poorly. Tom was startled to see it streak just above his head. If he had been quicker, he could have batted it down. The ball flew at a sharp angle toward the sideline, out of bounds near the thirty-five.

First down: Gus set up to throw downfield, then made a chest pass to Tad. Waylan's fullback ran for eleven yards. Suddenly the Fighting Irish were shouting at each other, arguing about coverage and defensive responsibilities. Waylan went for the kill against its unsettled opponent. Rapid fire play execution: plunges, bucks, crossbucks, end runs, mass runs. Waylan swallowed up chunks of yardage. McCann's lost its momentum, then its poise. More shouting. More Black and Brown gains. First and ten at the six yard line. A freight train of blockers cleared a swath around McCann's end. Jacob Rourke crossed the goal line and touched the ball down. Tad's kick after goal was good. Waylan 6, McCann's 0. Tom heard the Cheer Leader start the fight song: "Jake's our man, he's full of fight..."

On its next possession, Waylan kept up the pressure. The Black and Brown advanced downfield with a series of grinding runs. Inside the twenty, the Fighting Irish defense dug in. Two runs for no gain. On third down, Tad kicked a field goal. Waylan 10, McCann's 0.

The supporters sang, "Hail, hail the Black and Brown. Finest team, all around."

Only a few minutes were left in the half. The Irish return man caught the kick and dodged and juked Waylan's defenders until he reached midfield. Suddenly McCann's was re-invigorated. They attacked with a succession of runs up the middle. Now it was Waylan's turn to dig in to blunt the drive. From the twenty-five, McCann's attempted a field goal. Another shanked kick. Halftime.

On the sideline, Tom pulled the bottom of his jersey up to wipe his face. Eddie came over. They sat down to rest for a few minutes. Gus and Jesse were talking. Then Gus joined them and offered a canteen. Tom took drink and gave it to Eddie.

Tom: "What was Jesse saying?"

Gus: "We gotta open it up. Throw some passes. Run around the ends. They're holding the line."
Eddie: "We do need to try more passes."
Gus: "They're coming in fast. I don't have time to stop and throw. And they're marking our pass catchers close."
Tom: "We let up on that kick-off."
Eddie: "It put a scare in me when they got close enough for a field goal."
Tom: "We can't let up. These boys are tough."
Gus: "Toughest game I've ever been in."
Eddie: "What do expect? They're from Homestead. They fought the Pinkertons."
Gus: "Thank God Tad kicks like a cannon."
Eddie: "Thank God their kicker doesn't. Billy show up yet?"
Gus: "Haven't seen him."
Tom: "On their last possession, they were calling plays where Billy was supposed to be."
Eddie: "You think they know we're weak there?"
Gus: "They scouted us just like we scouted them. They know we're missing Billy."
Tom (squinting at the McCann's players on the opposite sideline): "Did that old man play?"
Eddie: "I didn't see him out there."
Tom: "I told you he was the coach. He ain't a football player."

Loomis blew his whistle to alert the teams to the start of the second half. Eddie got up. Tom raised an arm. "How 'bout a hand," he said. Eddie pulled him up.

Across the field, the Fighting Irish broke their team huddle.
"Faugh a ballagh!"
"Well, Eddie-boy," Tom said. "Once again into the breach."

McCann's received the kick-off and battered the left side of the Waylan defense with a quick sequence of runs. Turner was the linebacker on that side, filling in for Billy. They found our weakness, Tom thought. Billy was normally a reckless and physical defender who relished collisions. He hit runners head-on at the line of scrimmage and stopped them dead in their tracks. Turner played with less abandon. He always seemed to close in on the ball carriers from the side as they ran by and drag them down, giving up a few more yards per play than Billy.

An Irish back took a pitch-out and ran for fifteen yards. The breakthrough staggered Waylan's defense. McCann's rammed ahead for another first down with two short runs. Waylan regained its composure. Third down inside the twenty. McCann's kicked a field goal. Waylan 10, McCann's 4.

Throughout the second half, McCann's defense strangled Waylan's offense. The Irish tackles and linebackers quickly plugged up holes in the line. The ends and corners shut down plays to the outside. Pass coverage was tight. Tom noticed they weren't shouting and arguing among themselves anymore. The McCann's players were reading and reacting perfectly. They had used their halftime break well, sorting out misunderstandings about defensive assignments.

This game shouldn't be so close, Tom thought. If Billy was there and playing as he normally did, things would be different. He could break down a good defense with fearless, smash through the line, tackle-breaking runs. Sometimes brute force could change everything. Turner, Rourke and Tad - they weren't that kind of running back.

Tad was still delivering beautiful, long punts with his balletic kicking form, but McCann's was retaliating. They were moving the ball. Their shorter punts were enough to keep Waylan pinned in bad field position.

Tom's battle with his Homestead opponent was shaping up as a draw. On some plays Tom prevailed. On others, his opponent got the best of him. Tom had to give the smaller lineman his due: he was slippery on defense and a devil of a blocker. And he was showing no signs of tiring.

McCann's worked its way into field goal range again. Tom noticed that confidence and a sense of purpose had taken hold on the other side. The Irish saw a way to victory and were eager to get there. Their offense was now executing plays with smooth, ruthless precision. They aimed every run at the left side of Waylan's defense. Fending off his man, Tom watched blockers in shamrock jerseys blast holes to his left in the Black and Brown line. Their backs powered through for three, four, five yards before being tackled. He heard Jesse yelling from the sideline, imploring his boys to stop McCann's. Finally Waylan held. McCann's kicked its second field goal. Waylan's lead was cut to two.

Tom's opponent sat on the ground after the kick, breathing heavily. Tom offered him a hand. The player glared at Tom for a moment, then took it. Tom pulled him to his feet.

"You're a fine football player," Tom said.

"You're not too bad yourself," the lineman said.

"My name's Tom Hammond."

"Rooney," the Homestead player said. "Charlie Rooney."

Waiting for the kick-off, Tom realized the game was slipping away. McCann's had gained the edge on offense and defense. Not a big edge. But with the time left in the game, ten or twelve minutes, it would be enough to put them over the top. Unless Waylan could break their momentum.

The Irish made a substitution. The old man jogged into his position in the kick-off formation. He bounced in place full of nervous energy as he waited for Loomis to blow the whistle. What did this mean, Tom wondered. Would the old man help McCann's? A fresh player replacing a tired one? Or was this a token appearance, with his age making him the weak link? Tom felt his anger from the coin flip bubble up. If he had a chance, he would take a shot at this man; try to knock the grouch out of him. It would be a clean shot - hard but legal. The man was a player on the field now. He was fair game.

Waylan returned the kick to the thirty-four. First down: two yard gain. The old man was playing defensive back. A good place for him, Tom thought. He was out of harm's way unless a ball carrier broke free or Gus threw a pass. It was proof that he wasn't a serious football player.

Second down: tackle back right, mass run. Everything clicked. The Waylan blockers mowed down the defenders. Tom saw Turner round the corner. Finally, the big play Waylan needed. Five more points coming. Six if Tad made the kick after goal. McCann's couldn't overcome that lead. One man to beat - a sixty-year old defensive back. Turner should get by him with a quick move, or just run over him.

The defensive back charged at Turner, hit him on a thigh with a shoulder and wrapped his arms around his legs. Turner tried to jerk free. The other defensive back decked him.

A game-saving tackle by the old man. No hesitation making the hit. He was a serious football player after all.

A couple of exchanges of punts. McCann's offense had gone flat since their last field goal. Waylan still led by two. Waylan punted again. McCann's got another good return to the fifty-five. Suddenly the Irish had some fight in them. Their players were jumping with energy as they lined up, shouting motivating things to each other. Just like the end of the first half, Tom thought. McCann's gets fired up by a good kick return. Time to get to work. On the sideline, Jesse was clutching his stopwatch and yelling to hold them, yelling that there were only three minutes left.

McCann's hammered Waylan's left side with runs. They were executing plays at a blistering pace - run the ball, unpile, line up, run the ball again. In four plays they were close to Waylan's forty.

"C'mon Waylan!" Jesse yelled. "Two minutes to go."

Turner and the other linebacker cheated to the left. McCann's quarterback saw it and called a pitch-out to Waylan's right. Waylan strung the ball carrier out. He didn't gain many yards, but now McCann's had more room to work against Waylan's left.

Three more runs and McCann's had crossed Waylan's thirty.

"One minute, Waylan!" Jesse shouted. "Stop them."

An off-tackle run and a crossbuck gave McCann's a first down. Time's running out, Tom thought. They've got to kick it. The quarterback received the ball and scuttled to his left, centering the ball for a field goal attempt.

The teams lined up. Waylan packed its tallest players into the middle of the line. Tom was shoulder-to-shoulder with the nose guard. McCann's holder took a knee about five yards behind the line.

The kicker stood behind him. Tom assumed a stance like a sprinter in the blocks - low, compact, ready to charge. He worked his cleats into the dirt for traction. One play decides it all, Tom thought. Give it all you got. He watched the ball, the center's hands on top of it, out of the corner of his eye.

The instant the ball moved, Tom fired upward out of his stance. He smashed through the line between center and guard. The kicker struck the ball. Tom threw out an arm. He felt a smack on his open hand.

Tom hit the ground hard on his chest and belly. He rolled to his side and looked back. Players from both teams seemed to be frozen in place - standing, kneeling, piled on one another - all eyes fixed on a goal post he couldn't see. Watching...watching...watching. Suddenly the Waylan players thrust their arms in the air and cheered. The McCann's players grimaced and turned away.

The Waylan players congratulated themselves, elated yet restrained. A few shook Tom's hand or smacked him on the back, telling him he made a great play.

"You deflected it just enough," Eddie said. "It hit the post and bounced away."

Beyond the sideline, the Cheer Leader tried to get the fight song started. The supporters were too busy celebrating to pick up the tune.

The two teams mingled. The players shared a few words and perfunctory handshakes before separating for the opposite sidelines.

"That was a mighty fine play you made," the old man said in his distinct brogue. "A mighty fine play."

"All because you made that game-saving tackle," Tom heard himself say.

The old man waved a hand dismissively. "Ahh, it was just a tackle."

On the sideline, Tom took a moment to look over the field. The spectators were almost gone. The Fighting Irish were leaving. This was supposed to be the world championship. Tom had expected something special for the winner, maybe some kind of ceremony. It was no different than the aftermath of any other game. No celebration. No reporters scribbling notes. Stonebridge showed up briefly. He told Jesse the *Pittsburgh Sentry* would contact him about the prize money. That was it. Not even a trophy presentation.

Jesse told the players to gather their stuff, the carriages were waiting. Someone called to them - Sam Patrick in a bowler holding a Brownie camera. His brother Will stood next to him.

"Hey, it's the Patrick brothers," Tom shouted. "If you're both here, who's minding the tavern?"

"I left Lorena in charge," Sam said. "Now hold still. This is a historic moment. I want to make a picture."

Jesse and the players huddled together facing Sam. He looked through the viewfinder.

Chapter Thirty
Thursday, October 3, 1974

Clint arrived at the Waylan Athletic Club promptly at six. He had Vince with him. Almost nothing had changed from his visit a week ago - same two guys playing pinball, same guys sitting on the same stools at the bar watching TV, same guys sitting at a table talking. The only addition was a woman seated at the end of the bar. Joe stood on the other side facing her.

"C'mon. C'mon over here, Clint," Joe said, beckoning him over the woman's head.

"This is Shirley Hammond. Her father, Tom, played in the 1906 tournament."

Shirley was about sixty-five. She was large-boned and mannish-looking with gray-streaked, dull brown hair and a prominent jaw. Clint pictured her with a short haircut. He felt he had a pretty good idea of what Tom Hammond must have looked like. A glass of wine with a lipstick smudge on the rim sat in front of her. An old gift box, the kind you would wrap a shirt in, was beside it.

"I saw the announcement in the church bulletin," Shirley said. "It said someone was looking for information about a football tournament played in 1906. I guess that would be you." Shirley talked fast, with a twinkle in her eye and a mirthful voice. She seemed like a happy-go-lucky kind of person.

"I'm doing some research," Clint said. Shirley took the lid off the box.

"Maybe this will be of value. Pop played for a few years back then. He kept a journal about it. That alone should tell you how important it was to him. How many steelworkers do you know who keep journals? I saved it when he passed because, well, because it was him - his words, his handwriting, his thoughts, his experiences."

Clint opened the cover. Vince sidled next to him to take a look. Joe leaned over from across the bar. The first page read, *My Life on the Gridiron, 1904-1907.*

"That 1906 tournament, Pop talked about it often. He said they won the world championship but they never got a trophy for it and they never got the prize money."

Clint slowly turned the pages. The first dozen contained a narrative of the 1904 season. From the 1905 season through the 1907 season, the notebook was a journal. Beginning in August and running through December, Tom had made entries almost every day. He also sketched formations and plays, and pasted photographs and newspaper articles onto the pages.

"Looks like he decided to keep a journal beginning in 1905. To make sure he had a complete record of his playing days, he went back and summarized the 1904 season," Clint said.

The pages were crisp. The pencil hand-writing looked fresh. Other than the yellowing of the newspaper articles and yellowing on the edges of the pages, the notebook was in excellent condition.

Each entry had a heading with the day and date. Clint turned the pages until he came to September 1906.

"There's one of the articles from the *The Sentry*," Vince said, tapping his finger on the page. Clint felt crowded. He looked at Joe.

"This is Vince Gleason." Clint tilted his head toward Vince. "He's an amateur football historian, a real fanatic."

"You don't say."

"Maybe you could show him some of the things you got here."

"Well, come on." Joe walked out from behind the bar and motioned for Vince to follow him. "Let's start with these pictures over here."

Clint watched them for a moment; the keeper of the flame of Waylan football heritage and the enthusiastic student. He heard Joe say, "I think this is the oldest one." He was pointing to the framed photo Clint had taken apart in his last visit. "These fellows won a world championship tournament in 1906. That's the one your friend is researching. This was taken at one of the games. Has all their names on the back. Can you believe this little town used to be the home of the world champions? That wouldn't happen nowadays, a town this small having a top-level football team. Things have changed a lot."

"Weren't they called the Monsters of the Monongahela?" Vince said.

"How do you know that?"

Clint turned his attention back to the journal. The next several pages contained daily entries and more *Sentry* clippings. Clint found the entry he was looking for.

<u>Saturday, September 22, 1906</u>
The semi-finals were today. Homestead beat Ambridge 4 to 2 in the first game. We watched some of the game and came away believing we could whip either one. Monessen gave us a good fight. Tad kicked a field goal early to give us a 4 to 0 lead. Then Monessen scored a touchdown and the point after. They led most of the game 6 to 4. Billy played badly. No speed and he went down easy when tackled. Jesse took him out. He begged to go back in. Jesse relented but he didn't play any better. Without our top runner, we had a hard time on offense. Near the end of the game, Eddie caught a pass near the goal line. From there, Jake ran it in. Tad missed the point after, but it didn't matter. We won 9 to 6. Tonight we heard the Pittsburgh Sentry wanted the referees to disqualify us. They said the forward pass from Gus to Eddie was illegal. Fortunately the referees did not give in. I guess the newspaper isn't up on the rule changes like we are.

Clint glanced up and saw Joe and Vince standing in front of another picture.

"You probably don't recognize this team," Joe said. "You probably wouldn't recognize their name either. Ever hear of the Pittsburgh Pirates?"

"That was the Steelers before they changed their name."

"You're a sharp guy," Joe said. "Most people think it's the baseball team. Anyway, this is the Coalcrackers scrimmaging the Pirates in training camp in the 1930s."

"Waylan played the Pirates?"

"In a scrimmage, they did."

MIKE ROMEO

<u>Sunday, September 23, 1906</u>
Great jubilation today! We beat McCann's Fighting Irish of Homestead 10 to 8. It is amazing to think that someone considers us the champions of the world! The day started strangely. When we read the Pittsburgh Sentry with our breakfast today we saw they reported that Monessen won. I guess the newspaper thought its protest would hold. Jesse was angry and concerned that they wouldn't let us play. We didn't know what to expect when we got to the field. The referees were on top of the situation and the game went on. I'm pleased to say I had a "hand" in the victory.

Tom went on to describe the game: the intensity of play, Jake Rourke's touchdown and Tad's kick after goal, Tad's field goal, McCann's two field goals in the second half, McCann's drive in the closing minutes, their final field goal attempt.

<u>Monday, September 24, 1906</u>
We waited in great anticipation for the Pittsburgh Sentry to arrive so we could read about our glory. But the train didn't deliver it. Then someone said they heard the Sentry went out of business because its publisher died. Hopefully they only stopped it for a few days out of respect. The Sentry is the only paper reporting on the tournament, probably because they organized it.

Clint scanned the following entries for references to the tournament. In one after another, Tom wrote about Waylan's preparation for its next game or game itself. No mention of the tournament. Joe and Vince brushed by him to get behind the bar. Joe let him hold the artifacts back there, the old helmets and footballs. The kid gushed his usual exclamations every time Joe handed him something: "Wow! Cool! Amazing!" Joe was beaming. He was pleased to be showing the old stuff to someone who was just as fascinated by it as he was. Joe picked up the square-toe kicking shoe.

"Nowadays everyone says soccer-style kickers are better than straight-on kickers," Joe said. "What they fail to realize is that all soccer-style kickers do is kick. They don't play any other positions.

Their success is due to specialization. For the straight-on guys, kicking was their secondary responsibility. They also played a regular position. You give me a straight-on kicker who does nothing but kick and I guarantee you he'll have the same range and accuracy as a sidewinder."

Clint reread the three entries. In all his investigations, the last piece of the puzzle rarely fell into place as precisely as this one. There was almost always a ragged edge – a contradictory statement, timelines that didn't quite match, a piece of evidence that didn't fit. Tom Hammond's journal answered all the questions. Clint knew who won. He knew why the *Sentry* reported Monessen as the semifinal winner without providing any game details. He knew why Charlie Rooney and the Fighting Irish found themselves playing an unexpected opponent.

The reason behind the last two answers made complete sense: uncertainty about the new passing rules. Didn't Vince say it was unusual to play football games before the last weekend in September in the early 1900s? If he was right, then this tournament's games would've been among the first played under the new rules. Uncertainty could be expected.

Clint looked up from the journal.

"Amazing," he said. Shirley's eyes softened.

"It *is* amazing," she said. "You really get a sense of how much Pop cared about the game."

That wasn't what Clint meant, but he let it go.

Out of the corner of his eye, Clint saw Joe leading Vince around the back of the barroom, explaining the photos on the walls like a docent at a museum. Then he watched them disappear down a hallway. Back to the journal. An entry caught Clint's attention.

<u>Tuesday, October 9, 1906</u>
No prize money yet from the Pittsburgh Sentry's tournament. The newspaper went out of business. Jesse got in touch with their lawyer. He said everyone who felt the newspaper owed them money had to file a claim. A judge would decide who gets what. Some world

championship this has turned out to be. No story about our victory and no prize money.

"Shirley, can I borrow this?"

"Ooooh, I don't know about that. This old journal means a lot to me. I don't want to risk losing it."

Clint touched her forearm lightly. "I promise I won't lose it."

"Why do you need to take it?"

"This journal proves that Waylan won the tournament. I need to copy a few pages for my research."

"Show me the pages. I'll get them copied for you."

"Well, I want to read all of your father's entries for the 1906 season. I may find something else relevant to my research. I'll bring it back to you this time tomorrow, a personal delivery. Give me your address and phone number."

"Bring it back here and I'll pick it up."

"Whatever you want."

"Well, okay. You don't know how nervous it makes me to have this out of my possession."

"Don't worry, Shirley. I'll treat it with the same reverence that you hold for it."

"Give me your phone number, just in case."

On the drive back to Pittsburgh, Vince said, "You should've seen the stuff Joe showed me. There's a closet upstairs that's full of history - programs, newspaper articles, photographs, playbooks, you name it. He even has home movies of games going back to the nineteen-fifties."

"I knew you'd enjoy seeing it."

"Enjoy it?! Are you kidding? I feel like the guy who found King Tut's tomb. Joe told me I could come down on my own and spend as much time as I wanted going through everything."

"Beware of the curse."

"What curse? There's no curse."

"Then beware of the guy who confronted me down there."

Vince didn't reply. He had dozed off, still sleep-deprived from his all-nighter forty-eight hours ago. Clint drove awhile. He thought about the tournament – an obscure drama played out sixty-eight years ago by eleven teams in twelve games over two weekends. The teams were amateur clubs, mostly local and all unheralded. The games were contested on make-shift fields at county fairs. Such an inconsequential event and yet it rippled through time: the prize money still waiting to be awarded, a politician concerned about the dark secrets that might be revealed, an athletic club keeping its claim to glory alive, a family feeling dishonored over a game-fixing rumor, a woman treasuring her father's journal, an old player who may have lost his life over it.

Vince shook himself awake.

"Can you believe Waylan's football team has been in continuous existence since 1896?"

"Is that a long time?" Clint said.

"That's a very long time for a semi-pro team."

A little while later Vince said, "I was just thinking. You remember in the movie *King Kong* how they found him on an uncharted island where dinosaurs still lived?"

"I think it was called Skull Island," Clint said.

"Yeah, Skull Island. Waylan reminds me of Skull Island: an isolated place where a dinosaur from football's past still exists - a club team from the turn of the century."

References to Kings Tut and Kong - that was typical Vince, one of the world's eternal teenagers. Clint liked the analogies, especially the one about the movie. And just like in the movie, they were coming back with proof.

In his apartment, Clint read every entry in Tom Hammonds' journal for 1906. The last game was played on November 27. There was one more entry after that.

Friday, March 21, 1907
We heard from the judge today. He said our claim was good because we won the tournament. But we weren't owed money for goods or

services rendered, so we had to get in back of the line. The money from the newspaper ran out before our turn came up. Instead of eight thousand dollars, we got nothing.

Chapter Thirty-One
Friday Morning, October 4, 1974

She was slipping away, and he hated the feeling.

Clint was shaving. He always seemed to have moments of revelation when he was shaving. In his half-asleep, unguarded state his subconscious thoughts could express themselves before they were pushed into the deep background by his consciousness.

"What were you thinking," he said aloud to himself. "What are you doing?"

He had gotten the attention of this jewel of a woman. She seemed eager to be with him. Yet all he had done with the opportunity was eat lunch with her. They had been like business lunches, too, with talk about her job and his investigations and his career plans. No excitement. Nothing that threw off sparks. Now this guy with Steeler tickets was in the picture. How had Clint responded? He hadn't met her for lunch in a week. He hadn't even called her. Had breaking up with Gina messed him up that much?

She was slipping away and he couldn't say he blamed her. His talk about rejoining the army hurt things. At least he was honest. Give him points for that.

"Mr. Ronson, will you take the points or will you take Olivia?" the game show host said.

"I'll take the points," Clint said. The audience groaned.

"Awww, you took the points," the host said, a mix of sympathy and sarcasm. *"Questionable choice, sir."*

The thing was, he wasn't sure what he was going to do. His feelings about it changed from day to day. Maybe he would rejoin. Maybe not. If he did rejoin, he could do it on *his* timetable - next week, next month, next year. Whatever suited him. He could wait and see where things with Olivia were going, then make a decision.

Right now, Clint needed to turn things around with Olivia. He needed to call her. He needed to see her. He needed to let her know how he felt.

Olivia seemed happy to get his phone call. Clint's mood improved. She thought lunch was a good idea. His mood improved even more. She had an outreach meeting with a community group in the morning. She could meet him someplace after the meeting. How about the Polish deli on Smallman in the Strip? It was close to the meeting site. Clint said he'd see her there.

Olivia was wearing her Pittsburgh PD pullover with the khaki slacks and shiny black belt. Her blond hair swept across her forehead. She had small studs in her pierced earlobes. She looked fresh, vibrant. Olivia saw Clint and flashed him a big smile.

"How was your meeting?" Clint said.

"The usual. We updated them on crime trends in their neighborhood. Gave them advice on how to avoid becoming a victim. Opened the floor for questions. Seemed like it went over well."

Clint couldn't wait to share the news.

"I closed the football case."

"Really? Who done it?"

"The Waylan Athletic Club."

While they stood at the counter waiting for their orders, Clint gave her all the details about going to Waylan and getting Tom Hammond's journal. He told her how it answered all the questions about the tournament. They got their food and sat at the table against the window again.

"Did you run into that PI in Waylan? The one you said was pretty raw?" Olivia said.

"Turned out he wasn't a PI. He's the grandson of a player accused of trying to throw one of the games. I guess he was worried I would stir up something embarrassing to the family."

"Another subplot to the story," Olivia said.

"It gets better. Hammond wrote an entry about the athletic club becoming a party in a legal action to get their prize money. Then he made another entry saying the judge acknowledged they had a claim, but they didn't get any money. After I called you, I went to the courthouse."

"I would think the journal is proof enough, unless someone can challenge its authenticity."

"If the court documents named Waylan, they would validate the journal. My conclusion would be ironclad."

"What did you learn?"

"It was a bankruptcy hearing. The record lists the Waylan Athletic Club as an unsecured creditor."

"Explain it to me. My bankruptcy law is a little rusty."

"A secured creditor is someone who holds paper like a lien or a mortgage against the company. They get paid first. Other claimants are unsecured creditors. They get paid second. As a party trying to collect prize money, Waylan was at the tail end of the line."

"The money ran out before their turn came up."

"Right on. Tom Hammond said exactly the same thing in his journal," Clint said. "By the way, I made a copy of the journal to give to Vince for his help."

"That's all? No payment?"

"From what I know about Vince, that journal's worth more to him than any amount of money. I also called Terry McCann and told him the Fighting Irish didn't win."

"What did he say?"

"First he asked who won."

"Did you tell him?"

"Of course not. I gave him Walsh's number. I told him Walsh would tell him, if the client agreed to release the information. Then he said, 'I guess Charlie Rooney's memory was playing tricks on him. I told those guys you can't rely on anything he says.'"

"What he meant was *you* can't rely on anything he said."

"He probably knows Charlie recanted his story. He wants to cast doubt on it. He wants to make me question my conclusion. What he doesn't know how much additional evidence I have."

"Aren't you worried about the thugs who hang out there?"

"I don't owe them anything. Why would they have any business with me?"

"Are you sure they see it that way?"

"I can take care of myself against Jimmy and Psycho."

"Anything in the journal or the court records about the death of the publisher?"

"Just that he died."

"What about your big theory? That Harris was using McCann's to get the money?"

"If he has DeAngelo challenge my conclusion, I think it proves I was right. Otherwise, it's moot."

"And those cryptic verses that Ivanova gave you?"

"They're still cryptic."

"What now?"

"When I leave here I'm going to the law office to brief Walsh and write my report. Then I need to drive to Waylan to return the journal."

"Busy day."

Clint folded his arms on the table to lean closer to Olivia.

"I've been thinking…I'd like to take you out tomorrow night. Have a nice dinner somewhere."

Olivia's eyes went blank for a long moment. She glanced down, then back at Clint.

"Then I wouldn't have my lunch buddy," she said carefully.

He liked the way she said 'buddy,' like they shared something exclusive. But something else wasn't right.

"We could still eat lunch together," Clint said. "I've become a big fan of delis."

Olivia reached across the table and placed both of her hands on his, those big eyes looking directly at him.

"I don't want to change anything between us." She slowly drew her hands back.

Clint finally got it. Olivia wasn't talking about their lunches together. She had said 'no' in the tenderest way she could. What did it mean? Clint thought he knew. He wanted to hear her say it to confirm his suspicion. He wanted to ask her some questions, find out how she felt about him.

That would mean dissecting the relationship. Anything dissected is dead. Clint decided to change the subject to a safe standby.

"The Steelers play the Oilers next. What's your prediction?"
"They better damn sight win."

Chapter Thirty-Two
Friday Afternoon, October 4, 1974

Clint walked down Smallman to his car, turning questions over in his mind. Was Olivia put off by his talk about rejoining the army? Was it the guy who took her to the football game? Had she always felt their relationship was platonic? Maybe she saw Clint as the rock steady male friend she could confide in. Except she never confided in him about anything. Maybe he misread the whole thing, emotion clouding perception. Maybe they really had been nothing but lunch buddies.

Suddenly he was looking into eyes full of evil, psychotic glee. A hard object hit his ribs with the force of a punch.

"Don't make me shoot you," Psycho snarled. He motioned with his head. "Get in the car."

Clint saw Jimmy push open the rear door of a large brown sedan and step out. Another man who Clint had never seen before sat inside by the opposite door. Clint got in, followed by Psycho. Jimmy got in the driver's seat. The man by the door sized Clint up. He was big and beefy, with a square, fleshy face and heavy eyelids. Their eyes met for a second. The man gave Clint an acknowledging nod, like you would give to someone you catch staring at you on a bus. Then he turned his head to the window. Psycho shifted into the corner half-facing Clint. He held a pistol in his lap pointed at Clint's gut.

"Put your palms on your thighs and keep 'em there," Psycho said. "Move 'em, I shoot."

Clint complied. Hadn't he told Olivia he could take care of himself against Jimmy and Psycho? He didn't count on them getting the jump on him. Jimmy started the car.

"Relax," Jimmy said. "Somebody wants to talk to you. That's all."

"He could of called me," Clint wanted to say, but he didn't want to agitate his captors. That was the second rule if taken hostage. The first: Stay calm.

"Who you with in there?" Psycho said.

"An acquaintance," Clint said.

"That was a long lunch. I didn't think you were ever coming out."

"I was savoring my meal." The words slipped out impulsively. Clint momentarily winced at his lack of self-control. Psycho slowly tilted his head back and looked down his nose at him.

"You're funny, man," he said with a sneer. "I hope you keep your sense of humor. This could be very entertaining."

Jimmy waited for a line of traffic to pass. He eased the car away from the curb. They drove for a few minutes. No one said a word.

Jimmy had said to relax, that someone just wanted to talk to him. Nonsense, Clint thought. You don't kidnap someone to have a conversation with them. Didn't Walsh say that DeAngelo would play rough if he needed to? That Harris would destroy him? He thought Walsh had been speaking figuratively. Terry McCann must've passed the word to Harris after Clint called. Now Clint was experiencing first-hand the proof of his big theory; the payback for not saying the Fighting Irish had won.

Jimmy pulled into a convenience store parking lot. He got out and made a call at a pay phone. The call was short, ten to fifteen seconds, like a status report. The stop had to have been pre-arranged. Jimmy didn't tell Psycho and the big man what he was doing. Nor did they ask. Whoever Jimmy called must've been waiting by the phone expecting to hear from him. Clint wished he could call Shirley; tell her he wouldn't be able to return her journal today as he promised.

Jimmy got back in the car. They continued to drive in silence. Jimmy, Psycho and the big man seemed relaxed, as if snatching a guy out off the street was routine. Clint could see Jimmy's eyes when he looked in the rearview mirror. He made normal checks to the rear. He didn't seem to be paying special attention for anyone tailing him.

The thugs knew Clint was at The White Eagle. They must've known where he parked his car. Otherwise, how would they have known where to set up the ambush? Had they followed him? Did someone else follow him and call them?

"How did you guys know where I was?"

"The cops got informants," Psycho said. "So do we."

If he's telling the truth, he's got to be talking about DeAngelo's PI. Clint suspected he was the link between DeAngelo and McCann's. Who else could it be? Who else knew he was there?

Olivia!?

Jimmy drove into a run-down industrial area – crumbling buildings, potholes, abandoned cars along the curbs, not a person in sight. He turned off the road and passed through the gate of a barbed wire fence onto the grounds of an ancient factory; a red brick citadel with tiny windows. Piles of rusting industrial junk - steel drums, pieces of machinery, sheet metal - littered the weed-grown yard. Jimmy drove around to the back. Gravel crunched under the tires of the car. Another car was parked there.

"The boss is here already," the big man said.

"He drives fast for an old guy," Jimmy said.

Psycho got out and stepped back from the door. "Get out," he ordered Clint. "Put your hands on the trunk. Spread your legs." The big man came around and frisked him.

"He's clean."

Jimmy had walked ahead of them. He opened a door into the building.

The interior was a massive, gray space with shadowy corners. Faint sunlight came through the tiny, dust-covered windows. The air smelled musty and slightly oily. A stool sat in the middle of the floor in a stream of light coming from one of the windows.

"Have a seat," Jimmy said. "And don't be eyein' the place." Psycho moved to Clint's right front, about fifteen feet away. The big man moved to Clint's left front. Jimmy remained behind him. Clint heard footsteps to his right rear, someone walking toward them from out of the shadows. Psycho and the other man were looking in that direction.

"I'm always intrigued by people who won't go with the flow," the man walking toward them said. His voice was the low, rough growl of a longtime smoker. "What do they expect to get out of it, I ask myself. What makes them that way? Principles? Contrariness?"

The man approached Psycho. It was the mean-looking old guy Clint had seen at McCann's. He had three baseball bats resting on his right shoulder. He gave one to Psycho, then walked toward the big man.

"The thing is, if you won't go with the flow, you've got to be strong enough to stand up to the current." The old guy gave the big man a bat. He walked behind Clint. "Eventually, the current wears everyone down. Sometimes, it drags people down when they least expect it."

The old guy came around from Clint's right. He had given the last bat to Jimmy. Three attackers with baseball bats coming from three directions, one from behind. And Clint was a stationary target on a stool.

The old guy put his hands on his knees and got face to face with Clint.

"What do you know about the 1906 *Pittsburgh Sentry* tournament? Probably quite a bit, since you been chasing it down for the past few weeks. Let me tell you a few things you probably didn't know."

Another ripple from that inconsequential event, Clint thought.

The old guy stepped back from Clint. "A lot of money was bet on that tournament," he said. "One of the people taking those bets was my father. He worked for a big operator back then. He took bets, made loans, the same stuff that goes on nowadays. The biggest bettor was the man who owned the *Sentry*. The thing was, he was borrowing the money he was betting. He was taking out huge loans from my old man. Now, generally speaking, my father should've known better than to be making loans like that. But I guess he figured this man was good for it. After all, he owned a newspaper. He had to be loaded."

To Clint's left, the big man held his bat halfway up the barrel in one hand and smacked it slowly, repeatedly, into the open palm of the other. The old guy started pacing in a slow circle, all the while continuing his soliloquy.

"Now, if my father had known how desperate this man was, he might not of been such a generous lender. For starters, the man tried to fix the outcome of one of the games. A couple fellows had to pay him a friendly visit and tell him he couldn't do that. He could bet on his own tournament, but he couldn't rig the result. Not after he bet so much money." The old guy smiled and held out his arms, palms up, like he was pleading. "Can you imagine that? The crooks were making sure the tournament was being run straight."

"So why was he so desperate? I'll tell you why. Because he was broke and his newspaper was going under." The old guy practically shouted the words at Clint. He paused for a moment to settle down.

"I see it all the time," the old guy said. A man's business is failing. He needs some cash to keep it going. He thinks he can get it by betting on sports. He's been a fan all his life. How hard can it be to pick the winners? That's the lure of my little business. But the thing about betting on sports is…you never really know who's going to win. So when the man's team lost and he realized he was dealing with people who wouldn't take IOUs, he was overwhelmed by desperation. He killed himself."

Another mystery solved, Clint thought. Harris had committed suicide. Clint figured that by the end of this session, any remaining questions would be answered. Whatever good that would be.

The old guy was back in his face, practically shouting again. "Guess who was left holding all that debt? MY FATHER!"

The old guy turned away and began pacing in a circle again.

"A couple fellows showed up with baseball bats, took him for a little walk. They just wanted to impress upon him the urgency of making good on all those loans he handed out. The only problem was, they did their work a little too enthusiastically. Put him into a coma from which he never recovered. He died a few weeks later."

The big man continued to smack his bat into his palm. Psycho was making slow-motion cuts with the bat, like he was warming up for his turn at the plate.

"Of course, life turned into hell for me and my mother and sister. There she was, uneducated, no family, no friends, a four year-old son and a two year-old daughter to care for. It got about as bad as it could get for us. I didn't have the luxury of staying in school. By the time I was ten, I was hustling on the streets, trying to make enough money to keep us alive. You could say that tournament made me the man I am today."

Clint glanced at the two bat-wielding thugs in front of him. Jimmy was behind him. If Jimmy's first swing was at his head, Clint would be knocked out. Game over. But the first swing wasn't going to be at Clint's head. If they wanted to kill him quickly, they would've chosen some other method - gunshot or strangulation. No, they want him to suffer and struggle. They wanted the sadistic pleasure of seeing his dignity beaten away and hearing him beg for mercy, like their other victims probably did. How would it go? Would they pound him half to death, then dump him somewhere with an ultimatum to come up with the money? Or would they finish the job here?

Clint decided if he was going to go down, he was going to go fighting. Perched on the stool, he was an easy target. A thug could get the power of his whole body into a level swing. The force of each blow would break bone. The pain would be agonizing. The damaged body part would be a liability in the fight. Clint needed to hit the floor and roll before the first contact. Then the thugs would be aiming downward at a moving target. The power of their swings would only come from their shoulders. He needed to anticipate when the first blow was coming; look for a change in their eyes. Maybe the old guy would give a signal.

Once on the floor, then what? Maybe he could tackle the old guy. Put a strangle hold on him. Get the thugs to back off. On second thought, bad idea. The old guy would fight back. While Clint was struggling with him, the thugs could circle around him. What about the stool? Grab it and get to his feet. Use it to parry blows. Get against a wall to protect his back. If a blow broke a stool leg, he might have a sharp-pointed stick to use as a weapon. He could work his way to the door...

If his plan failed, he hoped someone would find the journal and get it back to Shirley.

Clint tuned his attention back in to the old guy. He was saying, "A few weeks ago, you show up, asking questions about the tournament and saying the prize money was waiting to be paid out.

And I'm thinking to myself, I have a right to that money. I deserve compensation for growing up without a father, for being forced into poverty, for being denied an education, for emotional pain and suffering, all because of that newspaper man and his damn tournament. Yeah, I deserve that money and a whole lot more."

Funny, Clint thought. I'm in the worst predicament of my life and all I can think of is how will Shirley get her journal back?

The old guy practically lunged back into Clint's face, closer than before. He was really worked up, shouting his words, his foul smoker's breath filling Clint's nostrils. Clint tried not to breathe.

"Then I find out the only thing standing between me and all that money is one of those people who won't go with the flow. We tried to make it as easy for you as we could. We introduced you to someone who played in the game. His word wasn't good enough for you. We offered you a little gratuity for your trouble. You still didn't do what we wanted. I'm asking myself, doesn't he understand? Doesn't he know what to do? Then I realized what was going on. You're too honorable. You're one of them who lives by some sort of code; makes you feel like you can stand up against the current. This time, the current's stronger than you are. This time, it's going to drag you down."

My big theory's wrong, Clint thought.

Clint dove for the floor. He instantly rolled, covered his head, rolled back, tried to locate the stool. Simultaneously he braced for the impending bat blows. Did he hear a noise outside, like a car skidding in gravel? No time to think. His brain was in its emergency mode, assessing input and sending orders in overdrive. He grabbed the stool and sprang to his feet.

Mental flashes fired in Clint's mind - amazement at not getting hit, the possibility of escape. He noticed the thugs were distracted by something beyond the doorway. The bats clattered on the floor as the thugs tossed them aside. Suddenly the door banged open. Cops rushed in and crouched in wide-legged stances, sidearms drawn, shouting commands.

"Get down! Everybody on the floor!" Jimmy and the big man quickly dropped.

"What's the problem, officers?" the old guy asked, trying to sound innocent and helpful at the same time.

"Down!!" The innocent and helpful act wasn't working. The old guy got on his belly with stiff, slow movements. Psycho hesitated for another moment, possibly looking for an out. A cop jammed his sole into the back of his knee, crumpling him to the floor. Another cop leveled his pistol at Clint.

"I said get down!" he yelled. Clint obeyed immediately.

Some of the cops kept their weapons trained on the prone men while others frisked them. They took pistols off the old guy and the thugs and slid them across the floor. Then the room was filled with the metallic zips of hand-cuffs being tightened. Clint felt his arms being pulled back and the cuffs clamp down on his wrists.

Clint saw Olivia come through the door. Her eyes swept the room. They stopped on Clint. She pointed at him.

"Let him go," she said. "He's the hostage."

A cop took the cuffs off. He helped Clint to his feet. Olivia came over.

"You need to come with us," she said. "We need to interview you."

"How did you know I was here?" Clint said.

"I saw them abduct you. I followed and called for back-up."

"You saved my life."

Olivia holstered her pistol and snapped the strap over it. She looked up at Clint sweetly.

"I couldn't lose my lunch buddy."

Chapter Thirty-Three
Friday, January 29, 1988

Be careful about what you wish for. Clint had heard that saying dozens of times. He never appreciated what it meant until right now. He had come to Pennington's hoping to run into someone he knew back in '74, maybe pick things up where they left off. That's exactly what was happening. Except instead of sitting across from a pert blonde, Clint was looking at the big head of Vince Gleason. And Vince was on a roll, talking about the cryptic verses as if thirteen years had not passed since their last conversation.

"You thought they were about the Baltimore Colts," Vince said. "Everything seemed to fit except one thing. That one thing was the main point."

"Refresh my memory."

"The team the quatrains are about: everyone who lost a championship game to them went on to win later championships; everyone who defeated them in a championship game never again won a championship."

"Now I remember. They would never win another championship until they paid tribute to the team in the verses."

"Right. When you first got the verses, what was it? A dozen years ago? They didn't fit the Baltimore Colts then. The Giants had lost two championship games to the Colts and they hadn't won another."

"They won last year."

"Righhhht," Vince said, nodding slowly to affirm that Clint was catching on. "It's not just that they won. It's who they beat. Vince laid the newspaper on the table. He tapped a finger on a photo of a quarterback. "This guy. The prince untrue."

"How do you know he's the prince untrue?" Clint felt weird using that term, like he was buying into the idea that those verses had hidden meaning. This whole thing felt weird - a chance meeting with a forgotten acquaintance and in a heartbeat they had picked up a conversation from years earlier. He looked around the room, hoping to see someone who resembled Olivia. A song played on the sound system - "What Have I Done to Deserve This" – synthpop with distinctive English accents, the Pet Shop Boys chanting the lyrics more singing them, Dusty Springfield providing guest vocals.

Vince was insistent. "Think about it," he said. "The Baltimore Colts drafted him, the number one pick in the entire draft. They staked their future on him. You know how valuable that opportunity is? To get the first pick of all the players coming out of college?"

"I know a lot of number one picks are flops."

"If a team chooses well, they can turn things around immediately. And the Baltimore Colts did choose well. This guy's amazing. But he refused to play for them. Said he would play some other sport instead. So they traded him."

"Rejecting the Colts, that makes him untrue?" Clint said.

"Rejecting the Colts after they picked him number one and pinned their hopes on him."

"So maybe there's a similarity between the verses and reality. Pure coincidence."

"Meaningful coincidence."

"Whatever you say."

Vince gave Clint a stony glare, like he was fed up with his continuing skepticism about the verses.

"Here's something that's not a coincidence," Vince said. "It's a fact. Every team the Baltimore Colts defeated in the final championship game, the Giants and Cowboys, have gone on to win a championship. Every team that defeated the Baltimore Colts, the Browns and Jets, have yet to win another championship. The Baltimore Colts are the only team in the NFL that statement is true for."

"How do you know?"

"You remember the system I came up with? The one where I could track every team that played in a championship and how they did in subsequent championship games?"

"The one you had on a bunch of three by five cards?"

"That's the one. I've been updating it after every Super Bowl."

Vince looked like he was waiting for an "attaboy" from Clint, some praise for his diligence. He got more skepticism.

"Now the Colts are in Indianapolis," Clint said.

"Doesn't matter. You remember how I defined a team? I said it was a combination of a franchise and a city. That way I took into consideration the devotion of the fans."

"So by your definition, the Baltimore Colts and the Indianapolis Colts are different teams?"

"Yes, which means the quatrains only apply to the Baltimore Colts," Vince said. "Given the underlying message of the quatrains, maybe the Indianapolis team ought to be concerned. They betrayed the devotion of the Baltimore fans."

Be careful about what you wish for, Clint thought.

"You going to ask me that question?" Vince said.

"What question?"

"Don't you remember? You asked, 'What's so special about the Baltimore Colts that the teams who beat them in championship games need to pay homage to win another title?'"

"Did I ask that? It's a great question."

"It *is* a great question. At the time, I said maybe it's because the Jets and Browns added insult to the defeat. And you said other teams have run up the score or talked trash about their opponents. Those teams have gone on to win additional championships. What makes the Colts so special?"

"I kind of remember it now," Clint said, even though he didn't.

"I've been pondering that question for years. I think I have the answer."

Clint raised his eyebrows to prompt a response. He didn't need to ask. He knew Vince was going to tell him.

"It's the horseshoe. The quatrains mention the talisman. Elena gave you a sketch of the talisman. It was a horseshoe. The horseshoe is the key."

"How?"

"Because it's an archetypal image. The horseshoe creates a psychic event for opponents. It gives them the foreknowledge to game plan and execute better. It unleashes the emotion that gives them the edge."

"I thought you were serious for a moment," Clint said.

"I am serious. You remember that book Elena gave us? The one by Carl Jung?"

"No."

"Man, you should've read it. I did. Over and over. I analyzed it. I dissected it. I researched concepts in the encyclopedia. I wanted to understand how Elena could have psychic thoughts. Specifically, I wanted to figure out how she came up with those quatrains. Then I realized, that book explains how the events in the quatrains could actually happen."

Nothing had changed with this guy, Clint thought. What is he now, thirty-five years old? And he's still talking about quatrains and psychic events. It was all nonsense. But for some reason, Clint wanted to hear the explanation.

"It all starts in the psyche," Vince said. "You know what the psyche is? Don't you? That part of the mind that relates us to our environment."

"Yeah."

"One of the ways the psyche does this is through the concepts of space and time, which themselves are creations of the psyche. That's why Jung says people can have premonitions of future events. He says under certain conditions the psyche can compress space and time to the point where it vanishes."

"What kind of conditions?"

"This is where the archetypes come in. According to Jung, the archetypes exist in everyone's mind. They are the organizers of the psyche. In certain emotional states, the archetypes create a condition in the psyche which lowers the level of consciousness and allows a person to become aware of unconscious ideas. Within those unconscious ideas, space and time may be compressed. It's nothing spooky or supernatural. It's just psychology."

"Theoretical psychology, maybe," Clint said. "What's this got to do with the Jets and the Browns and the Colts?"

"When a team begins preparing for a play-off or championship game, one of the first questions they ask is, 'How has my opponent done in recent post-season games?' That leads to asking, 'When did they last win a championship?' And if the team doesn't ask it, the sportswriters will. That's an angle they always bring up. For the Browns, the answer is the 1964 NFL championship game when they beat the Colts. For the Jets, it's Super Bowl III when they beat the Colts. As soon as you say the Colts, what's the first thing you picture?"

"Their logo."

"Exactly. The horseshoe on their helmet; that iconic, universally-recognized symbol of good luck. The horseshoe image enters the unconscious and activates the archetype of the loyal helper, which is often associated with the horse. That's why the horseshoe is the key. No other team wears a symbol that holds so much meaning."

"What about the Broncos?" Clint said. "They have a horse on their helmet."

"It's not the same. A horse rearing up through the letter 'D' doesn't elicit the same response as the horseshoe."

"So the horseshoe logo activates the archetype, which creates that condition in the psyche you were talking about..."

"Consider this," Vince said. "A team loses a game in an upset, especially an important game like a playoff or a championship. What happens the next time those two teams meet?"

"Revenge," Clint said. "Sometimes the game's a blow-out."

"Revenge is a powerful motivator because it unleashes intense emotions."

Vince took a sip of his beer. "Here's where my thinking comes in," he said. "If time can be compressed in the unconscious so that someone can foresee future events, what about past events? Couldn't they also experience something that already happened that they didn't actually live through?"

"Are you saying they're reliving the Colts' losses to the Browns and Jets?"

"No, not like that. My theory is that they unconsciously experience the emotions associated with the losses - the humiliation of a big upset, of having the score run up on you, of having someone guarantee a victory against you – and those emotions get conveyed into their consciousness."

"They feel the emotion but they don't know why?"

"I picture it like waking up from a nightmare," Vince said. "You know the experience. Your heart is pumping and you're full of dread and anxiety, but you can't recall the details of the dream. Anyway, with this experience they've tapped into some powerful emotions. They're like a team seeking revenge. They prepare for the game with more intensity and focus than ever before. They play it the same way."

"Like those teams are driven to avenge the Colts' losses to the Jets and Browns."

"Isn't that what the quatrains say?"

Clint expected Vince to tilt his head back and flash his smirk of superiority. Instead, Vince seemed to be studying him, trying to read Clint's reaction to everything he heard.

Then Vince said, "Speaking of preparing for a game, that whole process involves thinking about a future event. Trying to anticipate what your opponent's going to do, trying to think of ways to neutralize their strengths or attack their weaknesses. In a sense, concentrating on the unknowable. According to Jung, that's fertile ground for psychic activity, especially in a heightened emotional state."

Clint listened, not saying anything, trying not to show anything.

"We assume a good game plan is the product of thoughtful analysis. But a lot of judgment goes into it and a lot of that judgment is based on hunches and gut feelings. How many of those, the ones that play out, are instances of foreknowledge moving from the unconscious into consciousness? What about a player who precisely anticipates his opponent's next move. He counters it not by reacting to it but by acting an instant ahead of it. Was it instinct? Luck? Or could the player have had a glimpse of what was coming a moment before it happened? Did you see the Cleveland game?"

"Yeah."

"Remember how it ended?"

"You talking about The Fumble?"

"It was stunning; a freak play. Cleveland's sure touchdown, the game, the conference championship, the trip to the Super Bowl – all lost in the blink of an eye. Was it simply a brilliant act by a single player? Or could it be evidence of my theory?"

"Like the cornerback had a premonition?"

"Like unconscious awareness of the impending play guided his conscious actions. If he doesn't reposition himself before the snap where he did, if he doesn't look toward the backfield at the moment he did, if he goes for the tackle instead of the strip – Cleveland scores."

"Listen to what you're saying. All the work a team does to win games, all the drafting and trading for talent, all the planning and preparation, all the practice - you're saying all that can be wiped out by psychic activity. Doesn't that sound crazy to you?"

"I'm not saying it wipes all that out. I'm saying if those things are equal, it gives an advantage. Jung says there are important things in addition to those that can be measured."

"Like archetypes?"

"Think about this: Jung says scientific experiments are limiting because they force an answer to a specific question. He says they don't allow nature to express herself in her fullness. Well, a game is like an experiment. The rules are the parameters. The oddsmaker's line is the hypothesis – Team A will win by more than four and a half points. Then there's the null hypothesis – Team B will lose by less than four and a half points. They play the game. Someone wins. Someone loses."

"Or it's a tie."

"Or it's a tie. Whatever the outcome, we can accept or reject the null hypothesis. We feel like the two teams were forced to show us who is better and by how much. We credit the winning coach with doing a better job of manipulating and controlling variables like talent and preparation. But even coaches admit there're things in the game that are beyond their control, things like emotion and the mental state of their players and staff. In terms of football, that's part of the fullness Jung was talking about."

"If what you're saying is true, why haven't the Jets and Browns lost every single game since winning those championships?"

"Because teams don't prepare for every game with a play-off mentality," Vince said.

"You put some thinking into this," Clint said. It was a concession, not a compliment. He didn't know what to make of Vince's theory. Vince seemed sure about it. Clint couldn't trip him up with any of his questions. Clint didn't doubt the central premise, the ability of the psyche to influence human performance. He didn't know how it happened. Who really did? Vince's ideas made sense if you could buy into the existence of archetypes and the psyche compressing time.

"How would paying homage change things?" Clint said.

"I think it would take the edge off the angry emotions the players pick up on."

Vince didn't even need to think about that one. He had the answer ready, another explanation he had pondered long and hard...for years. Why bother continuing this conversation, Clint thought. Whatever mild curiosity he had about the quatrains was satisfied. He had given this chance encounter enough of his attention. It was time for some closing niceties. Tell Vince it had been good to see him and wish him luck, something like that.

"One more thing," Vince said. "I suspected the quatrains were prophetic. Now I know they are. With my system with the three by five cards, I see a pattern emerging."

Clint looked around the room again for Olivia, for any excuse to leave. He remembered Vince's fascination with Nostradamus. Hearing how Jungian psychology explained the outcomes of football games was one thing. But this new topic, Clint really didn't feel like getting into it. He looked back at Vince.

"Hey, it's been good to see you again…"

"Hold on," Vince said. "What would you do if you knew which team in a championship game was destined to lose?"

"You're going to place a bet?"

"Wouldn't you?"

"I had a bad experience with a bookie."

"I'm not going to deal with some shady operator. I'm flying to Vegas first thing in the morning."

"At least it will be legal."

"It has to be. I'm putting everything on the table."

"Are you kidding?"

"I never kid."

"It's your money," Clint said. "But here's my advice: don't bet over your head against the point spread."

"I won't be betting against the spread." Vince tapped on the photo of the quarterback again. "This guy's team is favored. I'm picking the underdog."

"You're crazy."

"'Cursed is he to thrice feel humbling defeat. Then his own glory would but once repeat'."

Clint had heard enough. "I got to go," he said. He started to get up. Vince grabbed his arm.

"I'll prove it. What's your phone number? I'll tell you how I did."

"I'll know who won."

"I'm going to tell you how much I made. What's your phone number?"

"I don't have a phone number."

"What about an address?"

"I don't have an address either. Right now I'm a transient."

"Someone's got to know how to get in touch with you?"

Clint jotted an address on a napkin.

"Here. They'll know where to find me."

Epilogue
Friday, February 5, 1988

A week later Clint was looking at a postcard showing an aerial view of Waikiki - brilliant blue sky, surf rolling up on the beach, high-rise hotels. He turned it over.

Clint,
Did I say those verses were prophetic? I meant profitable. Used some of my winnings to extend my weekend trip into a winter vacation. The weather's great here.

Aloha,
Vince

From the Anthem City

Like it on Facebook: www.facebook.com/FromtheAnthemCity